Swords Against the Moon Men

An all-new science fantasy adventure novel by the acclaimed coauthor of the Ancient Opar series, Christopher Paul Carey.

Hailed by author and science fiction scholar Richard Lupoff as a "masterpiece of science fiction" and a "pioneer work of the modern school of social extrapolation in science fiction," Edgar Rice Burroughs' classic lunar trilogy—**The Moon Maid**, **The Moon Men**, and **The Red Hawk**— tells the generational tale of humanity's fight for freedom against alien conquerors from the Moon. The hero, Julian, finds his soul perpetually reincarnated in the bodies of his successive grandsons, fated to confront—down through the centuries—the vicious Kalkars who have subjugated Earth.

The epic saga continues in this novel, **Swords Against the Moon Men**.

In 2076 AD, Earth has been conquered and humanity brutally enslaved under the cruel tyranny of the Kalkar invaders whose evil was spawned from Va-nah, the Moon's hollow interior.

Julian 7th—descendant of the great hero who led the first expedition to Va-nah and nearly defeated the Kalkars—receives a mysterious transmission from the planet Barsoom.

The desperate plea from the Red Planet swiftly hurls Julian upon a lonely quest into the heart of Va-nah where he teams up with an U-ga princess and a fierce alien quadruped, and launches a daring rescue to save a lost Barsoomian ambassadorial mission. The success of this mission depends on an unlikely alliance with the Warlord of Mars to assail the enemy's impregnable stronghold.

If Julian fails in this quest, humanity—and the entire solar system—will never escape the iron grip of the Moon Men.

SWORDS AGAINST THE MOON MEN™

As I fought my own combatant, John Carter moved with a celerity that barely seemed human...

THE WILD ADVENTURES OF EDGAR RICE BURROUGHS® SERIES

SWORDS AGAINST THE MOON MEN™

CHRISTOPHER PAUL CAREY

COVER ART BY CHRIS PEULER

INTERIOR ILLUSTRATIONS BY MARK WHEATLEY

EDGAR RICE BURROUGHS, Inc.
Publishers
TARZANA   CALIFORNIA

Swords Agianst the Moon Men
First Edition

Trademarks including Edgar Rice Burroughs® and Swords Against
the Moon Men™ owned by Edgar Rice Burroughs, Inc.
Cover art by Chris Peuler and interior illustrations by Mark Wheatley
© 2017 Edgar Rice Burroughs, Inc.

Special thanks to Bob Garcia, Gary A. Buckingham, Tyler Wilbanks, and
Scott Tracy Griffin, for their valuable assistance in producing this novel.

Number 6 in the Series

Library of Congress CIP (Cataloging-in-Publication) Data
ISBN-13:
978-1-945462-13-9
- 9 8 7 6 5 4 3 2 1 -

For my parents,
Henry Sherwood Carey, Jr.,
and Velma Ruth Carey

TABLE OF CONTENTS

FOREWORD

A bit of history might be of interest before reading *Swords Against the Moon Men*, the latest installment in the Wild Adventures of Edgar Rice Burroughs series. In April 1919, Edgar Rice Burroughs began writing a manuscript titled *Under the Red Flag*, finishing it in May of that year. The novel was an indictment of Communism, about which Burroughs had grave concerns (as illustrated in a comment at the bottom of the synopsis of *The Moon Maid* that he wrote to send out to prospective publishers: "This story is anti-communist and pro-peace-by-preparedness."). Burroughs was greatly disappointed that he was unable to sell the story, having received eleven rejections from various magazine editors who feared a possible public reaction due to the novel's strong political content.

Discouraged but not defeated, Burroughs rewrote *Under the Red Flag* in January 1922 with the idea of resubmitting it as a science fiction tale, changing place names and some character names, and rechristening the novel's protagonist, Julian James, to Julian 9th. He also rewrote the prologue, which then became the prologue for *The Moon Maid*, and added a short paragraph explaining the authority of the Twenty-Four, the governing council of the novel's villains. Burroughs did not submit the newly revised manuscript for publication at that time, holding it in abeyance.

Continuing to have hopes for the newly retitled *The Moon Men*, in June 1922 he began writing *The Moon Maid*, which would become a prequel to *Under the Red Flag*, creating a

Communistic race, the Kalkars, at the center of the Moon. *The Moon Maid* told the exciting story of Julian 5th and his love for Nah-ee-lah, and the enmity between him and Orthis, the novel's antagonist.

The Moon Men—now the story of Julian 9th and his rebellion against the Kalkars and Or-tis, a descendant of Orthis, as well as his love for Juana St. John—was repositioned to become the second volume in the trilogy. Interestingly, in *Under the Red Flag* Burroughs revealed that Juana St. John was the mysterious girl in blue dancing on the table of the Blue Room of the *Harding*. Burroughs deleted that information when he rewrote the prologue.

In April 1925, Burroughs began writing *The Red Hawk*, his final installment of the trilogy. Set in the twenty-third century of an America that has been reduced to a preindustrial state, the story focused on Julian 20th, his struggle to drive the Kalkars into the Pacific Ocean, and his love for Bethelda, who, in a surprise twist, is a descendant of Orthis, the antagonist from *The Moon Maid*.

Swords Against the Moon Men relates the story of Julian 7th, the father of Julian 8th and the grandson and reincarnation of Julian 5th. Julian 7th's exploits under the Kalkars and at the center of the Moon, in the land of Va-nah, are as exciting as Burroughs' original trilogy and reveal new interesting information about the lunar world. The novel also tells the story of Julian 7th's love for Voo-rah-nee, Nonovar of Vathayne.

Due to his completion of Philip José Farmer's *The Song of Kwasin*, the third volume of the Ancient Opar series, and his own additions to that series, I can't think of anyone besides Christopher Paul Carey who could have written this novel, which is as close to Burroughs as any I've read. I hope that it won't be the last novel that he pens set in Burroughs' worlds.

Robert R. Barrett

Wichita, Kansas

October 10, 2017

MOON MEN TIMELINE

March 4, 1866 John Carter is mysteriously transported to Barsoom (Mars).

1896 Birth of Julian 1st.

1914-1959 The Great War.

1916 Marriage of Julian 1st.

1917 Birth of Julian 2nd.

Armistice Day 1918 Julian 1st is killed in the line of duty in France.

1928 Jason Gridley invents the Gridley Wave and makes contact with Pellucidar.

1937 Birth of **Julian 3rd.***

1938 Julian 2nd is killed in the line of duty in Turkey.

1940 Earth receives primitive radio signals from Barsoom.

1959-1967 The Great War intensifies.

April 1967 Victory Day, marking the end of the Great War.

June 10, 1967 Mars Day, on which the first intelligible communication with Barsoom is established. Julian 3rd meets Edgar Rice Burroughs in the Blue Room of the Transoceanic Liner *Harding* and tells him the story of *The Moon Maid*.

March 1969 After being rescued in the Arctic on an expedition to hunt polar bears, Edgar Rice Burroughs meets with Julian 3rd a second time and is told the stories of *The Moon Men* and *The Red Hawk*. The President of the United States awards ERB the post of Secretary of Commerce.

April 10, 1970	Julian 3rd meets Edgar Rice Burroughs in Washington, D.C., and relates the story of *Swords Against the Moon Men*.
1970	Birth of Julian 4th.
1992	Julian 3rd is killed in the line of duty.
2000	Birth of **Julian 5th,*** whose story is told in *The Moon Maid* by Edgar Rice Burroughs.
2015	Barsoom launches a space ship for Earth but the vessel goes astray.
2019	The Barsoomian space ship falls within the gravity of Jupiter and communication with its crew is lost.
2024	On Earth, Lieutenant Commander Orthis isolates the Eighth Solar Ray, leading to the discovery of the Planetary Rays of Mercury, Venus, and Jupiter, as well as the Eighth Lunar Ray. The Eighth Planetary Rays of Earth and Mars have already been discovered.
December 25, 2025	Under the command of Julian 5th, *The Barsoom* launches from Earth on course for Mars.
January 7, 2026	Lieutenant Commander Orthis sabotages *The Barsoom*, hurling it toward the surface of the Moon. The space ship descends into a lunar crater, thus avoiding destruction.
January 8, 2026	*The Barsoom* emerges inside the hollow core of the Moon and sets down in the world of Va-nah.
2026-2036	The main events of *The Moon Maid*.

2036	Julian 5th returns to Earth with Nah-ee-lah, leaving Orthis behind with the Kalkars. Orthis begins construction of a fleet of Kalkar warships. The birth of Julian 6th.
2050	The Kalkars launch their assault on Earth. Earth stands defenseless against Orthis' electronic rifle and the International Peace Fleet is all but annihilated. Julian 5th designs a counter-weapon and sacrifices his own life, killing Orthis and destroying his electronic rifle.
2056	Death of Julian 6th.
2057	Birth of **Julian 7th,** * whose story is told in *Swords Against the Moon Men* by Christopher Paul Carey.
2076	The main events of *Swords Against the Moon Men.*
January 1, 2100	Birth of **Julian 9th,** * whose story is told in *The Moon Men* by Edgar Rice Burroughs.
2120-2122	The main events of *The Moon Men.*
August 12, 2409	Birth of **Julian 20th,** * whose story is told in *The Red Hawk* by Edgar Rice Burroughs.
2430-2432	The main events of *The Red Hawk.*

* Incarnations of Julian 1st.

THE MISSING JULIAN

I remember well the afternoon of April 10, 1970, not because of any official state business I was engaged in, although there was plenty of it. Only three years prior, the Great War that had raged for over half a century ended suddenly, and all the nations of the world, weary of the relentless bloodshed, rejoiced by throwing their weapons of destruction into the sea and ushering in a new age of peace. My recent appointment as Secretary of Commerce had foisted upon me great responsibility, as nations that had for so long pursued the business of burying their enemies in early graves now must engage in trade with fellow commonwealths that only yesterday had been their most bitter adversaries. Further, the first intelligible communication with Mars—or, as the inhabitants of the Red Planet call their home world, Barsoom—had been established in the very year of the Great War's cessation. The department I now headed had been swiftly charged with sorting out the financial complexities that went along with the incoming flood of scientific knowledge from Mars and its impact on our world's economy. In short, as the head of the Department of Commerce, I suffered a headache of interplanetary proportions on a daily basis.

But none of those weighty matters, world-changing though they might have been, answer for why I recall that particular afternoon above all others during that historic period.

No, it was because *he* visited me once again.

I had just retired to my office in Washington after a tiresome and insipid meeting of some bureaucratic commission with a typically self-important name and an equally ludicrous acronym. Having instructed my secretary to bar the door against visitors, I had nothing so much in mind as to close my eyes, lean back in my chair, and dream myself away to some far-off hinterland of the imagination. Perhaps my slumber would float me back westward over the continent and across the Pacific to my old bungalow at Diamond Head on Oahu, or maybe I would don an ethereal parka and snowshoes and trek across the glazen ice sheets of Antarctica in my dreamscape. Peradventure I would travel across the cold void of space to Barsoom itself and engage in the arts of war forbidden upon my own world and about which, I should perhaps be ashamed to admit, I was beginning to feel no little romantic nostalgia.

I was not even sure I had dozed off when a robin alighted upon a branch of the blossoming cherry tree outside my office window and began chirping all too cheerfully. When I opened my eyes, intending to get up and shut the window, I was astonished to find myself looking upon the sun-bronzed face of the man seated in the chair opposite my desk. I recognized him at once: his chiseled, clean-cut features, blond hair neatly cropped, and uniform decorated with the stars of an admiral of the International Peace Fleet.

"I'm sorry for startling you," the man said. "Your secretary said you once instructed him in no uncertain terms to escort me into your presence immediately if ever I happened to walk into your waiting room. When I saw you sleeping, I insisted that he not wake you. I know how taxing are the demands of your office."

"Ah," I exclaimed, "but now that you are here those demands seem as distant as the Red Planet itself."

My guest smiled strangely, as if my comment had by chance struck upon something already on his mind.

"It is odd," he said, "that only in your presence do I feel drawn to speak freely of my other incarnations. Perhaps there is a reason for it, though about that I can only speculate. Time, as I have told you, does not exist other than in the mind, and neither does space. And if that is so, as I know it is, then maybe you and I are somehow bound up in the ineffable panoply of reality itself."

When I shook my head, unable to comprehend his sentiment, he merely laughed.

"I cannot pretend to understand it myself," he said. "It is enough to know that it is the way of things."

I did not know how to reply, so I ended the silence that followed his strange pronouncement by asking, "What brings you to the capital? Surely you are on official business of the fleet and did not take leave of your duties solely to visit an old paper-pusher like me."

The admiral smiled at my self-assessment, and then rose and stood before the window, looking out upon the tree in which the robin that had so rudely awakened me still perched. He raised his arm and pointed through the branches, causing the bird to take flight. "There," he said in a whisper, as if to himself. "His office lies in that building across the street, precisely as it will stand one hundred and six years from now. Perhaps if I set it afire and burn it down...but no, someone will merely rebuild it and events will proceed as they must."

"Whatever are you talking about?" I asked.

The man ran his fingers through his hair as though to clear his head and a deep sigh escaped him, after which he resumed his usual composure. "You were wrong to suggest I came to the capital for any reason other than to speak with you." He walked slowly across the room and returned to his seat. "The dreams began almost immediately after you and I last met, as we flew over the Yukon coast aboard Captain Drake's cruiser. At first, all I saw was a woman's face, pale as ice and strikingly beautiful." My guest's head titled back and his gaze drew inward, as though he could see the ghostly visage floating before him even now. "Although the face haunted my dreams for weeks, summoning in me a feeling of intense familiarity, I could not for the life of me recollect to whom it belonged nor the circumstances under which I had known the woman. It was as if someone had drawn an impenetrable veil between us. And that, indeed, is the feeling I had—and that someone was very deliberately preventing me from drawing back that veil.

"As it turned out, I was not far from the truth, though it was almost a year before I knew for certain. Week upon week, month upon month, the visage came before me in my slumber, until I could no longer close my eyes for even the briefest moment without seeing it. My nights became sleepless. I feared I suffered from some mental ailment that would only end with my discharge from the International Peace Fleet and my permanent incarceration in an asylum.

"In my rare moments of lucidity, I began researching the symptoms of my condition. Fortunately, it was not long until Fate put before me an account of an unfortunate who had suffered an affliction similar to mine and found a cure. Knowing I had little time left before madness seized me forever in its grip, I took a leave of absence and arranged for transport aboard a flier of the International Peace Fleet that was being dispatched to patrol the Indian subcontinent. After being left off at the foothills of the Himalayas, I set off into the mountains with my Sherpa guide to locate the remote monastery of which I had read, where I hoped to find the one who might help me."

At this point my guest paused, as if gazing into the past. "I have already told you I am not like other people," he continued after a moment's reflection, "in so far as I can recall the events of many incarnations, both past and future, whereas others have only a narrow awareness of their present incarnation." Again I nodded, and he went on. "Do you remember, upon the occasion of our first meeting, when I told you I had no memory of the three generations that passed between my fifth incarnation— who was born in the year 2000 and was on board the first Earth ship to travel to the Moon—and my ninth incarnation—who was born in the year 2100 under the Kalkar occupation of the Earth?"

I nodded, for such an odd statement is not easily forgotten.

"Of course, I would not be able to recall the incarnations of Julian 6th or Julian 8th, for I am reincarnated only every other generation, each time in the body of my grandson. But why did my incarnations skip a generation? Why could I not recall the life of Julian 7th? Those were the questions the old abbot of the Nepalese monastery posed to me one frigid night on the Rooftop of the World.

"Although the monk's questioning did not cure me of my affliction, it served as the catalyst that eventually did so. That very night the abbot initiated me into an ancient meditative technique that has been passed down from one master to another for nearly a thousand years. As I pondered the man's questions, I began practicing the technique, which involved putting myself in a singular kind of trance that allowed me to examine my own consciousness beyond the imaginary boundaries of time and space. After a month of proceeding thus at the monastery, I was able to picture not only the woman's face, but her whole form. Soon thereafter, I awoke one morning with her name upon my lips. It was then that the floodgates of my memory opened and suddenly I knew every particular about my life with the woman just over a century from the make-believe construct we call the present."

By this time, I was on the edge of my seat. My guest must have seen the excitement on my face, for he too leaned forward in his chair, and said, "Should you like to hear the tale of Julian 7th and how he came to meet the fair maiden from my dream visions—a woman from another world?"

I said that I would and, after calling for my secretary to brew us a large pot of coffee, I bade the admiral to continue.

Chapter One

THE JOUST

I never knew my father, who died standing up against our Kalkar oppressors at the age of twenty. That was in the year 2056, only six years after that archfiend Orthis detonated the device that destroyed the airship upon which he and my grandfather stood. Thus ended the war to repel the Kalkar invasion of Earth, and so began the slavery of the human race under the cruel reign of the Moon men.

My mother told me that Father also died at the hands of an Orthis—or Or-tis, as the son of my grandfather's murderer and a Kalkar woman rendered his name. No less a devil was he, whose father betrayed all of humanity by giving to the Kalkars the bitter fruits of invention that grew from his brilliant though utterly corrupt intellect. With a force of a hundred thousand seasoned Kalkar warriors, as well as the deadly electronic rifle he had created, Orthis led his great armada of ships against Earth. Even after my grandfather, Julian 5th, destroyed Orthis' superweapon and the two men died together during that confrontation, the defenseless people of Earth stood helpless against the lunar invaders. The pitifully outnumbered cruisers of the International Peace Fleet fell within days, and Orthis' foul legacy took root in earthly soil as millions of Kalkars were transported to our world each year.

Or-tis was but a single putrid tendril sprouting from the profane seed his father had sown, twisted in his own unique way. Neither quite human nor quite Kalkar, he found little solace on either the Earth or the Moon, though he made his

1

Julian
7th

home upon the former, where he might inflict his vicious brutality upon the abject population of a vanquished planet. My father became the object of his venomous hatred solely because of the feud between their own fathers. But that is another tale. Suffice it to say that Or-tis murdered my father while I was still in the womb, and I was born into a world of slavery, darkness, and hate.

During the impressionable first few years of my life, my mother shielded me as best she could from the savagery of our Kalkar masters. Though we had little that was not taken away from us by the Kash Guard—as our immediate Kalkar overlords called themselves—we had each other, and that was enough. After all, I knew nothing different and, until the age of five, I was surrounded in the warm haze of love cultivated around me by my mother, grandmother, and aunt and uncle.

I still remember my grandmother's face, as pale as moonlight and surrounded by a swath of glossy hair as dark as the night sky—beautiful beyond earthly measure, and yet strained with deep sorrow whenever I would chance to come upon her alone. Always would she brighten when she looked up and noticed me upon such occasions, like the face of the Moon emerging from behind drifting clouds. At the time, I did not know or understand the cause of her sadness, for I had never known my grandfather nor been told the story of his passing.

My first real comprehension that the world outside our home was not a place of love and family—that it was, in fact, a savage world of servitude and oppression—arrived when the Kash Guard came to take my grandmother away. I do not know why they took her, nor did I ever learn her fate at the Kalkars' hands, for my family would not speak of it. All I know is that from that dark night, my life changed forever.

I peeked from out of the back room where my mother had hidden me as the Kash Guard stormed into our home, demanding that the widow of Julian 5th—"that spineless worm crushed beneath the Kalkar heel," as the soldier called my grandfather—come with them. I shall never forget the expression on my grandmother's face. I truly believe it was one of relief, as though some long-awaited dread had finally come and now she would no longer need have worry of it. Of course, I could not then understand why she would feel comforted by the arrival of the Kash Guard, whose presence I knew, even at that age, was something to be avoided if at all possible. Did not my mother put her arm around me and abruptly swerve to take us on an alternate route whenever we encountered the soldiers on the way to the market? And was I not quickly ushered into the house when the Kalkar officers showed up at my family's stables to pick out the horses my uncle broke for them?

I watched from my hiding place as my uncle, his arms crossed defiantly over his chest, got between my grandmother and the Kash Guard, saying that he was the head of the household and would go with them in her stead. The commander of the guard merely laughed and his men swarmed around my uncle, holding him by the arms. While my uncle was thus restrained and helpless, the craven cur of an officer struck him viciously in the face with his baton. I was proud to look on as my uncle casually spat out a tooth along with a mouthful of blood at the feet of his attacker, and then proceeded to smile brazenly in the face of what he must have believed was his own impending death.

Indeed, as I watched in horror from behind the door, the Kalkar raised his truncheon to deal the death blow to my uncle. But then my grandmother rose. Her head held high and proud, she stepped past my uncle and stood directly before the Kalkar commander.

"Wouldn't you rather see him live so that he might suffer?" she said calmly and slowly, as if speaking to a particularly dull-witted child. "He will spend the rest of his life knowing there was nothing he could do to prevent you from taking me. You will have broken his spirit and shown yourself to be superior."

The Kalkar lowered his baton, the expression of hatred on his face twisting into a cruel grin.

"Take the Nonovar to the interrogation chamber so that she might please the whim of the Twenty-Four," he said, and then he thrust the hard end of his club into my uncle's solar plexus. My uncle fell to the floor gasping as my mother and aunt wept, watching as my grandmother, her countenance regal and proud, strode out the front door surrounded by the Kash Guard. None of us ever saw her again.

The next morning my uncle, his face bruised and swollen, awoke me before dawn and took me out behind our house. He handed me a long, heavy piece of hammered iron and, taking a similar rod in his own hands, proceeded to teach me the art of fencing. It was, however, not the type of fencing that I later read about in a forbidden history book, where one fought for sport and tagged his opponent with the blunt end of a flimsy foil. No, it was my first lesson in how to kill a man as quickly, efficiently, and mercilessly as possible, without regard for the polite conventions of ceremonious swordplay.

From that day, when I was five years old and could barely hold up the length of iron, through early manhood, I trained relentlessly with my uncle, until my muscles hardened to steel along with my determination that I would one day avenge my grandmother. I swore to turn my skill with a blade against the members of the Kash Guard who had ripped her, along with my innocence and happiness, forever from my life.

For whatever reason, the Kalkar commander did not return to take away anyone else from my family. Perhaps he took my grandmother's words to heart, failing to understand that she had played upon his vile and coarse nature, heroically sacrificing herself so that my uncle might be spared a death sentence. However cruel and powerful the Kalkars might be, they are not a bright lot.

That did not mean the Kash Guard did not molest our household over the years as I grew up under their shadow. The males of my lineage had been cavalrymen since the early days of the founding of the old republic. Although the technological advancements of the passing centuries eventually made mounts obsolete in modern warfare, my family never lost touch with the tradition and continued to be proud and skilled equestrians. Thus, when the Kalkars invaded our world and we were denied the military service that ran in our blood, we turned to the only option we had left: breaking horses for our masters.

The Kalkars, though they used the sentient quadrupeds from the Moon as scouts, shock troops, and even mere beasts of burden, were not practiced animal handlers. Even had the Kalkars learned how to employ them as mounts, Va-gas, as the quadrupeds were named, were in short supply in the United Teivos of America, having been found to acclimate better in more tropical climes. Accordingly, the Kalkars found themselves reliant on the equestrians of Earth, such as those who propagated among my family line. This, of course, put us in the crosshairs of the Kash Guard on many occasions.

My uncle and I showed our contempt for the despots who ruled over us in a host of different ways. We did this despite knowing full well that if we pushed our minor acts of resistance too far we would be sent to a detention camp. There we would await a sham trial and be sentenced to toil for the rest of our brief and miserable lives in the mines.

Our favorite indulgence was to train a horse to perform with perfect obedience for its rider with the exception of a single trick, which was carefully concealed by the expected infrequency of the trigger. For example, several months might pass, possibly even a year, before the rider chanced to speak a certain uncommon but nonetheless inevitable verbal command to the horse, or prompted it in a unique way with the reins that was not expected to come up during the Kalkar's equestrian training. Then the mount would unexpectedly buck its Kalkar rider to the ground, after which it would stand tamely beside the fallen soldier and wait dutifully to be mounted once again.

Occasionally, word would come back to my uncle and me of the results of our mischief. In one instance, Fate shone upon us and we were lucky enough to witness the outcome of one of our little pranks in person when we encountered the rider and the horse we had trained at the market in town. How the Kalkar raged to find himself suddenly deposited headfirst in the market's sewage ditch! My uncle and I could not get quickly enough back home, where we drew the curtains and proceeded to roll on the floor in our unrestrained mirth. My mother and aunt looked at us as if we were both stark raving mad. But as joy was such a scarcity in our lives, they too were soon smiling and laughing with us, happy for any respite at all, however brief or ludicrous, in our wretched existence under the Kalkars.

Had the women but known of the reckless game we played with our lives, they would have doubtless scolded us severely, for the loss of my grandmother had wounded them deeply. Each day they prayed upon awakening, before meals, and at bedtime—and I am sure many times silently in between—for our safety. But my uncle and I were proud men, and if we could not resist our masters somehow, even with such small acts of rebellion, then there was no use in continuing our existence.

For all the risks we took to antagonize our Kalkar overlords, they needed my family for our equestrian skills. Since the end of the war against the lunar invaders, no new trains had been built and the railroads were already falling into disrepair. Furthermore, the grand airships of yesteryear no longer soared through the skies of our world, the power plants that fueled their engines from a distance having shut down in this new age of Kalkar despondency. Thus, not only was contact with other continents coming to an end, but travel throughout the North American continent as well. Only rarely did we hear news from other regions of the country, and even gossip from nearby towns came only at the speed of horse travel. Soon the horse became a precious commodity in the Kalkar collective, and so we Julians, practically raised in the saddle from birth, became invaluable as well.

And so it was that one day, when I was nineteen years old, I was in the stable at our little ranch on the edge of the ruins of old Chicago when young Henry, one of our hands, came running in to let me know a Kalkar was in need of my services.

"He says he's from the capital," the boy told me, "and from the ribbons on his uniform and the way he swaggers, I think he's important."

"All Kalkars think they're important, Henry," I replied, but I abruptly abandoned my stable duties and went outside. Though the Kalkars themselves are slow going by nature, they expected us to attend to them at a moment's notice. Anything less and they would dole out any number of punishments, whether it was increasing our taxes or taking our horses outright.

Henry was right about our visitor's deportment. When I emerged from the stables, the man gazed down from his mount and met me with a sneer. He did not carry himself with the typical slouch of a Kalkar and his eyes were bright and intelligent, if unequivocally arrogant and cruel. This man, with his tidy dark hair trimmed short and his uniform fitted and clean, was no slovenly Kash Guard.

Just behind the Kalkar on a small but stout pony sat a black-haired Earth man of Eurasian extraction. He wore a plain tunic and trousers, though these were also clean and well-tailored. His pony drew a small cart, on which I could not fail to notice a long wooden lance and a pile of what looked like plate mail. I had never before seen the latter, though my uncle had told me about how our ancestors had once worn it into battle.

"Good morning, Commander," I said to the Kalkar, biting back my hatred. "What may I do for you?"

"I'm told your name is Julian." The commander's words and belittling tone left me cold, as did the fact that he knew my name.

"That's right," I said.

"Good." The man's voice crooned in a way that sent chills up my spine. "The seventh by that name, no? Are you aware that my family has a history with yours? But then, I can see from the fire burning in your eyes that you already suspect who I am."

When I replied with nothing but a yawn, the man's haughty smile evaporated and a scarlet hue slowly crept over his face. He called for the man accompanying him, whose name was Baatar, to draw his mount forward and come alongside his own.

It was then I noticed Henry had come out of the stable and was standing directly behind me. By the Flag, the boy's arms were crossed over his chest in proud defiance of the Kalkar officer! Should the man decide to cut me down with his sword, I knew that Henry, though only a boy of twelve, meant to go down fighting at my side. But that, of course, I would not allow. If we were ever to escape the Kalkar yoke, we would need the courageous souls of future generations to lead the fight. I nodded at Henry to go back inside the house, but he only shook his head as the Kalkar and the black-haired man dismounted.

"I'm told you train the local Kash Guard in mounted combat," the Kalkar said to me. "Is that correct?"

I nodded, and the man stared down his nose at me as if measuring my worth. A cruel little smile slowly formed on his lips, and he ordered his retainer to attend to him.

Baatar removed a cuirass fringed with steel faulds from the cart and began helping his master into the corselet. After the Kalkar had donned his armor, he pulled himself back up into the saddle and Baatar passed up a visored helmet and the lance. The officer took the latter in hand, raised it vertically with an efficiency that bespoke of much practice with the weapon, and motioned for his servant to withdraw.

"Suit up and mount your steed, man," the Kalkar commanded me. "An Or-tis would like to keep his skill with the lance sharp and get in a little practice jousting—and who better to test my skills against than a Julian?"

Henry looked at me expectantly, pride more than fear showing on his youthful face, for he knew of the secret lessons in the arts of war given to me by my uncle—a schooling that had imparted to me an array of deadly skills I had purposefully withheld from the Kalkars I was forced to train. I told Henry to bring me my favorite stallion and my leathers, and he scurried off while the officer sat grim and terrible upon his mount.

The boy arrived swiftly with our finest steed, my old battered suit of brigandine draped over the saddle. I pulled down the pitiful excuse for armor—little more than a padded goatskin tunic and skirt of worn leather—and donned it. Within moments I was on horseback and Henry was passing up to me my tarnished old helmet and a splintered and scarred training lance.

As we rode out to the pasture behind the stable, my uncle emerged from the house. I could see him telling my mother and aunt, their faces strained with worry, to remain inside. Then he followed us out to the pasture and leaned against the wooden fence, for all appearances indifferent as he chewed coolly on a long stem of grass and looked out at us over the field. Though I knew he must be worried sick about me, I knew too that he was proud of both my horsemanship and my martial prowess. Besides, he didn't want to lose face in front of a Kalkar.

I ordered Henry to go stand beside my uncle, and then I rode out to the west end of the pasture while Or-tis—for that, I learned soon enough, was indeed his name—positioned himself to the east. I raised my own wooden lance high, testing its weight and eyeing with no little trepidation a little crack running against the grain from above the vamplate to about halfway down the weapon's length.

Or-tis motioned for me to ride out and meet him in the middle. When we were close, he lifted his visor and said, "When Baatar drops his hand, we shall each charge and try to knock the other off his mount. Don't fear, Julian, I don't plan to kill you." Then he smirked and added, "Although accidents are known to happen, even to the most careful." He snapped shut his visor and rode back to the other end of the field, while I returned to my end and turned my steed about to face him.

Or·tis

I whispered reassuring words to my mount and, gripping my legs tightly around his flanks, leaned forward and lowered my lance. I watched Or-tis do the same on his horse, his polished armor and lacquered lance gleaming beneath the noonday sun.

Baatar withdrew from the center of the field, raised his hand, and then dropped it low with a shout. The trodden ground rumbled with the sound of hoofbeats and Or-tis and I barreled toward one another on our charging mounts.

The world became a blur of green and blue but I kept my eye on that shining cuirass, which grew ever larger in my field of vision. With the experience of many a joust drilled into my bones, I dropped the reins just before impact to avoid choking and rearing my horse. With a terrible cracking sound, the tip of my lance hit home just beneath my opponent's breastplate. Wood splintered with violence, and I heard Or-tis cry out at the blow.

I seized back the reins and drew my mount to a halt on the opposite side of the field, frowning at the sight of both my broken lance and Or-tis, still in the saddle and bearing firmly his own undamaged weapon, wheeling about to face me.

Had this been an ordinary training joust, I might have called upon Henry to bring me a new lance. Even so, those that we had were in worse shape than the lance with which I had begun, the Kalkars never trusting my uncle or me with a for-midable weapon that we might use against them. But I knew this was no simple exercise, and already Baatar was raising his hand for the second round.

Behind Or-tis' servant I spied my uncle. No longer did he lean casually against the fence, his eyes now wide and hands balled into fists. Only for a second did I take in this sight, for now Baatar's hand was falling and I was once again charging toward the devil in whose veins flowed the blood of my grand-father's murderer.

I had but one fleeting chance of defeating my opponent and I took it. I had noticed how Or-tis, just before we met on the field, had raised the tip of his lance in the attempt to strike me in the faceplate of my helm. Doubtless he hoped he might break my neck in the process of knocking me from my horse. But when my lance struck him squarely in the breastplate, his own weapon had swung out over my shoulder and missed its mark. I suspected he would try this tactic again, especially given my shattered lance, which had lost half its length.

Again hoofbeats roared in my ears and I leaned forward on my mount, my pitiful weapon held straight out in front of me. Just before Or-tis and I met, I swung up the shortened beam of my lance, knocking aside his own lance, while in one fluid motion I swung round the butt of my weapon and smashed it into his helm's faceplate with my full weight behind the blow. When I turned about at the end of the field it was to see Or-tis lying facedown on the turf.

At first I thought I had killed the man, so still did he lie. Baatar ran out across the field and stood over his master, and something he held in his hand shone in the light of the midday sun. Now the servant crouched over the prone man, the sliver of glistening metal descending at an angle as if its holder meant to thrust it beneath his master's helmet at the nape of the neck.

Suddenly the arms of the fallen man quivered with what was clearly the spark of life, and whatever the shining thing was in Baatar's hand disappeared into a trouser pocket. Or-tis, with some difficulty, removed his helmet while his servant helped him back to his feet.

"Get my horse!" Or-tis shouted at Baatar as I dismounted at their side. The black-haired man ran off and some yards distant met my uncle, who had just recovered the reins of Or-tis' steed and was slowly walking the beast back to the center of the field.

Or-tis' eyes burned into my own and his gauntleted fist clenched as if he meant to strike me. Still gripping my broken lance, I stood up to my full height of six feet and two inches,

With a terrible cracking sound, the tip of my lace hit home...

my posture making it unmistakably clear I would knock him back down upon the turf if he so much as raised a finger.

"Such tactics are illegal in any fair joust!" he screamed at me, his face flushed with crimson. "You will suffer for it, as will your family! There is always some infraction that can be rooted out to send non-Kalkars to the prison camps!"

I grinned in the face of his threat and asked in a calm tone, "Do you not carry the blood of Orthis in your veins, and thus are you not part Earth man? By your own logic, one might wonder if that means you are also hiding something that might land you in the camps."

Or-tis stared at me for a long moment, trembling with rage. Then, as with any bully who has been called on his bluff, his blustering hostility collapsed from the blow to his bruised ego and he strode from the field. Baatar departed close at his master's heels, but not before he shot me a grin that made clear the antipathy he held for his master.

My uncle came to my side and we shared grim smiles, for we each knew this business with Or-tis was a long way from being over. But just where it would lead, neither of us dared even guess.

Chapter Two

A STRANGE TRANSMISSION

That night my family and I sat around the dinner table and ate in silence. With great pride, my uncle described how I had handled myself against the Kalkar officer, but my mother and aunt cared little for any portrayals of my supposed heroism. Instead, they responded only with heartfelt exclamations of relief that I had survived the encounter. After this, they grew quiet, and it was clear they feared what would soon come as a result of the joust. I could not blame them. We all felt the shadow of Or-tis looming over us and knew with certainty that it was only a matter of time before his wrath would fall upon our household.

After supper we drew the shades and gathered in the living room. By the light of a single candle, my uncle withdrew a stone from above the mantel and removed from the exposed niche a little triangle-shaped bundle of cloth. He carried this with reverence to the wooden table on which the candle rested and set it down upon the surface. Carefully, he unfolded the fabric and we gazed in solemn respect upon the tattered red-and-white-striped rectangle with its square of navy blue in one corner speckled with a field of stars.

It was Old Glory, the flag of my forefathers, carried by the regiment of Julian 1st, my ancestor, in a battle known as the Argonne in some land across the sea about which I know nothing. My family had guarded it for a century and a half, and one day I intended to give it to my son, should I live long enough to have one. It represented everything good that the Kalkars had taken from us, and I would gladly die to preserve it, as would any member of my family.

After renewing our spirits by gazing long upon this ancient symbol of freedom and duty, my uncle wrapped up the Flag and returned the little triangle of cloth safely to its niche. Our ritual complete, we all said good night to one another and agreed we would face with a smile whatever Fate brought us in the morning, no matter how evil or ill-starred.

The others had just gone upstairs to bed when I heard a quiet though unmistakable rapping at the window. I pulled up the shade to see the dark eyes of Baatar, Or-tis' servant, staring up at me in the night. Dread seized me instantly, for I had no doubt the Kalkar officer had returned to our farmstead to inflict upon my family whatever punishment his demented mind had cooked up in the intervening time since I had shamed him earlier that day. But if that were the case, why had Or-tis not simply broken down our front door and stormed into our house with a squad of Kash Guards? Furthermore, the dim candlelight cast through the window revealed Baatar's expression to be one of furtive caution, nor could I mistake the fear that streaked his broad face. All the same, I grabbed a rolling pin from a kitchen drawer while on my way to meet him at the door, should my assessment of the situation prove to be misguided and I have need for a defensive weapon, however crude its form.

The man entered the house swiftly, as if fearful of being discovered outside. I ushered him to the living room, where we sat at the table on hard wooden chairs, which together made up the room's meager furniture. The shades still remained drawn and the single candle burned in its holder on the bare tabletop, illuminating the face of my unexpected visitor. He was a handsome man, with intelligent, lively eyes set above high cheekbones. His English was excellent, though his accent revealed it to be a second language for him. I ordered him to explain the reason for his visit, and he lost no time in complying.

"My name is Baatar Tarkutai. Briefly, I must tell you something about myself, for only by understanding my personal history will you understand how I came to be here and the reason for my late-night visit.

"I was raised outside of the city of Darkhan on the Mongolian steppe," he went on at my encouragement. "At the age of fifteen, I was considered the best rider from my Teivos, having won all of the regional competitions. That was to be my misfortune, for soon the local commandant took notice of me and brought me to the capital. When he was transferred to London shortly thereafter, he brought me with him. I was there for two years, serving as the commandant's personal riding instructor, before a more important officer noticed me. This was Or-tis, my present master, who took me with him on one of the last transoceanic liners to take flight across the Atlantic Ocean. Or-tis, though he carried the blood of Earth people as well as that of the Kalkars in his veins, held a uniquely vital post in Washington. Or-tis oversaw the Kalkar intelligence service for the entire Western Hemisphere.

"Though I was at first merely Or-tis' riding instructor, soon my new master came to rely upon me for a variety of duties. I considered myself fortunate, for the Kalkar officers were mostly dumb brutes, more prone to lash out at those of more intelligence than to benefit from their counsel. Not so with Or-tis, whose mind was as keen as that of his treacherous forefather, Orthis, who had traded humankind's future in return for personal power and the satisfaction of his vengeance. And so it happened that I was often at Or-tis' side during his important dealings with those at the top of the Kalkar hierarchy, including meetings with powerful agents of the Jemadar in the intelligence service and even members of the Twenty-Four. That is how I first learned of the transmission from Barsoom."

"Barsoom!" I exclaimed, half rising from my seat. Of course, I knew that Earth had been in contact with the inhabitants of Mars in the years directly preceding the Kalkar invasion of our planet. In fact, it was my own grandfather, Julian 5th, who had commanded the space vessel that was to transport the first people of Earth to the Red Planet. But my grandfather's nemesis,

Orthis, had sabotaged that ship and caused its ill-fated landing in the interior of the Moon, after which he had allied with the Kalkars and personally led the invasion of Earth. Following the war, Earth had lost contact with Mars, leaving it but a distant, dreamlike myth in the collective memory of humankind. Thus, one may understand my astonishment at my visitor's pronounce-ment that Barsoom was again in contact with Earth after all these years.

"And what," I asked, "do the Barsoomians want of our Kalkar overlords?" I was well aware of the Martians' warlike nature, and a dozen of the darkest scenarios I could imagine suddenly rose up in a clamor within me.

"Ah, but the transmission was not intended for the Kalkars," my guest replied, a fleeting smile momentarily eclipsing the worry on his face. "No, the message was meant for you, Julian 7th."

I stared blankly at the man sitting before me, not compre-hending his words.

"More correctly," he continued, "I should say they wished to make contact with the lineage of Julian 5th, the great enemy of the Kalkars. But they are indeed aware of you personally, for their telescopes function far beyond the abilities of any possessed by either the people of Earth or the Kalkars who have come to occupy our world. Through their powerful lenses, the Barsoom-ians watched in horror as, twenty-five years ago, the great Kalkar armada launched itself from the Moon and swept down out of the skies of Earth to shatter our terrestrial civilization. Indeed, they have observed our world for generations, and even looked down upon this very farm."

I rose from the table and paced the room in silence for almost a minute, my mind racing with the implications of Baatar's strange tale. Was his story a deception? Or was it instead simply a fancy of his deranged mind? Life under the Kalkars, however, imparts one with a sensitivity to dishonesty, and the man before me betrayed no signs that he was speaking anything but the truth. Still, the man was Or-tis' servant and I knew I would be foolhardy to trust him without proof of his story's veracity.

"What you're saying is that my encounter with Or-tis this afternoon was no coincidence," I offered as I sat back down. "He came here to my family's farm because of the message, and now my family and I are in much danger."

Baatar nodded. "Or so I can only surmise, for I know little of the message's contents. I have only overheard my master discussing the transmission with a member of the Kalkar intelligence service. He spoke gravely the name of Julian, and of the Barsoomians' seemingly desperate desire to contact a living member of your lineage. That was all I overheard before I was discovered. I made hasty excuses for my presence and departed immediately, giving them the impression I was embarrassed at having been caught snoozing in the adjoining room. Brother High Commander Or-tis scolded me, but over the years I have given him no reason to suspect I am anything but his obedient servant, and therefore he dismissed me from their presence without punishment. That very night he informed me we would be leaving for the Teivos of Chicago in the morning.

"That was two weeks ago. The train broke down twice on our journey from Washington, which caused my master no little amount of frustration, for it was clear his mission in Chicago was of the utmost urgency. It is telling that our first stop in the Teivos was here at your farm this past afternoon. I can assure you, the Brother High Commander is here to root out any information you might have concerning the Martian transmission."

"But what could the Barsoomians want of me?" I wondered aloud. "I am but a common hand on a horse farm, with no power or prestige even among my fellow Earthlings."

Baatar had become more animated as he spoke, but now his shoulders slumped and he continued in a dejected tone. "I had hoped there was some truth to what I believe are my master's worst fears—that the Barsoomians conspire with you to lead a terrestrial resistance against the Kalkars. For only that can explain the urgency of his mission here."

"There is no resistance," I said. "I am but a slave."

Baatar shook his head wearily. "Then all is lost."

Together we sat in grim silence, devoid of any hope for the future of the human race. What could I, a mere farm hand, hope to accomplish against the invaders who had oppressed my entire species? Year after year, the Kalkars had come to our world by the millions and spread their tyranny across the globe. Nowhere upon the face of the planet was humankind free, nor did it ever seem likely that we would ever overthrow our cruel rulers in the face of their overwhelming dominion.

At last I roused myself from the funk that had settled over me and pushed myself up from the table. "I am tired of leaving my fate, and that of our whole world, in the hands of the brutal despots who rule over us! I would rather face certain death in the attempt to gain freedom for the people of Earth—even if that freedom will not be achieved in our lifetimes—than to continue on as a slave. If you risked your life to tell me of this secret transmission, then you must believe there is some way for us to reply to the Barsoomians' message. Tell me, man! Do you know the means by which we might accomplish the deed?"

As I made my impassioned speech, Baatar sat up straight and a gleam of hope flashed in his dark eyes.

"There is a way," he said, "but only if we are willing to move swiftly. We must leave tonight, for I fear that should we delay, Or-tis will move against you in the morning."

I rose to go upstairs and inform my uncle of my departure, but my guest protested.

"We must go now, and tell no one," he said. "Trust me. It will go better for them if they know nothing of our actions—for tonight we enter the hornets' nest and commit high treason against the Twenty-Four."

Chapter Three

AN UNEARTHLY PLEA

The ruins of a bygone era of glory sped past us as Baatar and I raced on our mounts toward the heart of Teivos. We made our way through treacherous passes, navigating the shattered remnants of once-soaring towers and crumbling heaps of grand edifices that littered the path before us. I led the way, and having dwelled in the Teivos of Chicago for my entire life, I was therefore able to avoid the neighborhoods and trails where we would most likely encounter Kash Guard patrols and sentinels.

After a handful of incidents in which, either through our own agility or good fortune, we narrowly escaped notice by Kalkar soldiers, we at last arrived at our destination. The building before us—though flanked by statues of majestic lions and adorned with stately pillars rising from its wide entranceway—had fallen into disrepair at the hands of the Kalkars. The moonlight revealed cracks in the stonework, and one pillar leaned precipitously, causing a portion of the architrave above it to collapse. Notwithstanding the dilapidated condition of the headquarters, I have long heard tales of the Kalkar leadership's decadence, all of which has been hearsay, of course, as we common folk know little of the secretive leaders of the Moon men. Even so, I was curious to discover whether there was any truth to such rumors, for the Kalkars proclaimed the accumulation of wealth to be anathema to their collectivist worldview.

Having come this far, I had no idea how we might hope to penetrate the building's defenses, for armed guards stood at

...Baatar and I raced on our mounts toward the heart of the Kalkar dominion.

every opening. These were no ordinary members of the Kash Guard, but rather those specially bred for size and strength, as were the hellhounds the soldiers held at bay. The dogs were ravenous specimens, trained by their lunar masters to hunt those of earthly blood. Occasionally, one of the canines would escape the Kalkars and run loose, terrorizing the neighborhoods of the Teivos. Though we complained to our masters about the stray hellhounds, they would do nothing. Our only recourse was to lock ourselves in our houses at night and in the daytime send out small groups of men armed with whatever feeble weapons we might improvise to track down the dog, such as wooden planks or, if we could salvage them from the ruins of the ancients, lengths of scrap metal. Then we would risk life and limb to kill the beast, for we knew that should we let it live, it would only one day go on to breed with other escaped specimens and form roving packs of hellhounds against which we would have no defense.

Baatar dismissed my worries with a wave of his hand and rode out boldly into the open. I had no choice but to follow Baatar into this den of fiends or to abandon our mission and return home to almost certain death at the hands of Or-tis. I did not hesitate, and prodded my steed forward across the broad plaza until I was dismounting beside Baatar and tying my horse to the post directly outside the capitol building.

As we proceeded thus, a group of soldiers marched out to meet us. Baatar was ready for them when they arrived, holding forth an oval medallion that gleamed with a silvery sheen in the moonlight. One of the soldiers took the emblem in hand and examined it closely, his brow beetling as if he were having a difficult time reading the inscription engraved on its face. Of course, I doubted the guard could read, as even fewer Kalkars could do so than my own people, some of whom could still recall the days before our ignorant conquerors set fire to the libraries. All the same, the soldier finally nodded his great head of shaggy yellow hair, although I am sure his response was simply due to recognizing the portrait of the Jemadar, the

Kalkars' supreme leader, impressed upon the medallion and not a testament to his literacy.

Satisfied with my companion's credentials, which doubtless Or-tis had provided to Baatar for the convenience of executing duties on his behalf, the Kash Guard escorted us inside the building. Here the squad's captain interrogated Baatar, who explained I was a worker he had conscripted from among the locals to help prepare the field office of Brother High Commander Or-tis prior to his arrival the next morning. The captain of the guard appeared well aware of Or-tis' visit, for he accepted Baatar's explanation without question and ordered one of his guards to lead us to the room.

We passed down several spacious though lackluster corridors before arriving at the office, which the guard unlocked and opened. Baatar flipped a switch on the wall and a lamp fixture overhead bathed the room in a stark white glow. This amazed me, for I had never before seen electric lighting, this being my first indication that the rumors of the Kalkar leaders' decadence were not exaggerations. After taking a seat in one of the chairs situated before a large desk, Baatar ordered me to pick up a broom that leaned in a corner and begin sweeping the floor. Then he sank down in the chair, yawned deeply, and closed his eyes. The guard glowered as I picked up the broom and began my chores, but he promptly departed without a word.

Baatar waited a full minute before rising and locking the door, the frosted glass pane of which prevented anyone outside the room from looking in and observing our actions. Next he went to a table against the far wall upon which rested a strange contraption of tubes, wires, and antennae. Attached to the device and sitting on the table before it was what I guessed to be a microphone, having read about such technological marvels in the yellowed and spotted pages of old forbidden books.

Baatar sat down on a chair before the table and flipped a series of switches, causing the device to spark to life, popping, hissing, and whining with such a racket that I feared it would draw the attention of the soldiers outside. Within moments,

however, Baatar succeeded in soothing the contraption's pro-
testations by turning a number of dials and flipping more
switches. Now he concentrated on adjusting one dial in particular, his head cocked as the oscillations of a low hum droned
in our ears. A peculiar burning smell unlike anything I had
previously encountered arose, but this I soon gathered was a
natural consequence of the warming of the glass tubes.

A chill went up my spine when I heard beneath the hum
the faint sound of a woman's voice arising from a small wooden
box positioned behind the microphone. I swiftly rolled the chair
from behind the desk over to the table on which rested the
transmitter-receiver and leaned in close to the device while
Baatar, sitting beside me, tuned in the signal.

The contrivance could only be a Gridley Wave apparatus,
named after the man who my uncle told me had invented the
device sometime around the year 1928. For some undisclosed
reason, Jason Gridley had kept his invention secret from the
world until 1945, when he shared a primitive version of the
apparatus with government scientists, thus allowing them to
send rudimentary signals to Mars in response to a series of
incomprehensible transmissions they had received from the
Red Planet. Years later, in 1967, an advanced version of the
apparatus was either supplied by Gridley or developed by the
scientists themselves—my uncle was not sure—at last permitting intelligible communications between Earth and Mars.

The woman's voice grew stronger as the hum receded until
finally it became so clear and distinct that, had we closed our
eyes, the speaker might have seemed to be in the very room
with us. My heart beat faster, hearing that melodious voice
uttering syllables that combined in strange, unearthly ways,
until I could contain myself no more.

"By the glory of the Flag!" I exclaimed. "How do I reply to
the woman?"

My companion moved his chair aside and motioned me to
slide in before the device, which I did with all haste. Baatar

The woman's voice grew stronger as the hum receded...

tapped a button on the microphone's pedestal. "Hold this down and speak to transmit," he said, "and release it to allow the Barsoomian to reply."

I waited for a pause from the speaker and then pressed the button. "This is Julian 7th, of Earth," I said in English into the transmitter. "Can you understand me?"

A period of silence followed my question during which I wondered if the woman was fluent in my tongue. If she was not, I would attempt to communicate with her in the singsong language of the U-ga of Va-nah. I had first begun to learn the speech of the human inhabitants of the Moon's interior as a young boy at my grandmother's feet, and later became fluent in the language after many lessons from my mother. If the woman on the other end of the apparatus spoke neither language, our conversation was fated to be brief, for I had never had the opportunity to learn the common tongue of Barsoom.

I imagined the woman must be stunned to finally receive a reply after weeks of fruitless attempts to make contact with Earth. I held my breath awaiting her reply, and I admit that I started when at last it came.

"I understand you perfectly, Julian 7th of Earth." Excitement filled the woman's voice, which was well-modulated and accented in odd ways that had never before fallen upon my terrestrial ears. "I am speaking to you from the fourth planet from the sun, which we call Barsoom and in your speech is known as Mars. I understand your situation better than you can imagine, having observed you from afar, so let us not speak of things that would waste precious time. I beg of your assistance in matters of great importance. Will you listen to my story, O heritor of the bloodline of Julian 5th, bane of the dread Kalkars of Va-nah?"

"I am more than eager to hear it," I replied, pressing the button on the transmitter. "Please, go on!"

"Very well, Julian 7th," came the voice from the box. "My tale, in brief, is as follows. Just over two earthly years ago, my people received a transmission from the satellite orbiting your world of Jasoom. The signal traveled to Barsoom from a crater leading to the heart of that moon. Within a year, our scientists were able to decipher the language of the U-ga, as the people living within the satellite called themselves. The one who made contact with us was named Tu-lav, the Jemadar—Jeddak, in my tongue, or King in yours—of the city of Vathayne. Tu-lav explained to us that Vathayne was one of many U-ga cities that had remained hidden when the Earth man Orthis led the Kalkar armies against Laythe, the last remaining U-ga stronghold known to the Twenty-Four. When Laythe fell, Vathayne and the other surviving U-ga cities bided their time in seclusion deep within the craters where they hid, knowing they were no match for Orthis and his disintegration ray. However, when your ancestor destroyed the gun that unleashed that devastating ray and the Kalkars proceeded to turn their focus on the verdant world of Jasoom, Vathayne and the other U-ga cities saw their opening.

"Once the vast majority of Kalkars had left Va-nah for Jasoom, Tu-lav and his allies struck from out of the shadows. Though the guerrilla forces of the U-ga took a heavy toll on their enemy over the next two decades, the Kalkar forces yet outnumbered them. And so it was that Tu-lav sent a transmission to Barsoom, seeking help from my people and warning that the Kalkar menace was poised to spread to the other inhabited worlds of the solar system. Knowing that Barsoom, having once been in contact with your own world and thus known to be populated, would likely be the Kalkars' next target, my city of Helium dispatched its greatest statesman to Va-nah within Jasoom's moon to open diplomatic relations between our nation and Vathayne. Already had my world repelled the unexpected menace of the Morgors from Sasoom, the fifth planet from the sun, and this time we wanted to be prepared in advance."

If I had been excited before, now I was practically mad with anticipation. Could it be possible that after the quarter century of Kalkar oppression, humanity had at last a powerful ally that might aid it in overthrowing its brutal masters? It was too much to hope, and yet why would the Martian woman single out the bloodline of Julian 5th, the Kalkars' greatest nemesis, if not to propose an alliance to defeat our lunar overlords?

"Several *teeans* passed," the woman continued, "a *teean* being roughly equivalent to a Jasoomian month, while we waited anxiously for the interplanetary vessel we had dispatched to deliver the Heliumetic envoy across the void of space to Jasoom's moon. At last came the message that the ship had arrived and descended into the crater that was home to the hidden city of Vathayne. The crew related how they had made contact with Tu-lav's people and expected to land in the city within the *zode*, or Barsoomian hour. That was the last transmission we received from the vessel. Now three more *teeans* have passed with no further word, and I am desperate to learn the fate of the ambassadorial mission."

I clicked on the microphone and said, "I am pleased and excited to hear of your world's efforts to form an alliance with the U-ga against the Kalkars, and more than crestfallen that the Barsoomian envoy has gone missing. But how in the name of three worlds could I possibly help your cause? I am but a simple farmer and breaker of horses. Though my grandfather, Julian 5th, fought valiantly against Orthis and his Kalkar legions, I have been little more than a slave my entire life, and so has it been for all of earthly humanity for the last quarter century under the cruel reign of the Kalkars."

"Have faith," came the reply from another world. "You are more resilient than you know. Have you not outwitted your enemy and made your way stealthily into his very seat of power unobserved?"

"How do you know that?" I asked. A little shiver ran down my spine as I imagined a goddess looking down upon me from the heavens and observing my every action.

"How else could you communicate with me than by using one of the enemy's interplanetary transmitters? My scientists do not need to triangulate your signal for me to know you are transmitting from the Kalkars' headquarters in the Teivos of Chicago. Only three transmitters are known to exist: two on your continent and another in the city you call London. You would, of course, use the communications facility nearest to you."

"But you must have known the Kalkars would intercept your message. Why take that risk?"

"As I said, I am desperate." I could hear the woman sigh over the faint static of the receiver. "I confess, my trepidation does not wholly revolve around the success or failure of the mission to Va-nah, though the outcome could very well mean life or death for the people of my world. No, I am personally invested in the well-being of the members of the expedition, and of one in particular.

"Already have my engineers begun construction of a new vessel capable of traveling to Jasoom's moon. But it will take five *teeans* to complete the ship, and once the vessel is launched, several more *teeans* are required to cross the chasm between worlds. By then, it very well may be too late for the brave members of the diplomatic mission. And for that reason, I implore you—no, I beg of you—to find a way to steal yourself aboard a Kalkar vessel traveling to Va-nah and discover the fate of the mission...and of he who is worth more to me than even life itself, he who is named—"

I did not hear the woman's final words, for at that moment the door to the office slammed open with a crash and in rushed two burly Kalkar soldiers wielding heavy truncheons. At their heels followed Brother High Commander Or-tis, a grin of triumph on his face.

Chapter Four

A TRAP!

O r-tis returned to the open doorway, stuck his head outside, and looked down the hallway in both directions. Satisfied that no one had noticed the disturbance caused by the entry of him and his men, he quietly closed the door.

Meanwhile, the Kalkar thugs came at us. Baatar and I scrambled out of the way, retreating to the back of the room. The Kalkars grinned malevolently, slapping their clubs against meaty palms in an effort to intimidate us. I grinned back at them, determined to meet my death in proud defiance, as my uncle had intended to do himself when the Kash Guard came to take away my grandmother some fourteen years ago. Baatar, though not smiling, showed no more fear of our executioners than I, and for that I was glad. Though we faced certain death, our spirits could not be broken. If the memory of our brave defeat was all the legacy we left behind, so be it. It was enough for me.

"Wait, wait!" Or-tis motioned for the Kash Guard brutes to stand down. "Don't harm them. At least not before I have obtained the information I seek."

He walked past the guards to the communications apparatus and pressed the button on the transmitter, speaking into it in an attempt to converse with the woman from another world. The hiss of static met him. Either the woman had broken the signal or waited on the other end listening silently. In the end it did not matter, for Or-tis switched off the device and the receiver speaker popped sharply and then grew silent.

"I heard a woman's voice before we entered the room," he said. "The technologists of the Twenty-Four inform me that the signal came from the direction of Mars. To whom were you speaking and what did you plot? Perhaps if you cooperate, Julian, I can arrange that your family won't end up toiling in the mines."

A grim smile crept over my face but I did not reward his threat with any other reply. Inside, however, I was sick with worry for my mother and uncle. If only I could get word to them, warn them before the Kash Guard came to take them away.

"Very well." Or-tis turned from me and wagged a finger under Baatar's nose. "And you, my longtime companion. You surprise me. All these long years you have feigned absolute loyalty to your master while you hid your resentment. All along you were nothing but a viper, coiled in the tall grass of deception waiting to strike me down. I almost admire your cunning. Should I not already know the vile nature of your ancestry, I might suspect Kalkar blood ran in your veins."

Baatar stood tall and did not quaver. "The spirits of my ancestors whisper to me even now," he said. "Nothing, they tell me, makes them prouder than to know that I face my death trying to free the world of the Kalkar taint!"

And with that he whipped out a small pistol from beneath his jacket and fired it point-blank at Or-tis.

The great nemesis of three generations of my family pitched forward on his face and lay on the floor unmoving.

For a moment everyone in the room stood stock still, as if spellbound upon the stage of some nightmare fantasia. But the spell lasted only an instant before the two Kash Guards came at us with their clubs.

I picked up the broom with which earlier I had pretended to sweep the floor and swung it at the nearest soldier. The big fellow blocked it with his truncheon, which he whipped up and thrashed at me with vicious glee, forcing my retreat.

Baatar was locked in his own death struggle with the other soldier, but I could do nothing to help him with my own hulking antagonist coming at me. The dance of death in which my antagonist and I were engaged carried us across the room until I stood backed up against the desk where lay the interplanetary communications console. In an effort to avoid a deathblow, I jumped to one side, only to see the Kalkar brute smash the apparatus into pieces with his club.

Now a rage seized me. It was one thing to have the fellow trying to murder me, but quite another to know he had likely silenced forever any hope of my world fostering an alliance with the inhabitants of the Red Planet. The brute very well may have sealed the fate of the human race. Now that the Kalkars had been alerted to the Barsoomians' plans, what hope did my people have of securing access to one of the two known remaining Gridley Wave transmitter-receivers, both of which would now be under even heavier guard?

With strength I did not know I possessed, I broke the broomstick I held over a thigh, then doubled the splintered halves together and, with all my weight and muscle, rammed the sharp ends into the Kash Guard's gut. The giant roared and barreled over in agony, for indeed had I inflicted a grievous wound to his abdomen.

While the Kalkar writhed in pain, I cracked him over the head with the broken sticks. Down he went like a fallen ox, but when I looked up my blood ran cold. There lay poor Baatar, supine on the floor beside his dead foe. My friend's dark eyes were cold and glazed with death. The Kalkar he had fought lay beside him, his skull cracked like an egg, a yolk of gray matter oozing out onto the floorboards.

Something changed in me upon seeing my friend lying there, his body broken and lifeless. This man from the other side of the globe had given his life to pursue the faintest of hopes, believing against the most outlandish odds that our foolhardy mission to storm the gates of the Kalkar high command and make contact with an alien world might somehow benefit the sorry situation of our enslaved species.

I thought of my uncle, and how the very morning after the Kash Guard carried my grandmother away to whatever hideous fate awaited her, he had taken me out into the pasture and begun my training in the arts of war. Were the endless drills in the most efficient methods to inflict dismemberment and death to my opponents simply perfunctory exercises, mere distractions to channel and release my pent-up anger and hate? I did not believe it. My uncle was above all a practical man. If he had trained me to kill, he meant for me to one day use my deadly skills in the effort to free our people from tyranny and oppression.

I had observed how Or-tis had looked cautiously down the hallway before locking us inside the room. It could only mean that Or-tis perceived his mission—to catch me and my companion red-handed in the act of colluding with the inhabitants of Barsoom—to be one of the utmost secrecy. It made sense. After all, Or-tis was the high commander of the Kalkars' intelligence service. He would not want to let slip even to a fellow Kalkar news of Barsoom's interest in allying with the grandson of the dread Julian 5th, slayer of Orthis and nemesis of the Kalkars. To do such would risk whispers of the alliance reaching the ears of my oppressed people, thus fostering among them hope—and possibly one day rebellion.

But what meant most to me at the moment was this: if it were true that no one else in the building knew I was here, I had the opportunity to escape.

I resolved then and there that I would not escape merely to save myself, or even my family. No, as I crawled out the window into the cold black night, I had something wholly different in mind—and wholly mad.

Chapter Five

A DESPERATE RUSE

I t is moments like the one I experienced as I left behind my dead friend in the headquarters of the Kalkars that change the course of history. You would do well to look out for such convergences of events—you who sit so comfortably in your office chair as the future of which I speak comes barreling relentlessly toward us. Or we toward it, although such abstractions bear little resemblance to the reality of the situation. Time itself is merely a mental construct designed to comfort our spirits as the vessels that bear them lie cast adrift in the vast and unimaginable sea of limitless reality. If our species rid itself of such delusions as time and space, we would be a happier lot, and the fear we hold of losing our finite consciousness amid the boundless scape of infinity would instantly dissipate.

Of course, as I fled the Kalkars' headquarters, I did not concern myself with such arcane musings. I knew only what I had to do—to make my way to the one place where I could make a difference.

Once again I traveled amid the crumbling skeletons of concrete and steel, the sundered relics of the once glorious metropolis of Chicago, which lay wracked and ruined after the tempest of the Kalkar invasion of a quarter century past. I could barely articulate even in my own thoughts what actions I would take once I reached my destination. All the same, I knew I must risk my life evading the Kalkar patrols and traitorous members of the human underclass who might turn me in for a crumb of bread or some other transitory reward. I would not call my decision one of bravery, for in reality I could do nothing else. If I took no action, the chance for humanity to forge an alliance with another world and cast off the Kalkars' shackles would evaporate, and that was simply not an option.

As a result of the damage inflicted upon Washington and the utter annihilation of New York City during the invasion, Chicago had become one of the largest districts in the United Teivos of America. Fortunately, the capitol building of the Teivos lay not far from where I wanted to go: the port where ships arrived from and departed for the Moon. Whether this proximity resulted from the local government's practical desire for convenient access to a transportation hub or rather because our Kalkar overlords feared a revolt of the impoverished citizens and wanted the safeguard of a speedy escape route, I did not know. I suspected both motivations might have been responsible. In any case, the fact that the lunar port was nearby served well for my purposes, for I intended to be on the next ship headed to the Moon.

It was, as I have said, a mad plan. But what more was there for me on Earth but a life of servitude and bondage? Could one even call such a life? Perhaps there were those among my kind willing to trade liberty for continued existence, but I could not.

Make no mistake; I did not blame my people for suffering quietly for so many years under the reign of the Kalkars. I had done so myself for the first two decades of my life, hoping I might keep my loved ones safe from the ire of our cruel masters. But now that I had experienced even the barest taste of freedom, now that I knew another world lay out there in the vastness of space ready to help my people in return for my assistance, I could not go back to my former life. I must seize the thin thread of hope dangled out by the woman from Mars. By the Flag, I must do the impossible or die in the attempt!

I passed down a darkened alleyway formed from the shattered remains of what had once been two towering buildings when suddenly I saw a dim form before me. The man-sized figure stopped in the shadows and called out first in the language of Va-nah, and then in English, "Who's there? Identify yourself!"

I guessed that the fellow, whose accent revealed him as a Kalkar, could see me only as poorly as I saw him. That he was alone, I was sure. When in a group, every Kalkar is an arrogant braggart—especially around Earth folk—but this man's voice carried an edge of fear, or at least startlement. I intended to use that to my advantage.

"I am a courier for the Twenty-Four," I said. "Come closer and I shall show you my identification and token of authority." Although I had, in fact, kept the silver emblem that had granted Baatar access to the capitol building, I had no plan to use it at this time. That, I hoped, would come later. For now, I meant to get what I wanted through other means.

Boot soles crunched in the darkness against the gravelly way as the pale form grew larger before me. I clenched my right hand into a fist and, when the stranger stood only a yard from me, I launched myself at him. My right fist caught him beneath the jaw and I drove my left into his belly.

The soldier cried out, heaved forward, and dropped his rifle, then fell to the ground at my feet where he lay still and silent.

After ascertaining that I had laid the soldier out cold, I went to work at once. First I relieved him of his uniform, and then took off my own clothing and donned that which I had removed from the soldier. My face does not resemble that of a Kalkar, as our lunar conquerors' features tend toward coarseness and are often disfigured with broken noses and wicked scars as a result of the brutish culture in which they live. Kalkars are also paler in complexion than Earth humans. But at six feet two inches tall, I could pass for a shorter-statured Kalkar, and though it was not common, upon occasion there were born individuals among their kind whose features bore the handsomeness and beauty of the U-ga of Va-nah. Therefore, I hoped my stolen Kash Guard uniform would do well enough to deceive any Kalkars I encountered into believing I was one of them. If it did not, I would soon be a dead man.

Thus disguised, I continued on, heading along the great inland sea that runs along the eastern edge of the Teivos. How long I traveled, I do not know, for both the thrill of my adventure and the fear of capture did wonders to free me from the lie that is time. It must have been only a couple of hours, however, for the dark blanket of night still fell about me when I came to my destination.

Ahead through a fence of barbed wire a sleek craft shone faintly in the moonlight. The ship lay moored on its side upon a massive landing stage, its body tapering to a slightly bulbous cone. Huge bay doors yawned open on one side of the vessel as dozens of Kalkar soldiers, working by torchlight, wheeled into its hold cartloads of what were doubtless supplies for the trip ahead.

I grinned at my good fortune. Even since the time of my youth, the Kalkars had noticeably decreased the frequency of their passage back and forth between the Earth and the interior lunar world of Va-nah. My uncle attributed this to the Kalkars' innate lack of ingenuity and industry, which he said had been bred into them by their unnatural form of governance, whereby those without talent and the spark of imagination were treated as equals, and more often superiors, to those who were gifted and resourceful. He claimed that this atmosphere of conformity hanging over Kalkar society stultified both social and technological progress. It was likely, he said, that only a handful among their kind retained knowledge of how to fly and maintain the vessels capable of traveling the void of space between Earth and its satellite. After all, it was only the scientific genius of Orthis that had allowed the Kalkars to travel to our planet. Following the death of that traitorous Earth man who had come to lead them, the Kalkars had neither the will nor the ability to maintain the fleet of space vessels they had employed to conquer our world.

The ship lay moored on its side...

...upon a massive landing stage...

At the time, I had accepted my uncle's explanation for the growing infrequency of ships we witnessed departing for and arriving from the Moon. Perhaps, I thought now, that explained the series of scorch marks scoring the exterior of the vessel lying at berth before me. These could have resulted from the friction of the Earth's atmosphere and specks of dust in the ether beyond impacting the hull at high velocities as the ship soared from one world to another. That the damage had not been repaired could be ascribed to either the Kalkars' habitual sloth or their lack of the knowledge and skill in metallurgy needed to repair their hull's armor plating. It would seem my uncle's theory was correct.

Then again, those blackened streaks looked suspiciously like the scars of battle.

I confess, however, that the latter theory only briefly flitted through my mind in my excitement at having espied the encampment. Whatever the case, I was lucky to have found a vessel in preparation for launch, though I did not know whether it would take off in the darkness of this same morning or rather sit upon its staging platform for days or even weeks before finally lancing forth into the heavens. I feared that any delay would give the Twenty-Four time to piece together my involvement in Brother High Commander Or-tis' death and that an all-out search for my whereabouts was imminent. Therefore, I would have to take matters into my own hands and ensure that the vessel that lay before me launched with all haste—and that I would be aboard her when she did.

I examined my stolen uniform one last time to reassure myself that I looked every bit the part of a Kalkar. My outfit consisted of the apparel of a low-ranking officer of the Kash Guard, as indicated by the plain trim of my cloak's white collar, the latter garment being woven out of wool dyed a blood red. Beneath it I wore a plain white tunic, cotton breeches, and a pair of well-worn, knee-high leather boots. A rifle slung over my shoulder, a half-exhausted ammunition belt, and a straight, heavy short sword sheathed in a battered goatskin scabbard rounded out my accoutrements.

That the fellow from whom I had filched my attire was stockier than I meant the clothing fit somewhat loosely. We were of similar heights, however, and the fact that ill-fitting pass-me-downs are often provided to the ranks of the Kash Guard gave me confidence that I could pass easily as a Kalkar, albeit a more handsome representative of the race. To ensure that my Earthly features did not raise any suspicions, I groped my hands about in the dirt, then scrubbed my soiled palms over my face and ran my grimy fingers through my hair. If there is one thing I have observed about the Kalkars' physical appearance, it is that they care little for the luxury of hygiene.

Pleased that I had done everything within my limited capacity to hide my humanity beneath a Kalkar veneer, I proceeded along the fence, which sloped down a hill to a heavily manned and fortified gate situated between two sentry towers. I was halfway down the hill when a guard in the nearer tower barked out a cry of alarm. I tossed my rifle to the ground, raised my hands above my head, and smiled to show that I offered no hostility. All the same, a group of burly soldiers marched out of the gate and up the hill to intercept me.

Feigning a Kalkar accent as best I could manage, I explained to the group's commander that I bore an important message from Brother High Commander Or-tis himself. This did not stop the soldiers from shackling my wrists, relieving me of my sword, and thoroughly searching my person. I smiled widely as they proceeded and said that beneath my tunic they would find a silver medallion on a cord around my neck. This, I explained, would testify as to the veracity of the message I bore, which was to be delivered only to the officer in charge of the encampment.

Soon one of the soldiers manhandling me produced the medallion from beneath my clothing. The commander examined it closely with his close-set, beady eyes. I could tell he could read the emblem no better than the officer of the guard outside the capitol building, but just as quickly as the other did he accept its authority. He immediately ordered his men to remove my shackles and handed me the medallion, which I once again placed about my neck. They did not, however, return my sword or my rifle.

The soldiers marched me down the hill and through the gate. I passed along the staging platform of the lunar-bound vessel to an outbuilding the other side of the yard, and within moments I was standing at attention in the office of the encampment's commandant.

The large brute rose from behind his desk and regarded me with black eyes peering through narrowed lids. Every inch of his seven-and-a-half-foot frame loomed over me as he tried to belittle me with his sheer physicality. I would have grinned up at him devilishly, for my spirit still rebelled against the murder of my friend Baatar, but I knew such an act would reveal my true identity. So instead I sobered my expression and bowed my head like any obedient Kalkar soldier would before his vastly superior officer.

"The seal of the high commander of the Bureau of Intelligence hangs from your neck," the commandant crooned in an almost mocking tone. "What is the meaning of your visit, Brother...Brother... What is your name, brother?"

"I am Brother Targav, a soldier from the district of Oak Park," I said, using the name of the Kash Guard who came each season to collect taxes at our farm.

"Well, what brings Brother Targav to the office of lowly Brother Zutan?" And having drawled out his question he thrust out a hairy paw and shoved me halfway across the room with what I assumed was only the smallest portion of his bull-like strength. I crashed into the soldiers behind me, only managing to remain on my feet because the men grabbed me roughly and held me up, laughing at me all the while.

Now I could not help myself and I laughed as well, though not at my own misfortune. No, I was thinking of what I would like to do to Brother Zutan should I ever have the opportunity to meet him alone in a darkened alleyway.

Still, I did not wish to cast off the Kalkar façade I had so carefully cultivated, for to do so would mean not only the end of my mission, but my very life. Therefore, when one of the men restraining me elbowed me in the ribs, I turned around and gave him a little present in return in the form of my hard knuckles driven forcefully into his jeering face. I have long prided myself upon the fact that I have no mean right hook, and I felt no little self-satisfaction when I saw the fellow I had struck lying unconscious at my feet and snoring softly.

The soldiers surrounding me—and there were twelve of them, all larger than I—made to subdue me, but then a strange noise arose in the room. Suddenly I realized that Brother Zutan was chortling with approval at my display.

"Brother Targav," he said, "you are a puny thing, but all members of the brotherhood are equal, are they not?" They were certainly *not*, I thought silently to myself, but such were the hypocrisies of Kalkar philosophy. "Who is any brother to judge you for your size," he went on, "when you can lay low a giant like Kargth in such a manner? I will talk to the Kash Guard in command of your district and see if I can arrange for your transfer to this base. You would like that, would you not, Brother Targav?"

"I most certainly would," I lied, for I could think of nothing more repugnant and nauseating than to live my life under the authority of the boorish Brother Zutan.

"Now," the commandant continued as he walked behind his desk and set down his substantial girth in an enormous oaken chair, "what message do you carry from Brother High Commander Or-tis? I understand he has recently arrived in the Teivos, though upon what business I know not." He paused. "Then, who is ever privy to his business other than the Twenty-Four?" He laughed darkly, but he looked around the room at

the shadows flickering in the lantern light as if someone might
be hiding in the darkness and listening in on our conversation.

I smiled coolly and sat down in a chair in front of the desk,
looking over one shoulder and then the other at the soldiers
standing behind me. Zutan took my cue and said, "Leave us!"
Instantly the soldiers filed out of the room, though they did so
more or less in a jumble, for the Kalkars show an amazing lack
of discipline for their position as the overlords of Earth. As my
uncle more than once told me, if not for the Kalkars' overwhelming superiority in arms we could easily rout them and wipe their
kind from the face of the globe. A couple of the soldiers, however,
retained enough dutifulness to remember their fallen comrade,
Kargth, and to drag his unconscious form from the room.

When we were alone, Zutan said, "Now, give me the message
or I'll have your flesh stripped from your bones and feed it to
the Va-gas."

As I had neither the need to delay nor the desire to end up
in the bellies of the intelligent talking quadrupeds of the Moon's
interior, I replied, "It is the order of Brother High Commander Or-tis that the vessel you are staging launches for Va-nah as
quickly as you can ready it—tonight, if at all possible—and that
I, Targav, will be a passenger upon it."

Zutan eyed me with an expression that could only be one
of suspicion, and I felt a little chill run up my spine that caused
the hair upon the nape of my neck to bristle. "Why?" was all
he said in reply.

"That," I said, "I am not at liberty to divulge, even if I were
privy to exactly why it must remain unspoken, which I am not.
It is enough that it is the will of the Brother High Commander himself. Do you not agree, Brother Zutan?"

Zutan frowned so darkly that I thought he would draw the
revolver that hung on his hip and put a bullet in my head. Then,
slowly, his downturned lips curled up at the edges, and again I
felt my neck hairs rise upon cold skin.

"So be it, Brother Targav," Zutan said. "The ship will launch within the hour. Report at once to your new commander. I am sure Brother Kargth, captain of the *People's Glory*, will be over-joyed to see you again."

Chapter Six

FAREWELL TO EARTH

After leaving the commandant's office, I flagged down a soldier and asked him where I could find Brother Kargth. The man, who had been among those who had witnessed me lay out Kargth on the commandant's floor, laughed and said the captain of the *People's Glory* was too busy preparing his ship for departure to accept visitors—especially if that guest was named Brother Targav.

"Perhaps he'll change his mind," I said, "when he learns that it is Brother Zutan's express wish that I am to be a passenger aboard the *People's Glory*."

The soldier's eyebrows rose. "As someone who has spent many years under the captain's command, I advise you not to disturb him if you value your hide. Get yourself aboard the ship and I will inform Brother Kargth."

It was then that I noticed the colorful embroidery on the collar of the soldier's cape. The man was an officer of some authority, and if he served under Kargth, it was perhaps wise that I should listen to him. I turned to do just that when a firm hand gripped my shoulder from behind and whirled me about.

"How is it," the officer said, "that a grubby soldier with no commission carries the seal of Brother High Commander Or-tis of the Bureau of Intelligence?"

I smiled widely and spread my hands. "Brother Or-tis does not care about who serves when there's a job to be done. He knows that all brothers are equal and selects the man he believes

48

will best benefit the state when a particular task arises. Who am I, a grubby soldier with no commission, to argue?"

The officer grimaced at me but said nothing. Though the Kalkars do in fact distinguish between officers and common soldiers—and in some rare instances even bestow titles to those close to the Twenty-Four, as in the case of Brother High Commander Or-tis—their notion of rank is a hazy one. The flagrant display of rank is, in fact, distasteful to them. Their core philosophy states that all adult male Kalkars are in essence equal. If one brother has fine embroidery upon his collar and another has no embroidery at all, it is only because the former is better equipped to perform certain duties for the state than the latter. In theory, the simple tasks assigned to the common soldier are supposed to be regarded as no baser or less worthy than an officer's more complex duties. The idea is little more than hot air, of course, as evidenced by the fact that the more brutal and vicious the individual, the higher placed he invariably is among the Kalkar regime.

The look the man gave me left no doubt in my mind that he understood I had played the Kalkars' own worldview against him. Still, he could make no reply, for to do so would be to admit he had undermined the state by declaring that one brother was intrinsically more valued than another, and that is something a Kalkar will never do—at least publicly. But then, most Kalkars are simply too dull-minded to even consider their doctrine, however dubious it might be, let alone to question it. They simply obey, as they have been told to do, and parrot the dogma that has been fed to them since birth.

That the name of the Kalkars translated to "The Thinkers" in the tongue of my own people was the height of irony. Indeed, that very name belonged to the populist faction that rose to power long ago among the U-ga and overthrew the nobility that had ruled the Moon's interior for millennia. But when I thought about the devastation the descendants of The Thinkers had inflicted upon our fair green Mother Earth, any humor I entertained from my caustic thought abruptly ceased.

All this I considered in but a moment, and relief swept over me when the officer stalked away with no further comment. I thanked God and the Flag and hurried off to the hold of the awaiting ship.

I arrived just as an infantry contingent was marching across the field and up the ramp into the belly of the *People's Glory*. I slipped in among the soldiers and soon found myself inside the vessel and climbing the rungs of a ladder leading to a narrow ledge overhanging the side of the hold. Jutting out just above the ledge and running almost the hold's full length was a bench upon which sat a long row of soldiers. The bench was but one of many lining both sides of the hold's interior, stacked one atop the other. All told, some five hundred men must have been crammed into the vessel. I could only wonder why such a large force had been levied to return to the Moon when the soldiers could be put to work here on Earth to address the many problems that faced the Kalkars' ailing Teivos.

While I pondered Kalkar inefficiency, an officer climbed up the rungs and proceeded to work his way down my row past the soldiers sitting on the bench. When he came to me, he stopped.

"Brother Targav?" he asked. When I nodded in acknowledgment, he said, "Come with me."

My heart about leaped into my throat, for I imagined the agents of the Twenty-Four had somehow succeeded in tracking me to the port and that my little game of deception had at last run its course. I managed to retain my composure when I rose, and it is fortunate that I did. Had I caused a scene in the midst of five hundred loyal Kalkar soldiers, it would have been a simple thing for my shipmates to knock me from the ledge and hurl me a hundred feet to my death at the bottom of the hold.

Furthermore, it would have been a pointless death, as my fears turned out to be unwarranted. When I questioned the officer, he replied that he only meant to escort me at the behest of the captain to a compartment at the fore of the ship. Of course, said captain was the same fellow I had knocked cold, and I could not imagine he harbored any kind feelings toward me.

When the hatch to the forward cabin swung open at my companion's knock, I found myself looking up into the sneering face of the giant Kargth. I was about to explain that I had intended no injury to the man when I struck him but had instead merely reacted reflexively to his elbow jab. It was by all means a bald-faced lie, but one I justified by the fact that the importance of my mission far outweighed any taint to my personal honor. In any case, the dark look on Kargth's countenance did not seem to harbor any patience for an explanation, truthful or otherwise. Thus it was a complete surprise to me when Kargth erupted in a roar of jubilant laughter, then slapped me on the back with a blow so hard I coughed and wheezed in the effort to regain my breath.

"Brother Targav!" he cried with unrestrained exuberance. "Welcome to the *People's Glory*! I will have use for a man like you back in Va-nah, what with the war ever raging against us!"

"The war?" I asked between coughs.

"Yes, the war!" Kargth exclaimed. "We shall drive the soldiers of Vathayne back into the crater out of which they crawled like a revolting swarm of pale-bellied rympths!" A rympth, I knew from my grandmother's stories, was a four-legged snake native to Va-nah.

"Oh, yes, of course, the war," I said. And then, with all the mock gusto I could manage, I shouted at the top of my lungs, "Death to the soldiers of Vathayne! Back into their dank, dark crater with them!"

Kargth bellowed with laughter and, eyeing me with a grin of approval, took his seat and strapped himself in. I followed his example and gazed out the two large teardrop-shaped portals situated directly above our reclining chairs. The sun, at last vanquishing the morning's darkness, was breaking over the horizon and casting its orange brilliance upon the scattered clouds overhead. The pilot called out for the engineer to activate the powerful motors of the *People's Glory*. Almost instantly, I felt the ship lurch beneath us as the buoyancy tanks filled with the Eighth Earthly Ray and we hove up into the air.

Some time has passed, at least in so far as we perceive it, since I first narrated the adventures of Julian 5th, my ancestor—forgive me, I mean my future *descendant*, from the vantage point of April 1970 as I presently relate this tale. Thus perhaps it is best that I should briefly refresh your memory as to the methods of propulsion that will one day be used to travel the void between worlds.

You already know, of course, that the Barsoomian scientists with whom Earth communicates on a daily basis have revealed the existence of a series of rays that behave in certain ways in reaction to particular heavenly bodies. The Eighth Earthly Ray, for example, can be used as a means of propulsion by the very fact that exhausting it earthward propels the vessel upon which such a motor is affixed away from the planet Earth. By exhausting the Eighth Lunar Ray in the same manner, one can slow a ship as it approaches the Moon and thus manage a safe landing, whether upon its strange surface or passing through a crater into its even stranger interior. All of the planets and satellites of our solar system, and even the sun itself, have such unique corresponding rays, and it is by such means that the *People's Glory* carried me and its other passengers through Earth's atmosphere and onward into outer space.

So it was that I watched the morning sky turn from orange to the deepest azure and finally to a velvet blanket of pitch black pierced by an unending field of glittering stars. I marveled as we left behind the fragile pale blue crescent that had until now always been home to my earthly form. What lay before me I did not know, except that it was vast beyond imagining.

I considered with some trepidation the enormity of space and how even the slightest deviation from our course would hurl us hopelessly into the cold and merciless reaches of cosmic infinity. It had been just such a wrong turn, guided by the hand of a traitor, that had landed my grandfather, Julian 5th, in the interior of the Moon. Ah, if only Fate had dealt humanity a different hand! Then the Kalkars would never have built a fleet of warships under the direction of the maleficent Orthis and launched them against the unsuspecting inhabitants of Earth.

That the destiny of an entire world might depend on altering a ship's course by only a few degrees was an even more terrifying thought to me than the possibility that our own vessel might be lost in the void. In desperation, I clung to the fact that it was ultimately a man's conscious decision—as misguided a choice as it was when Orthis sabotaged the controls of *The Barsoom* and plunged my grandfather's vessel toward the face of the Moon—that had changed the fortune of Earth. If Orthis, by an act of free will, could alter the course of the future, then so could another—and perhaps this time it would be for the better.

Such were my thoughts as the Earth grew smaller in the aft viewport and the pale, scarred face of the Moon loomed larger in the forward portholes. Several days passed as we rocketed toward Luna at more than twelve hundred miles an hour. On the fifth day out, I began to discern varicolored patterns upon the lunar surface. These hues became more vivid as we neared the satellite, until at last I could make out a rainbow of colors adorning vast swathes of vibrant plant life stretching across the cratered and mountainous landscape. The days passed until at last I could perceive the grotesque and twisted forms of trees, broad and thick-leaved. As the surface of the Moon waned and this vegetation passed into the Earth's shadow, I observed the colorful trees and plants wither, fade, and crumble into dust, until all that was left was a fine gray powder that lay heaped in moldering piles within the darkened area. I wished that I might remain above the Moon long enough to see it wax as my grandmother had once described to me, for what a wonder it would be to behold the vegetation springing to life and growing into full-sized trees before my very eyes!

As the Kalkar vessel was outfitted primarily as a warship and possessed no scientific instruments to speak of, I could only guess that a thin atmosphere surrounds the Moon, as imperceptible from the vantage point of Earth as the plant life itself. Only thus could I explain existence of the bizarre forests and tall grasses of unearthly tinctures that thrive on the satellite's sunward face. I wondered if any advanced forms of life might exist within the forest, but quickly dismissed the idea. Such life would see its entire environment utterly eradicated with the advancing shadow cast upon it from the Earth and would never have had the time necessary to take root in the first place. Even if animals or humanity somehow managed to migrate to the lunar surface via the craters that opened into Va-nah, they would have to exist in a state of permanent and precipitate nomadism, ever fleeing the oncoming darkness at an unimaginable breakneck pace. At one point, I did believe I saw what looked vaguely like a hairless antelope with a long reptilian tail spring out of the forest and leap high above a grassy clearing, but when I rubbed my eyes it was gone. I attributed the illusion merely to the intensity with which I had been gazing at the lunar landscape and thought no more about it.

The motors continued to exhaust the Eighth Earthly Ray behind our ship until the Moon's great face swelled before us and encompassed our entire field of vision. I looked with consternation to Kargth and the pilot seated beside him, but both men appeared unfazed by the speed with which the *People's Glory* hurtled toward the surface. When the pilot finally called the order to disengage the aft motor and activate the forward tank containing the Eighth Lunar Ray, I sighed with relief. Almost instantly I felt our forward momentum slow, and soon we leveled out and plunged into shadow, racing horizontally above the dark side of the Moon.

We traveled over the high ridges and deep craters for almost two hours while I sat on the edge of my seat so that I could better peer down at the surface through one of the forward portholes. I asked the pilot how he knew where to steer the ship. He indicated an instrument in front of him that resembled a dial gauge.

"It is a device invented by Great Brother Orthis," he said with some pride.

"How exactly does it function?" I asked.

The man shrugged. "Does it matter? I simply keep the needle within these two lines"—he pointed to a narrow V-shaped area between a series of graduations on the gauge—"and the ship goes where it should."

When I questioned the pilot further, he grew sharp with me. "Don't ask me how it works. Do you question why the Earth circles the ball that contains Va-nah?"

I could not help from laughing, for in fact I did question his contention that the Earth orbits the Moon. Fortunately, he misunderstood the cause of my mirth and believed I snickered at the absurdity of the examined life, which indeed is a ludicrous notion to the incurious, uneducated Kalkars.

Notwithstanding the pilot's debasement of the art of reason, I continued to ponder the mechanism. Finally, I decided it must be attuned to detect a specific signal emanating from a transmitter affixed to the ship's intended destination. The gauge was likely connected by hydraulics to the ship's exhaust separators, which were equipped to change direction according to the needle's position on the dial. Whether the transmitter was located at the edge of an entry crater or rather somewhere deep within Va-nah itself, I could not say. From what my uncle had told me, I knew the wave discovered by Jason Gridley for communicating with Barsoom had once also been used to relay messages to and from the primitive world of the Earth's hollow interior. I suspected the instrument on *People's Glory* had been designed to detect that same wave for the purposes of navigation.

The pilot pulled back on the throttle and the ship lurched up as we ascended high above a yawning crater. At the man's order, we all strapped ourselves back into our seats, and well it was that we did. Soon we swung about and the nose of our craft pointed straight down into the crater's dark mouth. I clutched the arms of my chair as if my life depended on it and felt cold sweat break out upon my brow.

I allowed myself to breathe more measuredly only after some unseen force seemed to pull us out of our precipitous dive, shallowing the severe angle of our vessel. Now we were circling the inside of the crater's rim, the circumference of our path steadily decreasing as the hole itself grew smaller in diameter. By the time we had corkscrewed down to the narrowest point of the crater, the circumference stabilized and the ship's forward lights shown down into what seemed a measureless abyss stretching before us.

We were in what my grandmother would have called one of the great Hoos of Va-nah ("hoos" meaning "holes" in the tongue of the U-ga). As I sat upon her knee as a child, she had told me how my grandfather believed the craters were in reality massive lava tubes that had ejected unimaginable quantities of magma from the Moon's molten core in some time-lost geological era. When enough magma was expelled that the volcanic activity inside the Moon subsided, the hollow core cooled, thus forming the inner shell that would one day blossom with life and become known to the inhabitants as Va-nah, or simply "the world." Until my grandfather's ship came to Va-nah and they were informed otherwise, neither the U-ga nor the Kalkars nor the Va-gas knew that anything existed on the other side of the Hoos besides an eternity of solid rock and the fiery gaze of Zo-al. The latter was the mythical deity the people of Va-nah invented to explain the sunlight that periodically shined through the Hoos, sometimes heating the atmosphere and forming devastating storms that swept down out of the heavens and wracked the land in their fury.

Down we spiraled into the vast lava tube, which must have been fully five miles in diameter. We proceeded in this manner for twelve or thirteen hours when I felt the ship roll strangely, then right itself again and come to a full stop. I did not ask the pilot for an explanation. I knew he would reply that what is simply is, and I would be none the wiser. I speculated, however, that we had reached the halfway point on the trip down the Hoos to the surface of Va-nah. Here a nexus of gravity and centrifugal force held the ship in abeyance. I realized my theory was likely correct when I saw the pilot activate the atmospheric thrusters and suddenly the ship glided out of the doldrums and continued on its way down the enormous cylindrical tunnel.

Or was it up? Now I could see light glancing toward us down the smooth rock face of the Hoos. Though the illumination did not carry the intensity and warmth of sunlight, it heartened me, for during the first part of our journey I had the unsettling feeling that the great lava tube was a tunnel leading down to Hell. Then again, perhaps the light I saw cast up from below truly was the refraction of Gehenna's infernal flames. Certainly the violet radiance was weird and unearthly.

An equal span of time passed as that which had elapsed when the ship traveled between the rim of the crater and the doldrums. All the while the light grew slowly but steadily brighter until without warning we emerged from the opposite end of the Hoos.

The sight that met us on the other side of the crater left me breathless. Mauve clouds, more beautiful than any atmosphere tinted by an earthly sunset, wafted in the sky above a vista unlike anything I had ever seen. On all sides the horizon curved upward like an immense bowl—if indeed it could be called a horizon, for no distinct skyline defined where either land or sea ended. Instead, one's field of vision simply faded into a violaceous haze.

The lighting proved to be equally outlandish. My eyes searched in vain for a source, but the diffuse illumination seemed to come from everywhere and nowhere at once. Finally, I gave up and decided that the soil and perhaps the vegetation itself must bear significant concentrations of radium. Later I learned I was only partially correct, for sunlight shining through the thousands of Hoos also contributes to the omnipresent radiance of Va-nah.

The ship skirted above the coastline of a quiet sea. A thick strip of black sand edged the vast body of water, while a lush forest of soft lavenders, violets, pinks, and yellows blanketed the landscape a short distance inland. I can assure you that it is one thing to see mountains and plains curve upward in the distance and quite another to see an entire ocean do so.

"Ah, a Bru-tan, I see!" Kargth exclaimed, taking notice of my astonishment. Bru-tan was the term for a Kalkar who had been born on the Earth. "Well, don't worry, we'll break the wonder out of you soon enough!"

The vindictive laughter that broke out across the cabin following Kargth's statement left me feeling anything but reassured.

Chapter Seven

A SOLDIER FOR THE KALKARS

We flew along for several miles while the sable sands and striking colors of verdant foliage raced below us in a chromatic blur. Suddenly, a great bay appeared ahead out of the lilac haze and rising above the inlet's precipitous cliffs loomed a massive fortress city.

An enormous wall, perhaps two hundred feet high, circumscribed the stronghold's towering edifices. The architecture, however, was plain and unadorned, a fact that did not surprise me given the stark, bland styles of Kalkar culture I had witnessed on Earth. Even so, the sheer immensity of the city astounded me.

I am not ashamed to admit that a wave of trepidation shuddered through me when I considered my odds at impacting in even the smallest way the supreme dominion of the Kalkars in Va-nah. What could I, a mere farmer and horse trainer from Oak Park, hope to do to weaken the Kalkars' iron grip on the inhabitants of both Va-nah and Earth? The enormity of my task threatened to overwhelm me.

Then I thought of the long line of military men from which I had sprung and the dark times during which they had struggled against equally bleak odds. I resolved that I would let neither fear of failure nor the extinguishment of hope absolve me of my responsibility to uphold honor and duty, even if it meant my demise. For should I be defeated and meet my death in the effort to secure freedom for my people, perhaps my memory would serve to inspire another to succeed where I had failed. I can think of nothing more selfish and cowardly than to stand by and do nothing, knowing that such inaction will doom forthcoming generations to a future of misery and hope-lessness.

While thus engaged in my reverie, I watched through the viewport as the pilot eased our ship over the wall and we began our descent. The atmospheric motors whirred as the *People's Glory* set down in an open court before the gaping doors of a drab hangar. Then the engines disengaged and I heard the hiss and creak of hydraulics as the landing gear took on the full weight of the vessel.

As we unstrapped ourselves from our seats, Kargth said, "Get yourself to gravity processing, Brother Targav, or you'll be as sick as a Va-gas that's dined on a rymph."

I recalled my grandmother telling me the four-legged snakes of Va-nah were poisonous, and yet I did not take the meaning of the giant's statement. "I feel fine," I said.

Kargth eyed me up and down. "Now that I think of it, you do bear some of the ugly features of an Earth man, Brother Targav. But even if you are a half-breed, you won't be immune to gravity sickness. Go on!"

The giant Kalkar shoved me toward the cabin door, through which the engineer had just exited the ship. I felt the pull of gravity that had been absent during our trip through space, but not to the degree that it had weighed me down on Earth. In fact, far from feeling ill, I felt rather pleasantly energized. But when Kargth's push brought me to the top of the thirty-foot ladder descending from the edge of the little platform outside the door, my newfound lightness caused me to misstep and I found myself hurtling to the ground far below.

Though on Earth the fall would have either killed me or left me seriously injured, I managed in the Moon's weak gravity to land on my feet undamaged. When I rose from my squat, I underestimated my strength and leapfrogged fully thirty feet into the air. This process repeated itself several times. By the time I was able to stop my wild jumping, I had crossed three hundred feet to the opposite side of the plaza.

Across the court I saw Kargth shake his head at me and then point forcefully to the hangar that lay before the ship. I nodded and proceeded to walk with caution to the building he had indicated.

The great doors of the space vessel's hold had been opened and a line of soldiers was filing out and marching into the hangar. I took my time and lingered while the other soldiers shuffled ahead of me. I wanted to observe what was in store for them before I willingly subjected myself to the mysterious procedure of "gravity processing."

Rope lines inside the hangar funneled soldiers into a large room. I managed to sidestep the area confined by the ropes without being noticed and climbed a set of stairs to an unoccupied second floor overlooking the staging ground where the soldiers were herded below. Here the men passed into a sort of tank-like chamber with metal walls that held ten soldiers at a time. On either end at the top of the tank were two nodes resembling the technological innovations of the ancients known as electrostatic generators, which I had read about in books my uncle had obtained for me. As each group of ten entered the tank, a soldier standing outside closed a hatch that sealed the men inside. Then the soldier signaled to a man across the room who was seated before a control apparatus of some sort. This cue prompted the latter to pull a lever on his gadget, causing a jagged line of greenish-yellow electrical energy to instantly spark across the gap between the two nodes.

At this point, another man positioned on the opposite side of the tank opened a second door through which the soldiers exited. I observed that these men walked with stooped shoulders and a heavy step, no longer carrying themselves with the sprightly poise with which they had entered the tank—a physical lightness of body that I myself still felt.

I could only surmise that the gravity processing of which Kargth had spoken amounted to a procedure in which the soldiers were returned to their normal lunar weights by some means of advanced science. I later learned that I was correct and that the gravity tank was yet another invention born out of the scientific genius of Orthis, my grandfather's nemesis. It was Orthis' solution to the problem posed by the Earth's higher gravity during his planning for the invasion of Earth by the Kalkars.

Since a person on the Moon weighs only one-sixth what he or she would upon the Earth, any Kalkar traveling to the latter world would be, if not crushed, then weighted down by the planet's far greater mass to a state of complete and utter incapacity. Orthis' answer to the quandary was to expose the person's mass to the appropriate type of Eighth Ray corresponding to the world on which he or she had just arrived. This allowed a Kalkar, for example, to retain a relative weight for his size when he traveled to Earth. In simpler terms, Earth's gravity would not crush him and he would retain the mobility and strength he had possessed before he had left the Moon. However, because of some arcane peculiarity of physics that I did not comprehend when it was explained to me, when the human natives of Va-nah return to the Moon, they must be expediently returned to their original lunar mass by means of the same technique effected in reverse or else they experience a form of illness that begins with the gradual onset of feebleness and ends with an utterly debilitating lack of muscular control. The same rule, I was told, does not apply to the inhabitants of Earth, who may travel back and forth between the two worlds with no ill effect upon returning to Earth other than a slight atrophying of musculature, which can easily be corrected by a routine of rigorous exercise.

The quadruped Va-gas, I was also informed, did not need to undergo gravity processing when they traveled to Earth for the simple reason that they were of a lesser mass than the Kalkars or the U-ga. They could, for instance, make bounding leaps of more than forty feet into the air while on the surface of Va-nah. When brought to Earth, they were naturally affected by the planet's greater mass and heavier gravitational pull. This reduced their ability to jump to that of an earthly antelope, but it did not incapacitate them.

Why the Va-gas should be of a lesser mass whereas the humans of Va-nah were of a greater was a perplexing mystery. Was it possible that one of these species was not native to the Moon? And if so, which one was the alien species, the lighter or the heavier?

I knew none of this at the time, of course, though easily enough did I understand the effect the tank had upon the soldiers who entered it. I immediately decided it would be best for me to evade such a procedure at all costs, knowing that my grandfather had experienced no ill effects while adjusting to Va-nah's lesser gravity, and that the greater strength he experienced while within the Moon's interior had in fact provided him with many benefits.

I crept back down the stairs and had just managed to slip outside the building without notice when a voice cried out from behind.

"You! Wait up!"

I started, fearing I had been caught dodging my mandatory turn in the gravity tank. Soft, rapid steps padded up behind me, and I started a second time when I turned to see who—or rather *what*—accosted me.

I had never before seen a Va-gas, as few, if any, reside in my Teivos. Moreover, though I was familiar with the quadrupeds' appearance from drawings, encountering one of the creatures in the flesh was a far different experience. I suppose I might convey the effect it had upon me by asking a simple question: how would you feel if your pet collie pranced up to your side with a porcelain cup in his paw and politely inquired whether it was tea time?

The face that looked up at me was proud and, though unusually broad, fully human in appearance, with large dark eyes, high cheekbones, and an aquiline nose. But that was all that was familiar about the creature, for its head rested upon a hairless, vaguely doglike torso, if the latter were, say, the size of a small pony. Its skin was the deep hue of a ripe plum. It stood about four feet at the shoulder, and perhaps five and a half feet to the top of the head. Each of its four powerfully muscled legs rested upon a three-toed paw, which explained the pitter pat of footsteps I had heard approaching me from behind. The hair upon its head was long and dark, but unlike a human's grew far back along the neck after the fashion of a mane. It wore a full-bodied garment with short legs, and interlocking geometrical decorations sewn around the trim of the collar and leg cuffs. A surcingle encircled its barrel chest and breeching was secured around its hindquarters, similar to a horse's tack. Attached to the surcingle on either flank was a small round shield decorated in bold relief with large symbols reminiscent of characters once used by the Chinese of Earth.

"Are you the one called Targav?" the creature demanded.

"Why...indeed I am," I admitted rather hesitantly in my startlement.

"Kargth has assigned me to you," the Va-gas said. "My name is No-ma-ro of the Sa-thans, though my tribe is no more and now I serve the Kalkars, who provide me with meat." No-ma-ro made a sound deep in his throat that I took to be one of disgruntlement. "Though it is not enough and my belly ever hungers for more flesh."

"Is that so?" I said, still in shock to be engaged in conversation with the strange and oddly garrulous creature standing before me.

No-ma-ro, for his part, did not appear to like my tone, for again he made the deep-throated sound and, trotting up to me, nudged me forcefully with his front side in a manner that made it clear he in no way regarded my species as superior to his own.

NO·MA·RO

"Come, Targav," he said. "I will take you to your barracks where we will get you a uniform that does not stink of Earth man." And with that pronouncement he brushed past me and, his head held high, trotted off in the direction of a broad avenue leading from the court.

I had to jog to keep up with the nimble, fleet-footed Va-gas, all the while striving to conceal the effect of Va-nah's lesser gravity upon my gait. My retarded pace apparently tested the patience of my guide, who stopped and turned back to glare at me every so often as we proceeded down the busy thoroughfare. Finally, he galloped back to me and, with a rather pony-like jerk of his head, said, "Get on!"

I complied, crawling up on to No-ma-ro's midsection and riding bareback. As we left the main road and cantered down a side street, my mount remarked, "You are as light as a cloud, Targav. Must we go back and put you back in the tank?"

"Oh, by no means!" I exclaimed, my mind racing to provide a rationale for both my lesser weight and why I had no need for further gravity processing. "Brother Kargth knows about my condition. In fact, it is why he's giving me special treatment. I am a Bru-tan, a half-breed, and a singular one at that. My constitution is unique and I do not require the tank. But whatever you do, say nothing of my lesser weight. Brother Kargth has a special mission in mind for me and will surely punish you by denying you meat if you divulge my secret."

No-ma-ro came to a halt and, stomping his front paw on the clay brinks lining the street, huffed loudly. "If Kargth denies me meat, perhaps I shall eat *your* flesh, Targav!"

I forced myself to laugh. "Of course I would never allow Brother Kargth to decrease your rations. We are friends, you and I, are we not? In fact, if you can keep our little secret, I will do everything in my power to ensure that you get more meat, not less. How does that sound, No-ma-ro?"

The Va-gas' head had been turned back as we carried on our conversation, enough so that I could see in profile a satisfied smile now stretching across one side of his broad face. "It sounds good," he said, "*very* good. But do not forget your promise, Targav, for if I grow too hungry for flesh, I know where I can get some quickly."

I reached down to stroke the Va-gas upon the side of his neck as I was in the habit of doing to reassure my old mare Betsy back at my family's horse farm, but then I thought the better of it. Though the experience of riding the Va-gas was not dissimilar from being mounted on a bareback pony, I would do well to remember that No-ma-ro was a rational, intelligent man, not an animal. At least, I thought quietly to myself, in so far as any man is rational when motivated by the urges of his belly.

No-ma-ro resumed his canter, and after passing down several narrow back streets and alleys that descended several of the terraces upon which the city was built, we emerged in a wide, level plaza filled with half a dozen companies of soldiers being drilled by their superior officers. My guide carried me along the edge of the square, and when we reached the entrance to a large, two-story building, he crouched down low to let me off his back.

"You, along with the rest of Kargth's company, are quartered on the second floor," he said once I had dismounted. "I will have a supply officer come by with a clean uniform. In the meantime, you will wait for Kargth, who will introduce you to your fellow cadets and initiate your training."

The Va-gas began trotting away but I called to him and he stopped.

"Where can I find you, No-ma-ro, should I be in need of your services?"

He raised a paw and pointed with one of his three toes to a tent adjoining the barracks. "There," he said, grinning devilishly. "A new recruit has joined our company. They say she is from the litter of the queen of the Go-thans, and Kargth has requisitioned additional meat so that the Va-gas of our company can celebrate the occasion. Do not disturb me. I shall be busy with the festivities."

I nodded and then watched him head off at a gallop to join his fellow Va-gas warriors to commemorate the arrival of the Go-than princess. If I understood anything about No-ma-ro from our earlier conversation, it was that meat is a very touchy subject to the Va-gas, and I did not want to be anywhere near one of the creatures when he was feeding, let alone a whole platoon of them.

The days and weeks that followed while I trained with the Kalkars passed by in a blur—if indeed one can measure so-called time with such terms as "day" or "week" in a land where no night exists to demarcate any unit of duration. For that entire duration, I feared I would be questioned about my professed role as an agent of Or-tis, but in this matter the Kalkars' habitual sloth and lack of curiosity worked to my advantage. If any questioned why I was there, no one bothered to mention anything about it to me, and though I suspect No-ma-ro remembered what I had told him, as far as I know he kept his word to me and said nothing. My payments of meat seemed to have done the trick nicely, not that I had believed the Va-gas held any particular loyalty to the Kalkars beyond the fragile bond created by the regular meals provided to him.

Kargth was a cruel taskmaster, and it turned out that some of my fellow cadets were even harsher in their hazing of me. Even so, I managed to come through the ordeal mostly unscathed as result of a single fortuitous circumstance: my earthly muscles afforded my aforementioned right hook a most injurious, if not lethal, potency. This, more than anything, earned me the Kalkars' respect, and under the watchful eye of Brother Kargth I rapidly advanced in both ability and pecking order among my peers.

Another thing that made me stand out among the soldiers was the friendly relationship I cultivated with the Va-gas warriors in our company. Prior to Orthis' arrival in Va-nah, the Va-gas had existed as a series of tribes competing both vigorously and viciously against one another in the struggle to obtain vital resources. When Orthis tipped the balance of power in Va-nah by teaching the Kalkars how to manufacture guns and ammunition, the way of life practiced by the Va-gas for countless eons suddenly vanished. Armed with only primitive spears, the quadrupeds were ill-equipped to put up any resistance. Entire tribes were exterminated before Orthis could put a stop to the genocide and explain to the Kalkars that the Va-gas would be of more use to them alive than wiped from the face of the land.

Orthis ordered his troops to round up survivors of the holocaust and imprison them in camps in the Kalkar cities. Here they were to be either fattened up and used as a source of meat or trained as infantry in the war against the people of Earth. Those lucky enough to be selected for the latter group became members of a reviled lower caste, for though the Kalkars permitted no class divisions among their own kind, they in no way regarded the Va-gas as human beings. Thus the quadrupeds came to be employed as expendable shock troops in the front lines during the invasion of Earth, chiefly in Asia and Africa. Their alien appearance made them particularly effective horrors to hurl against the people of my world.

My interactions with No-ma-ro had quickly convinced me that the Va-gas were a proud people—so proud that they endured the Kalkars' abuse in stubborn silence. I resolved to treat the Va-gas members of our company with the respect that was their due. Being a horseman, I also had an ulterior motive in mind.

In addition to deploying Va-gas warriors as scouts and suicide troops, the Kalkars often loaded up the quadrupeds like mere pack animals, strapping onto their backs all manner of supplies—with the exception of Va-gas meat, which the quadrupeds could not be trusted with as they are cannibals. My belief was not only that this was an insult to the Va-gas, but also that it served to undervalue the Va-gas' potential role in the founding of a highly effective Kalkar cavalry. Not, of course, that I wished to aid the Kalkar's military, but I had in mind that I might one day convince the Va-gas to turn on their masters and join humanity in common cause against the Moon men.

I went about achieving my goal first by presenting my plan to No-ma-ro, explaining that if he could convince his people to be ridden as mounts, the Kalkars would quickly come to appreciate both the skill and ferocity of the Va-gas warriors and therefore afford them better treatment. No-ma-ro was understandably skeptical, since no one comprehends the full scope of a master's cruelty like a slave. I asked him to humor me, but he outright refused until I illegally bartered two days' worth of my own rations from the camp cook for a supply of meat from the Va-gas pens. His belly now full, No-ma-ro finally relented to my request.

Over a period that might have spanned several days, had I only the means to measure it, I practiced alone with No-ma-ro in the plaza outside the barracks. Beforehand I had already fashioned an appropriate lance, which was heavier, sturdier, and longer than the thin, short lances used by Kalkars more after the manner of a javelin. I also made a primitive brigandine out of thin, lightweight sheets of exceptionally hard wood harvested from a unique variety of lunar tree. These I found discarded behind the barracks, the wood being used in the construction of the city's buildings.

The other cadets laughed and jeered when they saw me bestrode a Va-gas and arrayed in such a ridiculous armor. I waved back at them and smiled as I adjusted my equestrian talents to my strange new lunar mount. This only caused them to hector me all the louder, but I paid them little mind. I planned to get my revenge later.

When at last I felt I had mastered the rudimentary skills of Va-gas riding and had instructed and drilled No-ma-ro in the tactics I desired him to execute, we rode out together into the plaza and I called my entire company to join us. Kargth was present as well, jeering along with the other men. Though he had indulged me in my practice with No-ma-ro, considering it good for morale to see the men thus amused amid the tedium

The other cadets laughed and jeered when they saw me bestrode a Va-gas...

and hardship of cadet life, he nonetheless believed me a fool. Therefore I took especial pleasure in calling on him to take part in my little demonstration.

I instructed Kargth to take a hundred of his best men and arrange them on the far side of the plaza in a traditional Kalkar formation. This was a body arranged ten men wide and ten men deep, each soldier armed with a sword and a shield. Kargth stood at the center of the formation where he could direct it while being protected on all sides by his fearsome troops.

Meanwhile, mounted on No-ma-ro, I rode out to the side of the plaza that was opposite Kargth and his men. The four other Va-gas I had asked No-ma-ro to select ahead of time joined us. In whispers I consulted with all four quadrupeds, making sure they understood what they were to do. When they seemed sure of their mission, I lowered my lance, raised up my shield, and charged straight for the Kalkar formation.

Kargth ordered his men to march forward to meet us and they immediately complied. By this time, however, I had already cleared more than half the distance across the plaza. At the same time, the other Va-gas had swung far out on either side of No-ma-ro and me, arcing first away from us toward the edges of the plaza and then, as they neared the Kalkar formation, swinging back toward the center. We had timed our attack perfectly, for just as I crashed into the line of soldiers, the other four Va-gas struck the formation, two on either flank.

The result was pandemonium. Kargth's front line collapsed in retreat while the soldiers marching along the sides fled in a chaos of terror toward the center. Within moments No-ma-ro had leaped through the jumble of men, many of whom had been trampled by their own cohorts. I spied my target before me and again lowered my lance, ululating a savage war cry as I drove my weapon into the shield of a very surprised and stupefied Kargth. Down he went beneath me, and before I knew it No-ma-ro was leaping over him and exiting on the opposite side of the disorderly mass of panic-stricken men.

Fear shot through me upon hearing the screams and cries of the soldiers. I fully believed I had overplayed my hand, and that I might have seriously maimed or even killed some of the men. I had the sinking feeling that at Kargth's earliest convenience I would be put up against the wall of the barracks and shot, if indeed my commander had survived my demonstration of the effectiveness of the Va-gas cavalry.

Therefore I was justifiably relieved when I saw the giant officer emerge from the frightened throng and heard his great lungs bellow with laughter.

"Brother Targav!" he cried as he approached. "I shall never underestimate you again!" He gave me a slap on the back like the one that had left me sputtering a few weeks back when I had entered the cabin of the *People's Glory*.

"Then you won't have me shot?" I asked rather ruefully as I dismounted.

He slapped my back again and said, "You are hereby promoted to drill instructor. Begin training those cadets who can still walk how to ride the Va-gas like you do. This could make all the difference against the armies of Vathayne."

I was about to go do as Brother Kargth bade when suddenly a great boom shook the entire plaza and a series of ear-piercing sirens broke out all across the city.

Chapter Eight

THE WOMAN FROM THE SKY

C lear the plaza and protect the turrets!" bellowed Kargth. The mindless drilling my company had suffered since before my arrival paid off. The men who had only a moment before been in a state of disarray leaped up and obeyed Kargth's order. Along with the others I made for the tower rising from the southeastern corner of the plaza. High atop the battlement soldiers were rolling out a large gun and hoisting it skyward.

"There!" cried a soldier beside me, and my eyes followed the direction of his pointing finger.

Gliding high above the city to the northeast against a backdrop of pink and lavender clouds was what appeared to be a flock of rather large birds. I stopped running and gazed up at the sight as men ran furiously past me. Was it my imagination or did the forms resemble not birds but rather winged humans?

I strained my eyes but could not be sure. Did I see a box, a device of some sort, clutched in a talon of one of the flying figures? There was certainly a bulbous structure on their backs. Perhaps it was an inflatable bag that served to—

Before I could finish my thought there was a crack so loud I felt as if my eardrums had ruptured. To the north, a tower on the terrace directly above the court where I stood leaned forward sickeningly. Suddenly it was plummeting toward us in a roaring mass of stone, concrete, and steel.

"Radio bombs!" a man running past me shouted hoarsely over the din. "They'll kill us all!"

So much for Kalkar discipline, I thought, but then all thought left my mind as a tumult of debris from the collapsing tower rained down on the north side of the plaza. I ran south but fell heavily when a series of blows from behind slammed into me.

I got back up and discovered I was uninjured. The sturdy primitive armor I had been wearing for the cavalry demonstration had deflected the fusillade of debris hurled at me when the tower fell.

The boom of gunpower thundered from the southeast. The men on the turret had fixed the big gun's sites on the formation of fliers and fired.

I looked up and saw half a dozen of the winged forms plunging downward out of the sky.

The order to reload came from the tower above and my blood ran cold. Surely the aerial attackers were from Vathayne, the city in rebellion against the Kalkars that had received the Barsoomian ambassadorial mission. The fliers must be U-ga, like my grandmother who had been taken from me by the vile Kash Guard.

Now, far running from cold, my blood turned hot. I knew I must do everything within my power to take out the gun on the turret. Otherwise, the fliers of Vathayne were doomed to be swatted out of the sky like mere insects.

I ran for the tower and, upon reaching it, entered and scrambled up the winding steps, my lungs burning from the exertion. I emerged on the turret's top just as the gun was being ratcheted at an extreme angle toward zenith. The gun boomed and I saw a winged form spiraling down in a tailspin toward the battlement. It was a woman! Her wing had been clipped by the artillery fire and the gas bag affixed to her back no longer seemed to hold her aloft. Now, she would die, her graceful form crushed against the battlement's hard stone floor.

In a rage I mounted the turret, tore the gunner from his post, and thrust my sword through his heart. Without further thought for the man, I heaved the massive gun toward a defensive tower rising from the north on the terrace above. Another gun there was swiveling around and taking aim at the remaining fliers, who had drifted over the court below and were unleashing more devastation on the next terrace down. As fast as I could I primed the gun and then fired.

The gun jolted fiercely as its deadly cartridge discharged from the wide barrel, knocking me back and hurling me to the ground. I lay there stunned for a moment as if in the haze of a dream. The tower I had aimed at was crumbling in slow motion. At the same time I caught sight of a large bird preening its wing.

No—it was the woman from the sky! She was attempting to repair her mechanical wing. She looked up as I laid eyes upon her and our gazes met. I do believe she was the most stunning creature I ever saw, with her black raven hair streaming in the wind from beneath her silver helmet, and her deep dark eyes sparkling like onyxes amid her moon-pale face. Her figure, though feminine in every manner, looked strong and supple as she held up her damaged wing. That she had witnessed my action with the gun I was sure, for her look was one of concern for my well-being rather than a countenance of fear.

I stood up and reached out toward her, for every molecule of my being cried out that I must provide succor for this fair child from the sky. Then her eyes suddenly grew wide, and for an instant I believed my gesture had alarmed her after all. But no, she was looking past me, her lips parting as though she meant to scream in horror but had choked on fear.

Heavy hands seized me from behind. I struggled but could not break the hold of the two brawny arms that wrapped around me and squeezed with all the power of a monstrous python. I felt myself lift up and then I was lying once again on the stone ground trying to gather my wits.

"Traitor!" came the roar of my antagonist. "To think I once considered you my protégé!"

It was none other than Kargth, my Kalkar commander.

I tried to stand and draw my sword but the back of the giant's meaty fist slammed against my skull and I saw stars.

"Now, die like the poison-tongued rympth you are!"

I felt the viselike grip of the colossal Kalkar around my throat. I reached for my sword but found it trapped beneath my foe's heel as he crouched over me. Digging my nails beneath the giant's hands, I tried to pry open his iron grasp. Perhaps my earthly muscles would have succeeded even against the mammoth Kargth, but my strength waned as my lungs screamed silently for oxygen and he throttled me tighter and tighter.

I managed to kick my foe in the shins with the hard toe of my boot. For an instant the pressure eased and I inhaled a desperate gasp of air, but then the fingers tightened once more, and the mauve sky darkened to a sickly crimson and then the darkest gray as my vision faded along with my vitality.

With what little strength I had, I braced myself for the extinction of my mortality. Then, over the hammering beat of blood pounding in my ears, I heard a strange and familiar sound—the rapid, pattering trot of calloused toes upon stone. I had the vague sensation that something leaped over me and then I heard Kargth cry out in astonishment.

Suddenly my lungs burned as they filled with blessed air. My vision cleared and I saw Kargth lying prone on the battlement, a hook-ended Va-gas spear sticking out of his back like a flagpole.

"Come, Targav," said No-ma-ro, lifting me up onto his back with his powerful arms. "Let us seek meat elsewhere. I grow tired of going hungry while the Kalkars save the best flesh of the herds for themselves."

"Wait!" I cried. "The girl—she must come with us!"

I cast my gaze about in search of her, only to find the woman standing on the edge of the parapet, her broken wing now mended and her gas bag buoying her up onto the tips of her toes.

She looked back at me, her onyx eyes glistering with hope, her lips curling in a glorious smile. And then she leaped from the edge, carried up high on a gust of wind and back into the clouds of the roseate sky.

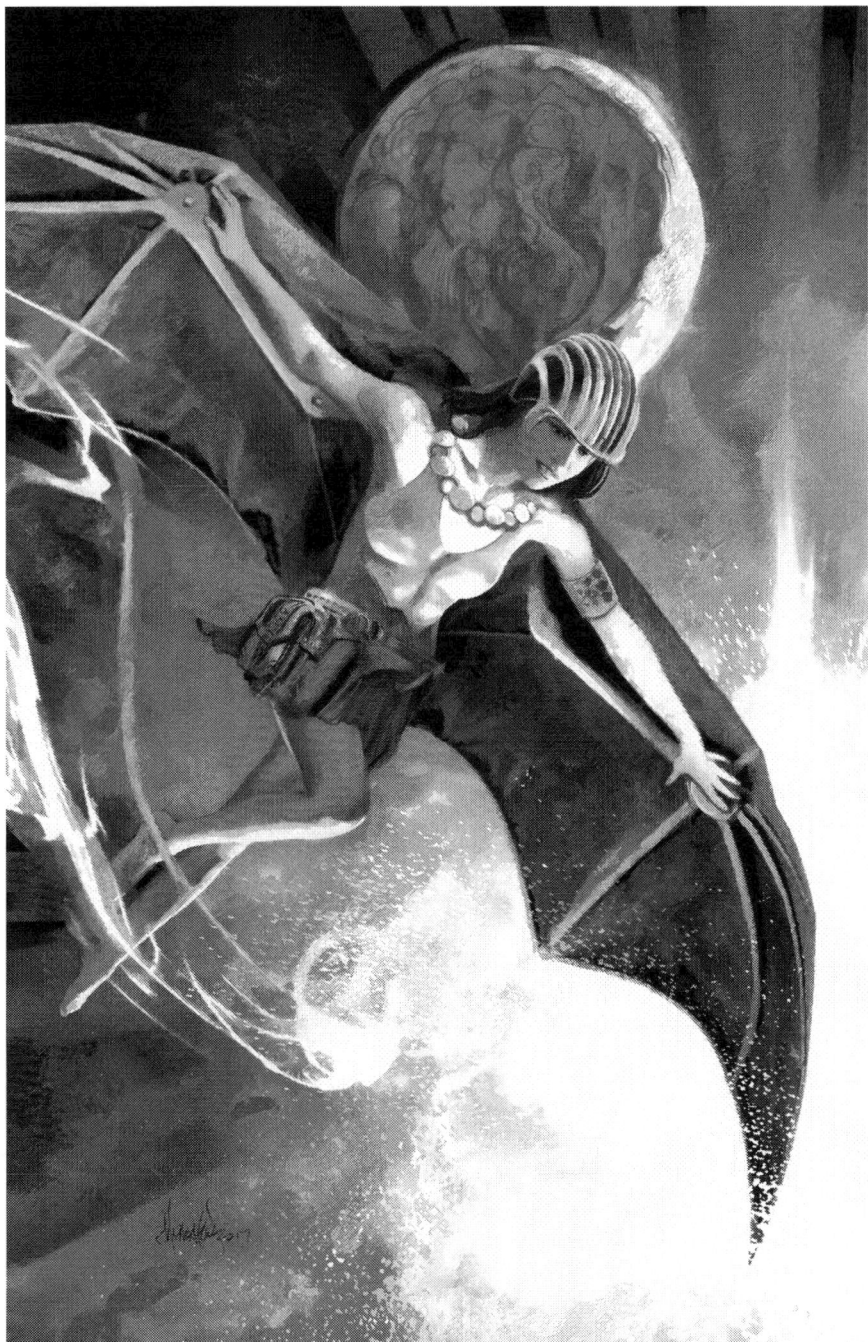

And then she leaped from the edge, carried up high on a gust of wind...

Chapter Nine

FLIGHT AND FIGHT

No-ma-ro retrieved his spear from Kargth's corpse and then bolted down the winding stairs while I held on for dear life to his heaving flanks. I did not know where the Va-gas was taking me, but neither did I care as long as it was far away from this foul den of the Kalkars.

I called for No-ma-ro to stop at the foot of the tower while I leaped off and knelt beside the body of a soldier who had been killed by the collapsing tower, relieving him of his pistol and rifle. Across the plaza I spied my lance lying in the open court. I remounted my Va-gas companion and directed him to recover the abandoned weapon, which he strapped to his side by means of his harness.

By now most of the soldiers from my barracks had fled to the terrace below. There they engaged in the desperate effort to dig out the injured and the dead from the rubble of a third tower that had fallen to the radio bombs of the winged warriors. Those soldiers who yet remained on our level had not witnessed the fight with Kargth on the turret and so paid us no more heed than they did any of the other men in the plaza. No-ma-ro simply trod from the court with me astride him without incident.

We mounted terrace upon terrace as we climbed the back streets that wended their way up the steep rise of the mountain fortress. High above and far to the north, the tiny winged figures of the aerial attackers receded against a majestic backdrop of luminous pink clouds. I could only hope the woman from the turret was safely among the group of fliers.

When we arrived at the wall we found a gaping hole choked with debris, the result of another assault by the fliers and their devastating bombs. None but the severely wounded were alive to see us as No-ma-ro navigated the carnage and carried us beyond the boundaries of the Kalkar city. The Va-gas made for a lush woodland running along the high plateau, assuring me that our enemy would not follow us there, and soon we were galloping down a forest trail and leaving our former lives as soldiers for the Kalkars far behind.

When it became clear that no one pursued us, No-ma-ro slowed to an easy canter and I had the opportunity to discuss our new situation with my companion.

"Why, may I ask, did you save my life back on the turret?" I inquired. "If you desired to desert the Kalkar forces amid the tumult of battle, you could have done so with far less risk to yourself without bringing me along."

"You were the first human to treat me humanely," the Va-gas said.

I laughed at the irony of the quadruped's reply, as the words for "human" and "humanely" translate fairly well into English from the universal tongue of Va-nah.

"What do you find humorous?" No-ma-ro asked. "Do you mock me, Targav?" And then he added beneath his breath, "If that is indeed your name."

"Far from it, my friend," I responded. "I'm merely express-ing my delight that you, in turn, are the first Va-gas to treat me, well...like a Va-gas."

No-ma-ro nodded curtly, as if he approved of my statement and we had come to some sort of understanding.

We loped along the trail for some time amid a breathtak-ing array of lavender hues as I waited for the Va-gas to say more. Finally, I could no longer hold back what was on my mind.

"No-ma-ro, why did you question my name back there? Do you believe I am someone other than I have claimed?"

"When we first met," he said, "I told you to get a new uniform that did not stink of Earth man." He stopped on the trail and made a motion that was the Va-gas equivalent of a shrug. "When you bathed and changed into a fresh uniform, you still carried the stink of your world. That is how I knew you were not a Kalkar."

"And you would trust an Earth man more than a Kalkar?" I asked.

"I will trust anyone for as long as he continues to provide me with meat."

"I see," I replied, unsure whether No-ma-ro's statement was an attempt at humor or a candid declaration of his expediency. "Well, my real name is Julian. And perhaps your trust in me is about to come to an end, for truthfully I am not much of a hunter."

No-ma-ro looked back over his shoulder and regarded me with a sour expression. "We shall have to make do on the woodland fruits until we get to Vathayne. Then I shall have use for you, Ju-lan of Earth."

"We're going to Vathayne?" I exclaimed. "Whatever for?" I could think of nowhere I would rather be at the moment, but I could not imagine a Va-gas would be well received by the U-ga, who bred the quadrupeds for consumption.

"It can be no worse there than among the Kalkars," he said. "Besides, I have heard rumors about Tu-lav, the Jemadar of Vathayne who leads the rebellion. It is said that by his order the Va-gas of Vathayne are treated as equals among the U-ga." No-ma-ro's stomach growled with hunger, and he added, "But even more importantly, there will be meat. As much as one wants, they say."

"Oh? And where did you gain this intelligence?" I did not want to shatter my friend's dream of endless servings of juicy Va-gas steaks, but I feared he was the victim of a mere rumor and I wanted at all costs to avoid ending up on his dinner plate when he found out the truth.

"I overheard it from a servant of the Go-than princess," No-ma-ro replied. "He said that in the land of Vathayne, Va-gas do not eat Va-gas. Instead, meat is grown artificially in vats and provided in great quantity to the Va-gas who dwell there. Therefore, there is no need to devour the flesh of our own kind."

"If what the servant told you is true and Vathayne is indeed a Va-gas paradise, why didn't he accompany you?"

"He would have but he died in the assault. But not before he told me where lies the land of Vathayne. We made plans to leave the Kalkar city together and to bring you along to speak to Tu-lav on our behalf, for the Jemadar will surely look kindly upon an Earth man, whose people are also great enemies of the Kalkars."

"I hope you are right, No-ma-ro," I said. "I should like nothing more than to join Tu-lav's rebellion and bloody the nose of the Kalkar collective."

No-ma-ro grinned wickedly. "War is good. It is what my people live for." Again, my companion's stomach growled fiercely. "But meat is even better, so we will go to Vathayne and feed on the unending supply of flesh from the vats."

Feeling it would be unwise to argue with the hungry belly of a Va-gas warrior, I said nothing and we continued on.

Under the ceaseless luminosity of the eternal lunar day, surrounded as we were by the weird and unearthly flora and geography of the Moon's interior, I soon lost all sense of how long we had been traveling and how far. Craters vast and small rose before us only to vanish in the dense jungle almost as soon as we passed them by. Though No-ma-ro was not much of a conversationalist, I was glad for even his meager companionship amid the loneliness of the unending wilderness.

During our journey through the forest, I observed countless varieties of plant life, many that would have been unimaginable even in the wildest dreams of an earthly botanist. One of these would have resulted in our deaths had not No-ma-ro already been familiar with it.

This was a particular variety of carnivorous tree, called a roo-den in the language of Va-nah. It reproduces by dropping a strange sort of net composed of vegetable matter, which is weighted down in several places along the fringes by heavy coconut-sized fruits covered in spiked members. The roots of the tree can detect the vibrations of a creature coming down the forest path and are sensitive enough to know when prey passes directly underneath the tree's branches. At this point, the tree releases its net, which falls down on top of the animal. The heavy fruits weigh down the mesh, trapping the prey long enough for the fruits' sharp members to extend and burrow deep down into the soil. These members grasp the roots of the mother tree and then retract, pulling taut the net and restricting the prey's movement. The acidic lining of the net dissolves the flesh, bones, and organs of the trapped animal over a lengthy period, providing nutrients for the nascent tree, which rapidly grows tall like its mother and eventually produces its own spawn capable of hunting prey.

No-ma-ro showed me how to recognize the trees before we passed under them, though on more than one occasion they nearly did us in, since the deadly roo-dens had adapted to grow along curves in the forest trails. When I learned of this aspect of the trees, I inquired of my friend what kind of game frequented the trails, since I had so far seen no evidence of animal life in the forest other than once when I thought I had spied a small deerlike creature leap across the path far ahead of us.

The back of the Va-gas twitched under my thighs in a manner reminiscent of a horse shaking off flies. "The roo-dens eat the bodies of the mur-laks," he said, his tone making it clear that a mur-lak was something to be despised. When I asked him what sort of creature the latter was he replied, "Let us hope we do not encounter one." Although I pressed him on the matter, he would say no more.

After many sleeps—I could find no other way in that nightless world to measure duration other than noting the periods of our slumber—the trail emerged from the deep woods and ran along towering cliff tops overlooking a vast sea. Once again the sight of an ocean curving upward in the distance, with neither horizon nor definitive end, proved an astonishing spectacle for my earthly eyes.

We camped beside the path between the forest's edge and the precipice, listening to the sound of the ocean lapping the thin, rocky band of shore far below. Our bellies full on fruits and berries we had picked from the trees and surrounding vegetation, we lay down to get some rest.

In my restlessness, however, I failed to woo Morpheus, though it was not for want of trying. In my mind I counted sheep leaping over a fence, as my mother had taught me when I found it hard to sleep as a child. When that failed, I metamorphosed the sheep into leaping Va-gas, but the image proved so ludicrous I found myself even more wide-eyed than before.

I could not keep my thoughts from the woman from the sky. Always her face loomed before my mind's eye, dissipating any image I conjured to relax my awareness and open the gates of dream. I wondered who she was and if I would ever see her again. Having watched as the Kalkar gun shot her down out of the luminous heavens, I worried that she would be dead before I ever had the chance to once more gaze into those black onyx eyes or look upon that brave smile.

The thought of injury to her person inflicted by the same race responsible for so much carnage on Earth made my blood boil, and I renewed my determination to find the hidden city of Vathayne so that I might join cause with its citizens and aid them in sending the Kalkars to their doom. The Kalkars were the scourge of two worlds, and for the sake of all intelligent life everywhere I would stop at nothing to accomplish their complete and utter annihilation.

Even amid my anger, that lovely face floated before me, as if to reassure me that good yet persisted in this universe of war, bloodshed, and slavery. Thus comforted, sleep came at last and I dreamed. I found myself winging through lilac skies alongside the woman with the raven hair. Below us the lavender hills of Va-nah shook and buckled, and when we flew farther we looked down upon the Kalkar fortress from which No-ma-ro and I had fled, and watched the entire city fall from the mountainside to be swallowed by the sea.

It was a glorious sight to behold, and I wanted only to remain in my dream with the winged woman for all eternity. Therefore, it was with great annoyance that the most irritating grunting noise intruded upon my well-earned slumber and woke me.

I felt torpid upon awaking and it was all that I could do to open my eyelids the barest fraction of an inch. Even so, the violet light that entered my eyes burned with such intensity that I was forced to press my lids back shut. Further, I was experiencing the strangest tickling sensation in my throat. Bother, I thought—all I want to do is sleep!

Finally, no longer able to abide the irritation in my throat, I forced my sleep-numbed fingers to my neck, the surface of which felt oddly ridged and bulky like...like nothing so much as—fingers wrapped tightly around my gorge!

With a surge of horror, I realized that the grunting noise from my dream was no mere auditory hallucination. No, it was I! I myself was making the very noise that had awakened me—all because someone was violently choking me to death!

I forced my burning eyes open, and I am not ashamed to say that I screamed. Who, I ask you, would have not? For when I opened my eyes, what I looked upon was *my very own visage* staring back at me—the face of Julian 7th!

In a flurry of wild terror, I beat my fists against my doppelganger's face. Though its features resembled mine in all detail, its flesh was sallow and wet, its eyes as dull as those of a corpse. As the thing's clammy grasp attempted to suffocate me, I drew back my leg, positioned my foot beneath my double's stomach, and thrust with all my strength. My attacker released his hold

...staring back at me—the face of Julian 7th!

and flew off me, landing on his back upon the bed of lavender moss on which No-ma-ro and I had been sleeping.

The thing that lay before me was naked and covered in a thin layer of puss-like ooze. While the creature lay supine in its startlement from my kick, I snatched up my sword and drove it into my monstrous double's heart. Or where its heart would have been had it been human. The effect, however, was the same, and my double writhed in its death throes for mere seconds before becoming still.

It was then that I noticed the hideous creature strangling poor No-ma-ro in his sleep beside me. Just as I had been attacked by my double, so too had the Va-gas been assaulted by his. It took only an instant for me to leap to his side and drive my blade through the back of my friend's repulsive twin. The creature fell to one side, thrashing about as if experiencing a violent seizure, and then ceased moving.

As soon as I had dispatched his attacker, No-ma-ro jumped up and shook himself like a wet dog, attempting to rid himself of the revolting slime the creature had deposited on him.

"Mur-laks!" he cried, and then trotted to the forest's edge and began dragging fallen branches and dry brush to the mossy bed where we had lain.

"Whatever are you doing?" I inquired.

"We must burn the bodies, unless you want to see more of our twins sprouting from the mur-laks' putrefying flesh."

Needless to say, I leaped up in all haste and began aiding my companion in his task of gathering wood and kindling. With a flint and iron that No-ma-ro kept in his equipment pouch, as well as a small amount of gunpowder removed from one of my rifle's bullets, we managed to light a small fire, which we nurtured into a full-fledged bonfire. Once the blaze was raging hot, together we lifted the bodies of the mur-laks and hefted them into the flames. A pungent aroma rose when the carcasses caught fire and began sizzling and crackling, not unlike the smell produced when a particularly moldy batch of mulch hay is set aflame.

"Now what in Hades were those things?" I exclaimed.

"I have told you, they were mur-laks," No-ma-ro replied in his typical curt fashion. I was not about to let the fellow give me the silent treatment again, so I demanded that if he did not explain the creatures, I would refuse to move on from this dread area of the accursed forest.

No-ma-ro huffed heavily from the great bellows that were his lungs. "Very well, but if the mur-laks return and strangle us to death, do not complain to me about it."

I assured him that my dead corpse would be as silent as a stone were such an event to transpire. He cocked his head and for a moment looked at me through narrowed lids, as if trying to decide whether I mocked him, but at last he went on.

"The mur-laks are a type of plant peculiar to this region of Va-nah, as far as I am aware. At least, I have never encountered them elsewhere nor had any from my tribe until we migrated to this area when I was but a foal. We lost a quarter of our tribe to the frightful creatures. A mur-lak creeps up silently while its prey is asleep, often taking the form of a small lizard or a worm. Its body releases a sweet flowery aroma that deadens the senses of its prey, ensuring that its victim remains unconscious. Then the mur-lak extends from its body a grass-like stem, at the tip of which is a slender needle. This pricks into the victim's flesh with two-fold purpose, both injecting a poison into the prey that makes it remain asleep and taking a sample of its blood. From the blood the plant somehow learns the essence of the creature it has stuck with its needle, allowing the mur-lak to transform in only a short time into its victim's twin."

"But how," I asked, "does it gain mass if it begins as a creature the size of a small lizard?"

"A hollow root reaches down into the soil, which the mur-lak draws into itself and swiftly transforms into a mockery of flesh and organs."

I shuddered, wondering what circumstances had led nature to develop such a hideous abomination. I recalled the deerlike creature I had spied earlier and asked No-ma-ro about it.

"Yes," he said, "it must have been a mur-lak. Now, may we go?"

"Almost," I said. "I have one more question. Why did you bring us into this forest if you knew the mur-laks infested it? Surely you must have known the simulacra would prey upon us!"

"I told you the Kalkars would not pursue us if we entered the woods," he said. "Was I not correct? Besides, passing through the woods is the only way to reach Vathayne. Is that not where you wish to go?"

I told him that it was but warned that if he was holding back any more pertinent information, he had better be forth-coming with it now or I wouldn't be so quick to save him next time the mur-laks struck.

The Va-gas looked at me as if he were considering my threat in all earnestness. "How do you feel about getting wet, Earth man?" he asked.

I asked No-ma-ro what he meant, but he only grinned and said, "Let us leave behind the forest of the mur-laks and I shall show you."

Chapter Ten

A LUNAR SEA

We continued down the path, which ran for some distance along the summit of the towering, sea-girt cliff. It might have been a day by earthly reckoning or possibly as much as a week—for who can say in timeless Va-nah?—before the trail began descending the craggy wall. Though I felt reassured to leave behind the sylvan habitat of the deadly roo-dens and the hideous mur-laks, the way along the cliff was no less nerve-racking. Soon the path narrowed considerably, oftentimes to such a degree that I found myself hugging the cliff face while the rocky soil broke away beneath my heels and tumbled down the precipice for what must have been fully a mile or more until it reached the slender shoreline below. How No-ma-ro managed the climb I do not know, though I joked with him that he must be half mule and that I was tempted to ride him down. Of course, he did not understand the reference.

After we had climbed to approximately the halfway point, I pressed my companion on our plans for when we would reach the little band of shore along the cliff's base. His answer both astounded me and was cause for great trepidation.

"We shall sail across the great sea," he said matter-of-factly.

"But where will we find the resources to construct a boat?" I protested. "We have neither axe nor hammer, and where will we obtain the wood? Though the beach is far below and it is difficult to make out details of the vegetation that clings to the cliff, I see no evidence that such undergrowth will provide the timber necessary to build a seaworthy vessel."

"Trust me, Ju-lan Sev-ath," he replied, which was as near as he could come to pronouncing my full name. "We shall sail across the sea."

As I looked back up the harrowing trail that skirted the steep rock, sheer exasperation overwhelmed me at the thought of enacting our climb in reverse.

"I'll trust you, No-ma-ro," I said. "But heaven help you if you are wrong, for I will make you carry me back up to the top!"

The Va-gas grinned, and I do believe he took great satisfaction at seeing me so out of sorts.

When at last we set foot at the bottom of the cliff, I looked along the shoreline in despair. Though leafy foliage grew along the bluffs, I saw no trees we might hew down to construct a boat, even had we possessed the necessary tools.

No-ma-ro for his part appeared unfazed and trotted over to the lavender-hued undergrowth, where he plucked a large ripe purple fruit from a flowering plant and took a bite out of it. He continued eating the fruit until he had consumed all but the core and then cast away the remains.

"That will do just nicely," he said, looking up at an enormous, feathery leaf growing from a hefty stalk. "Here, hand me your sword."

I did as he commanded and watched as he crawled into the scrub and began hacking away at the base of the plant with my blade. The leaf fell with a crash upon the thicket, for it was indeed a massive frond, fully fifteen feet in length and just under half as wide.

"That," I said, as the truth of his intentions dawned on me, "is our boat? Why, it's hardly a sixteenth of an inch thick! It will surely tear and sink into the sea beneath our weight!" I was crestfallen, as there was nothing more to do but begin the arduous climb back up to the summit and reenter the frightful forest.

No-ma-ro handed me back my sword and said simply, "Strike the leaf with your blade."

So angry and dejected did I feel that it was with much relish that I swung my sword with all my strength down upon the thin, almost transparent frond.

As the blade struck and bounced off the leaf's iron-hard surface, my inadvertent cry must have been heard even more than a mile above by the hideous creatures of the woodland. Indeed, the leaf itself resounded like an iron bell tolling stridently above the gentle surf and far out across the placid waters.

"The leaf is as hard as steel!"

"And lighter than the winged fliers of Vathayne." With his utterance, No-ma-ro squatted back on his hind legs and, grasping the stem with his fore-paws, lifted the enormous leaf over his head and hurled it into the sea. I fully expected the leaf to sink, but I was yet again surprised, for it floated on the water like a flower petal that has fallen gently onto the surface of a pond.

I stood there with my mouth agape, admiring the form and structure with which nature had endowed the leaf. Even the sleekest example of a canoe could not have been designed better. The laminas of the leaf bowed up on either side, creating an area between them that did in fact resemble the hull of a canoe, flat on the bottom and nearly perpendicular on the thwarts. The leaf's apex rose from the bottom like a curving tongue, which leveled out to make a little deck at the bow, and the hewed-off end of the stem served the same purpose at the stern. A more seaworthy craft I could not imagine.

"Well done!" I exclaimed to my companion. "I won't doubt you again."

I waded out into the surf and dragged our boat back ashore, after which we proceeded to gather an abundant supply of fruits from the copious trees growing along the cliff's base. These we loaded into the craft, along with a number of large, hard-shelled pods that grew on a particular variety of tree. A sort of natural plug stoppered each of these pods at the stem; one simply had to pull on the stem to pop off the plug and gain access to the slightly sweet-tasting nectar at the core, which on average amounted to about a quart of liquid per fruit.

Thus provisioned, we hauled our leaf-boat out into the shallows and climbed aboard. Using oars fashioned from the stems of the same species of plant from which we had obtained our canoe, we pushed ourselves off from shore and soon found ourselves plying the calm waters of the lunar sea.

Though I had lived most of my life on my family's farm, I had once set out in a small boat upon the great inland sea that stretches along the eastern edge of the Teivos of Chicago, having been ordered by the Kash Guard to cross to the other side to attend a sick mare belonging to a Kalkar officer of some import in another Teivos. Therefore, I had some familiarity with the feel of an oar cutting the water. So it was that I remarked to No-ma-ro that, despite the strength of my earthly muscles, the oars moved rather sluggishly in the sea. The Va-gas merely shrugged, for he knew nothing different. Only later did I learn that I could lay the blame for the water's peculiarly high viscosity on centrifugal force operating on the surface of the Moon's hollow interior.

Despite the listless sea, I felt we made good progress, though of course I had no measure for the passage of time in this sunless world other than the callouses that grew thick upon my palms and the aching in my arms and back from the repetitious act of rowing. I was, however, thankful for the lack of the sun ruthlessly beating down upon us, as well as for the mild temperature of the soft ocean breeze, for the climate ranged from ten to twenty degrees Fahrenheit cooler upon the sea than on land, where eighty degrees was the norm.

No-ma-ro had assured me before our departure that we had enough provisions to cross the sea to the land of Vathayne, so when I noticed our supplies beginning to dwindle I remarked upon the development to my companion.

"Perhaps the servant of the Go-than princess who told me the way to Vathayne was mistaken about the length of the voyage," he said, gazing at me somewhat strangely, I thought. Was that the glint of hunger I perceived in the dark eyes of the Va-gas?

I moved away from my companion to the boat's aft, where we kept the food provisions. Still keeping my eyes on the Va-gas, I tossed him one of the remaining pieces of fruit.

"Chew on that while you row," I said, "and keep your mind on the flesh vats of Vathayne. The endless supply of meat that lies ahead ought to keep you motivated."

"Do not worry, Ju-lan," No-ma-ro said, still fixing me with that peculiar look. "The thought of meat has not left my mind."

I shuddered and, returning to the task of rowing, leaned my shoulder into my oar with a renewed sense of urgency.

It was not much after this uncomfortable episode when I heard a deep rumbling from the sky sternward. I looked back to see a mass of dark purple clouds rolling down the curving sheet of the sea behind us, lit up every few seconds with terrific flashes of lightning. The breeze against our backs had recently picked up, causing small, choppy waves to break against the stern and increasing the difficulty of our rowing and our efforts to maintain a straight course ahead.

"Zo-al is angry!" cried No-ma-ro when he noticed the oncoming storm. "We are lost!"

"I don't believe in losing," I said. "Not while I still live, in any case, and I certainly don't intend to go down without a fight, especially against your temperamental storm god. Now row harder!"

Though fear had stricken the Va-gas, he did as I commanded, and together we bent our backs into the rising gale.

The waves swelled beneath our craft, and we were forced to secure our useless oars to the bottom of the boat. We clung tightly to the edges of the thwarts as we rose up high on the crests of waves and then, our stomachs turning, we plummeted down into the deep troughs, where we could see nothing but towering walls of water. Using ropelike vines we had procured from the vegetation along the shoreline, I tied myself as best I could to a knot on the stem-like projection jutting from the stern while my companion similarly affixed himself to the bow.

The purple sky darkened to almost black, but the lightning now struck all around us, illuminating in brief flashes of brilliant intensity the terrifying sea that raged about us. The clouds opened and deluged us with sheet after sheet of icy rain. I marveled that our improvised craft had so far managed to stay seaworthy, but I could not believe it would remain so for long. The violence with which our boat crashed down upon the waves' troughs seemed to increase with each occurrence, and often I found myself in the air, clinging desperately to the feeble vine that was my lifeline.

Once, as we rose up fifty feet on a wave, I saw in a flash of lightning what I thought might be a colossal mountain projecting from the sea. When we were lifted up again I could see nothing, however, and soon I convinced myself I had only glimpsed but another massive wave against the darkened heavens.

The booming and cracking of thunder created such a din that I could no longer feel smug about the lunar inhabitants' belief in the dreaded Zo-al, the godlike beast said to emerge from deep within the Va-nah's craters when he grew angry. Fully could I understand how the terror generated by the frightful storms had given rise to the belief in that all-powerful demon. In reality, the tempests were but natural phenomena created by the unequal sizes and distribution of craters opening from the Moon's interior onto its surface, and through which sunlight heated Va-nah's atmosphere in an uneven manner. But amid the clamor and chaos of the appalling storm, even I began to doubt as my hindbrain seized control of my rationality and endeavored to wring all sense from it.

Then the inevitable occurred. As a wave wrenched us savagely into the air, I felt the line securing me to the stern break

The booming and cracking of thunder created such a din...

and I was hurled into the frigid sea like so much flotsam. I sank down, deep below the water's surface. Down, down I went, and farther still. My lungs ached for air as my limbs thrust and kicked me in a direction that I hoped was upward. Submerged as I was, I found the waters strangely calm, but they bore the heaviness of oil so that I could not discern whether I made any progress in my torturous effort to reach the surface.

I thought my lungs would burst and still I swam through the endless depths. The pain in my chest became so terrible that I almost looked forward to the blissful release from life that a single intake of water into my lungs would bring. But whether due to my upbringing or my very nature, I am a tenacious soul, and I held on to life with every fiber of my being. Well it was that I did, for only seconds later my head broke over the surface and I was breathing in blessed air, as well as gulping down several mouthfuls of water.

I must have been once more at the crest of a wave, for there it was again, illuminated in a lightning flash against the backdrop of the dark, turbulent sky—a mountain in the middle of the sea! It was not a mirage, I was sure, for I blinked and in the light of another fiery bolt I saw it yet again. I threw every ounce of my strength into my breaststroke and made for the island massif.

At times the clamor of the storm grew suddenly silent as I sank back under the waves, but always I struggled back to the surface and inhaled life-giving air. Often I knew not the direction in which I swam, but then I would rise up on a crest and again catch a glimpse of that soaring peak. Each time it appeared a little closer, until at last I dared to entertain hope.

The waves battered me without mercy, rapidly draining my vitality even as I drew nearer to my goal. At one point I felt something long and scaly rub against my thigh, and a new kind of terror seized me. I truly think I might have perished had it not been for that brief encounter with the unknown monster of the lunar depths, for it gave strength to my flagging muscles and renewed my determination to reach the island in all due haste.

Between the crashes of thunder and over the splashing of the waves, I heard at last the roar of breakers upon the shore. As I paddled with my legs, one of my toes touched the sandy bottom beneath me, and a moment later my whole foot found purchase. I tried walking through the shallows, but so fatigued was I that my feet failed to hold my weight and I fell back into the water. Turning upon my back, I allowed the breaking waves to carry me ashore, where I lay upon the black volcanic sands while the water lapped over my exhausted form and at last sleep overcame me.

Chapter Eleven

CAPTURED

I lay unmoving in my slumber where the sea had deposited me for as long as it took the clouds to brighten to their normal pink and the waves to recede several yards from my sandy bed. When I awoke, every muscle attached to my frame hurt and it was only the overwhelming desire to alleviate my intense thirst that finally motivated me to attempt to stand. This I managed to do feebly, and I staggered down the slope of the beach and drank of the sea. The water was only very mildly salinized and therefore potable, if not quite as satisfying as the semisweet liquid from the cores of the hollow fruits No-ma-ro and I had provisioned in the boat.

When I had quenched my thirst and felt my fortitude returning, I set off down the beach to explore my new surroundings, keeping an eye out toward the sea in case I might spy our boat upon the water. I did not know whether a Va-gas could swim, but I had a hard time envisioning it and feared the worst for my former companion.

As I strolled along the lunar shore, I studied the great massif I had glimpsed when carried high upon the waves amid the tempest and that now loomed above me on my right. That the mountain was volcanic in origin I had no doubt, shaped as it was like the other craters I had observed in Va-nah, though towering to a much greater height. I wondered whether it might be one of the Hoos leading to the surface of the Moon, those colossal vents that in some dim age had ejected magma from the core of Earth's satellite and created the inner world of which

I was now a resident. For as far as I could see, the mountain's base stretched along the shoreline, and as I proceeded on my way, its treacherous flank only continued to wind out before my vision. Truly was it a massive crag.

I had gone some distance when I spotted something long and narrow floating listlessly in the shallows. I waded out into the sea and retrieved the object, which turned out to be my lance. I had secured the weapon to the bottom of the boat as the storm hit, but it had apparently broken loose. Finding it heartened me, for I had lost my sword and rifle in the raging tempest, and the bullets in my pistol, which I still wore in the holster at my hip, had been soaked and were at best unreliable if not entirely useless.

When I returned to the shore I caught sight of a small, dark recess at the base of the massif. As this was the first variance I had observed in the unbroken face of the rocky foundation, I walked over to examine the opening. I could see nothing within its pitch-black interior, so I stepped inside and called out. My voice echoed deeply and I had the sense that a vast cavern stretched before me. Further, the fresh air from outside blew easily into the grotto, for which fact I suspected the existence of a tunnel leading to another opening to the surface somewhere beyond the reaches of the cave.

As my first objective was to find a source of nourishment and the cave was unlikely to yield such, I began walking back to the beach, resolving to return and seek shelter there should another lunar storm strike the island. I had gone only a few steps when an unnerving chittering sound came from out of the dark mouth of the cavern behind me.

The hair on the back of my neck rose erect and a chill ran down my spine as for a moment I froze in place. Then, clutching my lance in both hands, I whirled about to confront whatever had made the sound.

Instantly came a clattering of what sounded like many appendages beating rapidly against the hard stone floor of the sea cave. I raised my lance toward the noise and crouched just as a mighty force barreled into me. Still gripping my lance, I flew through the air and landed on my rear in the sandy area just outside the cavern.

I kicked myself backward, still seated upon the sand, as the strangest creature I had ever laid my eyes upon emerged into the light of the eternal lunar day. I had only the barest moment to take it in—a crablike, wolf-sized body with six beady eyes forming a half-crescent around the front of a beaked, avian head—before one of the beast's fore-pincers stabbed down into the sand just as I rolled out of its way.

I came up on my feet and swung my lance like a baseball bat at the thing's birdlike head. The hard wood of the lance hit with a loud crack against the chitin that seemed to plate every inch of the monster. The creature reared back on several spindly legs, its fore-pincers now raised again and aiming to strike, but already I was running out of its reach.

Something about the crablike nature of the monster made me think it would do quite well in the water. Therefore, instead of heading for the sea, I ran along the crag and then bounded up its side as quickly as I could without dropping my precious lance. I looked down the steep face of the rock to see the lunar crab skittering after me upon its long, jointed legs.

I climbed higher, but the creature ascended swiftly and I knew it would soon overtake me. I positioned myself on a narrow but stable shelf some forty feet up from the mountain's base. What I hoped to achieve against the monster from my perch I did not know. I had only the lance as a weapon, which would have served me well were I mounted upon a horse or a Va-gas. Here on the precipitous ledge, I might do little with the lance but enrage the crab-thing as it clambered up and attacked me with its powerful, razor-sharp pincers.

As the lunar crab scrambled up directly beneath me, I jabbed down the lance with the force of both of my well-muscled arms. The lance's steel tip merely glanced off the hard, slick chitin

I had only the lance as a weapon...

that armored the creature's underside. I tried to lift the lance back up but the crab-thing grabbed it by one of its pincers and nearly pulled me from the ledge as we engaged in a furious tug of war for possession of the spear.

Knowing I was doomed if the lunar crab deprived me of my only weapon, I risked being grabbed by the monster's other pincer and kicked the creature fully in its hideous, many-eyed face. Just as I did so, the lunar crab pulled upon the lance with the tremendous strength of its pincer and, losing my footing, I fell directly toward the beast!

My feet landed forcefully upon the creature's underside, which it had exposed as it reared at me with its claws. Taken by surprise at having my full weight upon it, the beast lost its own hold upon the rock and flipped upon its back as I grabbed on to its hard-shelled belly. Together we careened down the rugged mountainside. I found myself holding on for dear life, riding the lunar crab as if it were some monstrous bobsleigh.

The creature screeched something awful as we slid down the steep slope, its jointed legs flailing and trying to find purchase so the crab might turn itself over. Fortunately, it did not succeed, even as its slide came to a sudden stop and the creature lay belly up, writhing upon the bed of ebony sand at the mountain's base. I stood up from the monster, one foot pressing down upon its chest, and raised my lance, which I had managed to cling to despite our wild ride down the mountainside. With all my strength I thrust the tip of the lance into the crab-thing's gorge.

The monster's razor-sharp mouthparts, resembling those of a terrestrial arthropod, thrashed with fury at the lance as the beast's screeching deafened my ears, but the damage had been done. I had inflicted a mortal wound to my hideous foe, which soon lay still other than the occasional reflexive spasm of its segmented limbs.

I stepped back from the monster and gaped in surprise as I looked up at the beach. Standing before me in a semicircle was a group of armored men bearing drawn swords.

The newcomers could not be Kalkars, as they were all handsome specimens with fine and well-proportioned features, each soldier being of the same stature as an Earth man. Their complexions were as pale as my grandmother's, and I could only assume the men were U-ga, members of the human population of Va-nah. My grandmother, Nah-ee-lah, had sprung from this same noble race, which had been hunted down and subjugated by the Kalkars for centuries, or perhaps even millennia, before Laythe, the last openly known U-ga city, had ultimately fallen to its enemies with the help of the traitor Orthis.

Overjoyed at having found a population of U-ga apparently living under their own authority upon this remote island in a vast lunar sea, I smiled broadly and extended my hand in the universal sign of friendship.

A stern-faced man stepped forward. His gleaming visored helmet appeared more ornate than those of the other soldiers and I could only assume he was the leader of the group.

"You have slain the Jemadar's personal mo-lah-kar," he said gravely. "You will come with us to Vathayne to be tried in the court of Tu-lav—or if you resist, you will die here upon the obsidian shores of La-fal-nah."

Chapter Twelve

IN THE COURT OF THE MOON KING

I had never before heard of a mo-lah-kar, but it was clear that the crab-thing I had killed seemed to be quite precious to Tu-lav, the Jemadar of Vathayne. The soldiers lost no time in relieving me of my pistol and lance, and proceeded to bind my wrists with a kind of rope that resembled silk but was as strong as iron. I protested, stating that I had only dispatched the beast in self-defense, but my complaints were ignored. The leader ordered his men to place a noose of the same material around my neck and the soldiers led me back to the cave where I had first encountered the mo-lah-kar.

Although not happy about being thus restrained, I was not worried. I thanked both Providence and luck that the lunar storm had deposited me upon the shores of the very hidden kingdom I had sought, for who can say which of those two cosmic forces blesses us when we are met with such fortuitous circumstances? I knew that once I explained to the Jemadar of Vathayne how his people's allies upon the distant planet of Barsoom had set me upon my mission, all of the charges against me would be dropped and I would be welcomed unreservedly as a friend. After all, I was the descendant of Julian 5th, who had battled the maleficent Orthis and ultimately sent the fiend to his death.

Therefore, I offered no resistance to my captors and accompanied them in good spirits. We entered the cave and proceeded across the level stone floor until darkness consumed us and I could see nothing ahead. Before long my shoulders were rubbing against rock on either side, and it became clear that we had filed into a narrow tunnel at the back of the cave. A draft of cool sea air blew through the tunnel from outside the cave, giving evidence to the theory I had posited earlier that a passageway in the grotto must eventually open somewhere upon the surface.

The tunnel floor began to incline and wind gradually to the right as we continued on. Soon I realized I could make out the faint outline of the man climbing ahead of me, which became more defined the farther along we traveled. At first I was at a loss to explain how I could see within the tunnel, as I could perceive no distinct light source, but as the illumination brightened I came to understand that the rocks surrounding us must contain radium. Thus, in the same way that the surface of Va-nah is bathed in a gentle light produced by radium-rich soil and rocks, so too was the tunnel we trod illuminated.

My leg muscles grew weary as we climbed ever upward within the bowels of the colossal crag. I attempted to engage my captors in conversation, introducing a host of topics ranging from the geological origins of the mountain to the finery of the soldiers' trappings and accoutrements. The men responded only with stony gazes and cold silence.

The tunnel wound on with mind-numbing monotony until I could only surmise we must be nearing the summit of the soaring mountain. Suddenly we came to a large, heavily reinforced door composed of silvery metal. The leader of the soldiers produced a metallic cube from a bag hanging from his belt and the door swung open of its own accord. The man ahead of me tugged on the rope about my neck and led me through the doorway.

When I emerged upon the other side, I gasped at the sight before me. I was standing on a terrace overlooking the interior of a massive crater, which plummeted endlessly downward until it faded into utter darkness. Surely I was within one of the Hoos, the enormous dormant volcanic lunar vents that bored through two hundred and fifty miles of lunar crust until they emerged upon the surface of the Moon.

But the sight of the unfathomable crater, though indeed it was spectacular, was not what took away my breath. No, it was the cyclopean metropolis that had been constructed along the curving sides of the great abyss that left me agape. I had never seen such a sight, which in its vastness and complexity seemed to defy all sense of scale. I could hardly conceive that human hands had constructed such a marvel of architecture and engineering.

Tiers of enormous buildings circled down the face of the crater, the broad avenues and boulevards running between the structures abounding with pedestrians. Both U-ga and Va-gas filled the busy streets, the sight of the latter species reminding me of what No-ma-ro had said concerning the easy acceptance of the quadrupeds among the people of Vathayne.

At one point, on the level directly below our own, I spied a crablike mo-lah-kar being led on a leash by its master, who yawned as if bored with his task as he directed the beast down a narrow side street and then vanished into the crowd. My eyes could not deny the fact that the fearsome creature had been domesticated. I suddenly understood something of the sentiment expressed by the leader of my captors when he had accused me in the harshest of tones of having killed the Jemadar's personal mo-lah-kar. I wondered if my act of slaying the repulsive creature that had attacked me would fill the king of Vathayne with as much abhorrence as if I had ruthlessly killed a man's pet hound back on Earth. The idea seemed absurd, given the frightful appearance of the lunar monster and the fact that I had acted only in self-defense, but then I knew next to nothing of the culture and customs of Vathayne's citizens. I affirmed that I would do well to keep such cultural deficiencies in mind if I hoped to strike up an alliance between Tu-lav and my oppressed people back on Earth.

My captors led me across the terrace to a wide protuberance of stone jutting from the crater's side like a gargantuan tongue.

We mounted the natural bridge, crossing far out over the dizzying heights of the Hoos. A strong breeze whirled down upon
us from the summit of the extinct volcano. I gazed up and saw
a flock of winged human figures, like those that had besieged
the Kalkar city from which I had come, gliding overhead upon
the air currents. The soldiers escorting me continued on unper-
turbed while I tried to hide my concern that a particularly
powerful gust might hurl us over the brink to our deaths.

At last we passed over the mile-wide chasm and dismounted the bridge on the crater's far side. Here loomed a towering,
fortified castle carved from the stone face of the volcano's throat.
High upon its summit on one side stretched a wide and flat
horizontal surface that resembled a landing platform. Although
it was devoid of aerial vehicles or the personnel and equipment
necessary to operate an air fleet, I surmised that it might be the
area from which Vathayne both launched and received its force
of winged fliers. Perhaps from my vantage I merely could not
see the openings in the deck from which the fliers and support
personnel might emerge, and I wondered whether the lack of
outbuildings upon the platform might be indicative of concern
for an aerial attack on the city by Kalkar dirigibles.

A contingent of cavalrymen stationed before the castle,
mounted upon Va-gas and holding high their shining lances,
rode out and met our party, and then proceeded to escort us
through an immense gate into the courtyard beyond. We crossed
over a drawbridge spanning a defensive ditch that had been
excavated deep into the terrace and then climbed an elevated
road that spiraled up the castle's base to a great double door of
some gleaming lunar metal. Two of the cavalrymen accompanying us raised golden horns to their lips and trumpeted to
announce our arrival. The towering doors swung open, drawn
by soldiers on the other side, and our group entered the fortress,
crossing the bailey to an imposing stone keep. A portcullis set
in its face drew up and the smaller party that had captured me
passed inside while the cavalrymen withdrew on their Va-gas
mounts.

The soldiers led me through a grand foyer to a high, arched door flanked by guards, who saluted the leader of our group and opened the gate so we might pass. I found myself in a large and stately throne room whose walls depicted in bas-relief the regal likenesses of what I gathered to represent the kings and queens of Vathayne over many generations. Before the soldier at my side forced me to bow my head, I caught a glimpse of four thrones resting upon a dais at the far side of the chamber, the center two of which, raised higher than the others, were occupied by a man and a woman, both of whom I judged to be just past middle age. Being U-ga like my escort, the pair exhibited marble-white skin and raven-black hair. The woman, her body lithe and her face displaying a cold unearthly beauty, looked vaguely familiar to me, though I could not fathom where I might have met her and so dismissed my observation without further thought. I was brought to the foot of the dais, where I was commanded to kneel. Not wanting to offend my people's future allies, I assented, at which point I was told I was permitted to raise my head and look upon the royal countenances of Tu-lav and Val-eev-mah, the Jemadar and Jemadav—that is, Emperor and Empress—of the free kingdom of Vathayne.

I looked up to find the Jemadar scrutinizing me with an expression of distrust, if not outright scorn. He regarded me for only a moment before beckoning the leader of my escort to ascend the dais and take his seat upon the throne to his right, an order that the soldier promptly obeyed.

"Who is this outsider you have risked bringing within our sacred sanctuary, my son?" Tu-lav said, his tone clearly laden with contempt for my presence. I raised my brows—not only upon gathering that I was the object of the Jemadar's suspicions, but also upon discovering that I had been captured by Tu-lav's own kin, the Javadar, or Prince, of Vathayne.

"He is a trespasser who has slain one of your moh-lah-kars—the royal guardian who protected the entrance to Vathayne at the base of La-fal-nah," the Javadar said. "I have brought him here, Father, so that you may pass judgment upon him, as the ancient law decrees."

"I see no need for me to pass judgment," Tu-lav replied. "The law is clear. This spy slew my guardian while attempting to infiltrate Vathayne. Like all spies, he must die."

"Don't I get a trial?" I asked, increasingly anxious at the conversation unfolding before me. "I can explain my presence here quite easily. I am by no means a spy. In fact, quite the contrary. I was sent to Vathayne upon a mission of the utmost urgency—a mission that has bearing on the success or failure of the war you wage against the Kalkars. An ambassadorial entourage from Barsoom has gone missing and—"

The Jemadar made a motion with his hand and the soldier beside me struck me forcefully with the back of his hand, leaving my cheek flaming with pain. Although I knew full well the deference I must at all costs show to the monarch before me, I am not one to suffer such a humiliating blow without answer, no matter who commands the deed. Immediately, I leaped up and struck a clean blow with my fist to the offending soldier's chin, laying him prone upon the ornate tiles of the throne room of the Emperor of Vathanye.

The guards instantly seized me while Tu-lav, rising from his seat upon the dais, issued my death sentence. "Kill him!" the Jemadar cried. "I want to see his Kalkar blood run thinly like the water it is."

One of the guards restraining me drew his short sword and was about to drive it into my abdomen when a woman's voice sang out loudly in the melodious tongue of the U-ga.

"Belay my father's order!" came the voice from the back of the chamber. "This man saved my life—he is no Kalkar spy!"

The soldier held his sword in abeyance and looked to the Jemadar for guidance. Tu-lav merely scowled and sat back down as a beautiful young woman, wearing a gauzy sleeveless tunic and a silver circlet upon a head of long jet-black hair, strode past me. As she took her seat upon the throne to Tu-lav's left, she turned to face me. I gasped in astonishment. It was the woman from the sky! That day upon the turret in the Kalkar city, I had unknowingly rescued Tu-lav's own daughter, the Princess of Vathayne, from certain death.

Although I might be struck dead in an instant by the soldier's raised sword, I knelt with bowed head before the woman whose words had granted me at least a temporary stay of execution. Such humility and deference did the mere sight of her inspire in me, for never before I had seen a creature more regal and fair.

"Rise, warrior," came the woman's voice. "Know that the authority of Voo-rah-nee, the Nonovar of Vathayne, will protect you until your story has been told and its merits have been judged true or false. Now speak! I am anxious to hear the tale of the man who singlehandedly saved my fliers from being shot down out of the skies above Kalkar City No. 472."

I rose and, smiling wide with gratitude, bowed to the Nonovar, which meant Princess in the tongue of the U-ga. "I am Ju-lan Sev-ath," I said, for there was no use in speaking a name the locals could not pronounce. "I come from a world beyond Va-nah—Earth, of which doubtless you are aware, though it was unknown to the people of Va-nah only a few short decades ago. I thank you for hearing me out, Nonovar."

Voo-rah-nee gave me a nod and a smile, gestures that both heartened me and summoned up a strange, unidentifiable feeling in my chest. The Jemadar, however, frowned and said, "Ju-lan," pronouncing my name both slowly and with a tone of suspicion. "I have heard that name before. Are you related to the Earthman, he who was called Ju-lan-fit, who brought the dread malefactor Orthis to Va-nah and in so doing aided the Kalkars in their conquest of our world?"

"Ju-lan-fit was my grandfather," I said, using the U-ga pronunciation for Julian 5th. "But he was as much a victim of Orthis' wickedness as the inhabitants of both Earth and Va-nah.

It was the woman from the sky!

In fact, it was Ju-lan-fit who slew Orthis in battle and spared both worlds of his further aggressions."

Tu-lav sneered at my statement, and I could feel the already palpable tension in the room grow yet more taut. "Both worlds spared?" he exclaimed. "You dare tell such a brazen lie in my court when all here know only too well that both Va-nah and Earth abide in the thralldom of the Kalkars?"

"Trust me," I said. "It would have been worse had he lived."

"Trust you?" Tu-lav's mocking laughter echoed off the walls and ceiling of the cavernous chamber. "You, in whose veins run the blood of Ju-lan-fit, the outsider who handed Orthis our world and caused the extinction of Laythe, the last U-ga city to reign in open defiance of the Kalkar scourge?"

"Father!" Voo-rah-nee cried, her cheeks coloring to a deeper cream in her anger. "We will hear out this man's story. I—no, you, as well, my Jemadar—owe it to him for risking his life to spare the fliers of Vathayne from the guns of the Kalkars." Then, addressing me, she said, "Go on, Ju-lan Sev-ath. Fear no more interruptions until you have had your say." With this last utterance, she locked an icy glare upon her father.

"Well," I continued, "I am but a lowly trainer of horses who—" Quizzical eyes stared back at me and I had to explain that a horse was a beast of burden similar to a Va-gas but without the lunar quadrupeds' sentience or high intelligence. Smiling encouragingly, Voo-rah-nee nodded and I went on. "I was contacted by an emissary from the city-state of Helium upon the planet Barsoom, who sent a transmission through the ether from her own world. The woman sought my help to locate an ambassadorial mission that had traveled from Barsoom to Va-nah after opening up diplomatic channels with Vathayne."

Voo-rah-nee shot her father a questioning look, but Tu-lav merely shrugged, leaning back in his throne and yawning as if he were bored with my story.

"The Barsoomian space ship made contact with Vathayne as it passed into a Hoos and made its way to Va-nah, but that was the last time the Heliumites heard from the vessel. The Barsoomian emissary who contacted me, knowing I was the descendant of Ju-lan-fit, the great enemy of the Kalkars, implored me to steal myself onto a Kalkar transport ship and travel to Va-nah to investigate the disappearance of the Barsoomian ambassador and his party. To achieve my goal, I was forced to pose as a Kalkar soldier. That is why I was in Kalkar City No. 472 when the fliers of Vathayne attacked."

The Nonovar rose and addressed the Jemadar. "The stranger tells a plausible story, Father, though I know nothing of contact between Vathayne and this outer world of Barsoom. Tell me, my Jemadar, is there truth in his words? Have you been in secret communication with these Heliumites of which Ju-lan Sev-ath speaks?"

"Of course not, Daughter," Tu-lav said. "Every word this spy utters is a lie. He is a danger to Vathayne."

"And yet I have seen with my own eyes his acts of bravery and honor," Voo-rah-nee said. "Do you think *I* am a liar and a threat to our people?"

Tu-lav's entire countenance changed suddenly and now an expression of unadulterated love for his child lay writ clearly upon his face.

"You, like your mother, are one of the two great treasures of our kingdom," he said. "I do not question what you believe, only that what you saw in the chaos of battle in the Kalkar city may have other interpretations. Perhaps this Ju-lan acted thus to gain your sympathy so that he might enter our city under the guise of trust, when truly he means to sow our destruction. But my heart grows soft where my daughter is concerned. Therefore, I shall order this man to be placed under arrest until I can ascertain either the truth of his story or his guilt."

"The man who saved the lives of my fliers will not be thrown into the dungeons like a common criminal," Voo-rah-nee declared.

Tu-lav threw up his hands in defeat and smiled at his daughter. "Very well, my dear Voo-rah-nee," he said. "He will be placed under house arrest in the keep's apartments." Then his expression darkened and he regarded me. "But if this man exhibits even the barest hint of treachery, he will die beneath my own blade."

Chapter Thirteen

WITH THE NONOVAR

The apartments where I was confined were lavish by the standards I was used to under the Kalkar regime back on Earth. My rooms took up an entire floor of the keep, and included a bedroom, a dining room, a small lavatory and washroom, an open area equipped with various devices to aid in exercise, a spacious library containing an assortment of books on history and science, and a parlor where I could either receive guests approved by the house guard or relax in solitude.

I spent much of my time in the library, acquainting myself with both the antiquity of Vathayne and its present-day culture. My studies revealed the Vathayneans were an ancient people whose fortress-city had been constructed long before the rise of the Kalkars. For eons they had dwelled within the massive Hoos that was their homeland, cultivating a society ruled by a powerful Jemadar and shepherded by a noble class devoted to the steadfast principles of fairness, rational philosophy, and the rule of law. As the city's influence expanded within Va-nah over the millennia, Vathayne founded several colonies that rose to prominence. Together with other outlying cities that had arisen independently, the colonies formed a mighty empire that was divided into ten vast provinces, each ruled by a Jemadar. In that age, great ships of the land, sea, and air traversed every corner of Va-nah, and a healthy competition grew between the provinces that gave rise to an age of prosperity and enlightenment.

But even as the empire to which Vathayne belonged blossomed with riches both material and cultural, a small group formed that decried any who had more education and wealth than its own members. Soon the group formed a secret society that began spreading its message among the masses and instigating vicious attacks against both the universities and the government. In an ironic turn, the members of the group called themselves "The Thinkers," or in the universal language of Va-nah: Kalkars. Over a long period, The Thinkers sowed their bitter seed of hatred, intolerance, and ignorance, until finally they ushered in a bloody revolution that swept across all of Va-nah and resulted in the murder of the Jemadars and the vast majority of citizens from the noble class. The revolutionaries took over the reins of government, but being unschooled and brutish, they knew nothing of the art of governance and the once-enlightened culture of the U-ga rapidly fell into decadence and disorder. In the vacuum of power created by the Kalkars' revolution, the Va-gas, who had been bred merely as a source of meat by the humans of Va-nah, rose up against their masters, further precipitating the decline of the U-ga into barbarism.

Due to its isolated location upon an island far out on the lunar sea, Vathayne managed to escape the total destruction that followed in the wake of the Kalkars' rise to power. If other cities survived, they were unknown to the Vathayneans. Some nobles from the empire's shattered cities, however, did manage to flee the Kalkars' onslaught. These fugitives went on to found new settlements that waged an ongoing war of resistance against the Kalkars.

In the history books I found mention of Laythe, the city of my grandmother's birth, which fought valiantly to defend its independence until Orthis came and armed the Kalkars with the superior weaponry of Earth. The judgment of the historians of Vathayne was not kind to my grandfather. As he had commanded the Earth mission to Va-nah, Julian 5th was recorded as a villain of the highest order. History is oft said to be written by the victors, but I can attest that this is not always so. Moreover, when it is written by the losers, it can be just as misplaced and condemnatory.

Now I understood Tu-lav's antipathy toward me and my family. Like every citizen of Vathayne, he had been taught to vilify my grandfather, regarding him as the devil who had unleashed death and destruction upon the last vestiges of civilization remaining openly within Va-nah. Could I blame the Vathayneans for believing what they did? After all, they had no way of knowing the complete story, having had no contact with Earth or knowledge of how Orthis had sabotaged my grandfather's mission to Barsoom and the details of his lieutenant's subsequent treachery. As far as Tu-lav knew, Julian 5th was complicit in the plot to deliver Va-nah into the hands of the Kalkars, and indeed may have ordered Orthis to carry out that evil act. I was likely the first person ever to have challenged the official history of those events. Why should I, the grandson of the U-ga's most notorious enemy, be believed?

Realizing the hopelessness of my situation, I sank into a despondency that was relieved only by regular visits from Voo-rah-nee, the Nonovar of Vathayne. Upon these occasions she would call upon me in my quarters for the purpose of gathering evidence in my defense in the hearing to be convened by the Jemadar's court. There in the parlor we would sit, sipping from tall crystal glasses a sort of milky tea derived from some variety of lunar plant while Voo-rah-nee questioned me about the history of Earth and the cruelty imposed by the Kalkars against its inhabitants. She believed the best defense I could offer would be to present to the Jemadar and his court with the true history behind my grandfather's sojourn in Va-nah, in the hope of illustrating that no benefit had come to my family or the people of Earth as a result of the mission. To the contrary, we would present to the court in detail the story of how Julian 5th had striven to his last breath to defeat Orthis and the Kalkars and to wipe their scourge from the solar system.

Notwithstanding the depressing topic of our ongoing discussions—for recounting the bleak history of Earth and the enslavement of its current population is by no means a pleasant task—my heart lifted each time I heard the doorbell chime to announce the arrival of the Nonovar. Voo-rah-nee listened with patience and deep empathy as I told my story, responding with compassion to the darkest parts of my narrative but always ending on an optimistic note, proclaiming that the court could do nothing other than clear my name upon hearing the truth of the matter. I was less hopeful the court would accept my version of events, but her enthusiasm was infectious and heartened me nonetheless.

Though we spent much of our conversations deliberating tactics for my pending trial, I also had the opportunity to question Voo-rah-nee about the wonders of life in Vathayne. Being a city of unimaginable antiquity by terrestrial standards, Vathayne boasted innovations unheard of not only upon present-day Earth, but also across modern Va-nah as a whole. One of these inventions was the radio bomb, which reminded me of a terrifying weapon that had been used on Earth prior to that fateful year of 1967, when the half-century of war abruptly ended and the era of pacifism and universal disarmament that followed unknowingly left the globe defenseless against the coming lunar threat.

I had seen the Vathaynean fliers employ their radio bombs to devastating effect as they soared through the roseate skies over Kalkar City No. 472. Voo-rah-nee explained that the boxlike devices I had spied clutched in the hands of the fliers transmitted a signal to a small, lightweight, radium-fueled missile. When in combat, the flier would release the missile and then manipulate the controls on the device to guide the bomb to its target with startling precision. The radio bombs struck terror in the hearts of the Kalkars, especially when employed on the battlefield against ground troops, as the explosive missiles were often directed to chase down strategic targets, such as the infantry commander, who, even when mounted on a Va-gas, rarely succeeded in evading the flaming terror from the sky.

I also took advantage of my conversations with Voo-rah-nee to inquire about the U-ga's belief in reincarnation, which I had

gathered was the center of her people's worldview and pro-
foundly affected many aspects of their culture. Of course, I was
particularly interested in the subject due to the predilection in
my family line for recalling our own past and future lives. In
this peculiar aptitude, I confess, I have always been something
of a dud. Though at times I have had brief flashes of other
lives—vague, dreamlike visions of images flitting momentarily
before my mind's eye and then vanishing just as quickly—these
transitory experiences provided me with no insight into where
or from when they had originated. They might have been mere
figments of my imagination as far as I was concerned, leaving
no more impression upon me than the unexplained moment
of déjà vu has upon any person with a sound and rational mind.
Still, I knew my impotency in this regard was in no way indicative of the singular ability of certain individuals in my direct
ancestral line to recall multiple incarnations from both the past
and future. In particular, I had heard much in my youth about
Julian 3rd, who was said to have been so gifted in this talent
that he had foretold with uncanny accuracy the invasion of
Earth by the Kalkars, though if he knew anything of the future
beyond that event, I was unaware of it. A pity, I thought, for if
he had, he could have saved me much suffering and grief!

I believe you will understand from what I have just told
you why the U-ga's belief in reincarnation so interested me.
Voo-rah-nee's response to my inquiry left me no less intrigued.

"Do not the people of Earth recall their previous incarnations?" the Nonovar asked when I put my question to her.

"They do not," I said. "Well, in any case, most do not. My
familial line is an exception, and I am told that there are other
cultures that believe in the cycle of a soul's birth and rebirth in
a new body, though the new incarnation is not always human.
Often, it is said, depending on the individual's spiritual progress,
or rather lack thereof, the soul may be reborn into a much inferior creature, say a slug or a worm." As I did not know the
U-ga terms for the latter creatures and Voo-rah-nee was thus
uncertain of my meaning, I used a substitute that she could

understand and explained that one might be reborn as a rympth, one of the four-legged snakes of Va-nah.

Voo-rah-nee recoiled in horror at my suggestion. "Say that it is not so, Ju-lan! I cannot bear to think that I am speaking with a man who might one day be incarnated as a creature so repellant!"

"Then, in Va-nah," I said, "reincarnation is not regarded as a means of spiritual transformation? On Earth, you see, those who believe in reincarnation see it as a means of working out their moral deficiencies so that one day, if they have purged themselves of their imperfections, their souls will no longer be incarnated into new bodies and will instead move on to join the godhead and experience the ultimate fulfillment and bliss."

"It is hard for me to fathom what you mean when you speak of *belief* in reincarnation," she replied. "For the U-ga, it is simply a fact of life. You speak the truth when you say your people have no memory of their past lives?"

When I reaffirmed that this was indeed the case, Voo-rah-nee shook her head of midnight-black hair in exasperation. "How terrible! To live such short lives and have no hope of immortality!"

"Oh, there are many on my world who believe in immortality—just not immortality of the physical variety."

"I do not understand. What other kind is there? Is that not the very definition of the term?"

"On Earth, many believe in spiritual immortality," I said. "Physical immortality, however, is regarded as nothing but a myth."

"But what kind of immortality can a spirit have other than to be incarnated in a physical body? Surely a spirit cannot exist in a discorporate form—if a soul did not seek out a body, it would simply drift away upon the windy breath of Zo-al. And even if it did persist, what a horrible life it would be to exist forever as a specter!" There is no term in the U-ga tongue for a ghost, and I gathered that the word for "soul" carried quite a different connotation in that language. Voo-rah-nee, however, coined a colorful metaphor on the spot that might be translated literally as a "shadow with no substance," which I have rendered here as "specter."

"Well, perhaps it is not such a bad thing," I said wryly, "as long as one has other specters with whom one can mingle."

The Nonovar shuddered. "I do not know of such things."

"But you, in fact, can recall your past lives?"

"Of course," she said.

"Who, then, was your previous incarnation?" I asked.

"I was a Nonovar in my last life as well," she replied, reassuming the regal poise she had for a moment let lapse in the intimacy of our conversation, "though in other incarnations I was a commoner and in yet others a slave. Always are the U-ga of Va-nah reborn in our children's children, though often not in our direct grandchildren, as you have told me you have been. Sometimes we are reborn many generations hence into entirely different circumstances."

"Do you have memories of your future incarnations, as I have told you some of my previous incarnations are said to have had?"

"No." She smiled. "As far as that goes, you are unique."

I wondered about that. Why should it be that I was different from all other U-ga in that regard? For that matter, why should I, an Earth man, remember my other incarnations at all, even in fleeting visions? I had met no one else from my world—other than my grandmother, who was a U-ga from Va-nah—who had such an ability. I put the question to Voo-rah-nee.

"It is an intriguing mystery," she said. "Perhaps it is because two of your incarnations have spent time in Va-nah. It could be that there is something about Va-nah—a radiant field, similar to the planetary rays that space vessels use as a means of propulsion—that has affected you beyond the limits of space and time. Or it may be due to the fact that your grandfather conceived a child with a U-ga woman. Your soul, having inhabited a body that carries U-ga blood, may have somehow been affected. As for why your incarnations have awareness of their future embodiments, I cannot say. Again, possibly it is a result of your mixed heritage, a synergy of sorts, where neither Earth man nor native of Va-nah alone has the ability, but a person of both bloodlines does. Or maybe something will transpire in one of your future incarnations of which you yet have no knowledge. This factor or event, whatever it is, may have changed something in your soul. I have read in a work of the ancients how time does not truly exist as we experience it—that is, as if we are moving forward upon a line. Instead, the line of each of our lives exists beyond time, which is merely an imaginary concept. It is our consciousness, our soul, if you will, that travels across the line. And who is to say that one cannot move backward as well as forward along it, or even experience the line all at once?"

I had to admit that it was an intriguing hypothesis, and one that explained much about the singular ability of my ancestors and, to a much lesser degree, myself.

"I have a vested interest in the veracity of your notion," I said.

"And why is that?" asked the Nonovar of Vathayne.

"Why, if your theory is correct that my ability is due to something that will happen in one of my later incarnations, then my imminent fate is considerably less gloomy than I have supposed it to be of late." When Voo-rah-nee looked at me quizzically, I continued, grinning: "It means a romance lies in my future—one that will result in at least one child who is destined to give birth to my grandson, into whose body my soul will be reincarnated."

The white china cheeks of the Nonovar colored, but I could not fail to notice that, though she lowered her eyes from mine, she smiled. Neither could I avoid observing that my heart beat faster upon seeing the woman's reaction to my statement, as inexplicable as my own response was. After an awkward moment in which my mind drew a complete blank and I could think of nothing to say, Voo-rah-nee let out a little laugh and changed the subject to a discussion on the merits of the works of some dry, longwinded philosopher of the ancients whose name I have since forgotten.

Upon another occasion Voo-rah-nee told me that in a short time I would be called upon by someone who very much wished to see me. I supposed it was some court-appointed lawyer she had arranged for my defense and promptly put all thought of the visitor out of my mind. Imagine my surprise when I went to the parlor upon hearing the chime and opened the door to find the savage face of a Va-gas grinning devilishly back at me. And not just any Va-gas—it was my old friend and traveling companion, No-ma-ro!

"Greetings, Ju-lan Sev-ath!" he said, brushing past me and trotting into my quarters like he owned the place, inspecting the tapestries that hung on the walls and sniffing the upholstery of the furniture. "They have put you up not like the criminal they accuse you of being, but instead like the Jemadar himself! Not that I am complaining about my own living arrangements, mind you. The vats provide all the flesh I can eat, and my tent is warm with the bodies of my many wives!"

For some time I could only grin back in stupefaction at my Va-gas friend, so surprised was I at his unexpected arrival. At last I found my tongue and asked him how he had survived the raging tempest upon the lunar sea and made his way here to Vathayne.

"It is to you I should ask the same question," No-ma-ro said, "for how anyone could live after being hurled into those storm-wracked waters I do not know. Of course, I survived because I managed to remain strapped to our boat. Had I not, I would have sunk into the depths like heavy stone, since like most of my people, I don't know how to swim. I can only thank Zo-al, the maker of storms, for sparing me and casting the boat upon the shores of this island. There I was found by a Vathaynean patrol, led through a tunnel system to the city, and conscripted into the ranks of the cavalry after vowing to obey the will of the Jemadar."

"Wait a moment," I said, perplexed, recalling the hostility of the party that had captured me. "You made a simple vow of obedience and the soldiers of Vathayne welcomed you with open arms?"

"Indeed!" exclaimed No-ma-ro. "And as I've said, they have provided me with all the flesh I can eat! Truly is Vathayne a paradise."

As much as I was glad for my friend, it galled me to have been treated so very differently by the Jemadar and his soldiers.

While I was standing there chagrinned, the chime rang once more and I welcomed a smiling Voo-rah-nee into my quarters. Almost immediately she must have noticed something was bothering me, for she said, "Are you not happy to see your friend?"

I smiled and said I was very glad for that fact, but the Nonovar sensed my deception and regarded me skeptically. Still, she remained quiet, not wanting to offend my quadrupedal guest.

No-ma-ro must have sensed the tension between Voo-rah-nee and me, for he padded for the door and made his good-byes, saying his belly was rumbling for more flesh from the vats and that he would return to visit me at a later time.

When the Va-gas had departed, Voo-rah-nee scrutinized me and asked, "What is wrong, Ju-lan?"

"It's nothing," I said. "In fact, I feel somewhat foolish even entertaining the thought. It's just that I must wonder why I, in whose veins flows the blood of the U-ga of Va-nah, am regarded with such suspicion and being put on trial while a savage Va-gas who worked directly for the Kalkars is immediately rewarded with his every desire."

"Ah!" Voo-rah-nee exclaimed, "I understand now," and she lightly touched her hand to my arm, sending a tremor through my entire frame that I did not immediately understand. "It did not help that you slew the Jemadar's mo-lah-kar," she went on. "But there is another reason why No-ma-ro has been welcomed whereas you have been imprisoned. We have a saying here: 'Friendship with a Va-gas begins and ends with his belly.' For countless generations my people bred the quadrupeds for their meat, treating them as an inferior species. Who could argue with the notion? Were they not disgusting cannibals who consumed the flesh of their own kind? And did not they attack the U-ga and eat the corpses of our people? Then came the discovery of the flesh vats and we learned that a satisfied Va-gas is a happy Va-gas. They held no inherent hostility toward the U-ga, just as we held no instinctive ill will toward them.

"Now we U-ga of Vathayne are at peace with our Va-gas brothers and sisters, and we have joined together for mutual defense and so we might wipe the dread Kalkars from the face of Va-nah. In this way have science and education saved our two peoples, as they have produced the technology necessary for the invention of the vats. But should the flesh vats fail... then the loyalty of the Va-gas will instantly vanish. Without a source of meat to placate them, they will turn on the U-ga of Vathayne and feed on us as they tried to do before. Or worse, they will fly back to the Kalkars, who will breed more of their kind so that Va-gas will feed on Va-gas, and the Kalkars will cultivate the survivors as warriors to send against us."

I shook my head. "What are you saying? That the Jemadar trusts No-ma-ro over me only because a satiated Va-gas is a loyal Va-gas?" The notion disquieted me, knowing as I did that No-ma-ro had exercised his free will to abstain from eating me on our long journey through the mur-lak-infested forest and over the open sea, though I could not deny he had often *looked* like he wanted to feed on me.

Voo-rah-nee nodded and smiled sweetly. "You must understand there is no reason to take it personally. It is simply because you are a U-ga that my father does not trust you."

"Welcome to the City of Brotherly Love," I said wryly, but my sarcasm slipped right past the Nonovar.

"Are you ready to continue discussing the case we are building for your defense?" she asked. "The trial is scheduled for only one *ula* from now." An *ula* was the lunar equivalent of a month, for while there were no heavenly bodies in Va-nah with which to demarcate the passage of time, the U-ga had come up with an ingenious method of doing so by observing sunlight from the surface of the Moon illuminating the bottoms of the Hoos. The time it takes for this light to fill up a certain designated crater, to darken, and to fill with light again they call a *ula*, or a sidereal month. This period is further divided into an *ola*, which in Earth time amounts to about six hours and thirty-two minutes, while ten *ulas* make a *keld*, or lunar year, corresponding to about two hundred and seventy-two earthly days. Therefore, Voo-rah-nee was telling me I had only about four earthly weeks before I would be put on trial for espionage, the verdict of which would determine whether I lived or died.

"Yes, let us continue," I said cheerfully, and we seated our-selves as was customary in comfortable chairs facing one another across a large table, its obsidian surface cluttered with an as-sortment of legal tomes and documents we had been consult-ing.

"One point that we have not yet addressed," I went on, "and something I believe may have no small bearing on the prejudice of the court against me, is the Jemadar's claim that he has no knowledge of the diplomatic mission from Barsoom. If the members of the court believe the Jemadar's statement on this matter, they will have no choice but to rule against me."

"I have questioned my father about this," Voo-rah-nee said, "and he has assured me in no uncertain terms that he indeed has no awareness of any diplomatic mission from beyond Va-nah, whether from Barsoom or elsewhere. Perhaps you have been deceived by this woman. After all, do you have any verification that she was telling the truth?"

"I am here, am I not?" I said rather testily. "The woman who transmitted the message told me of Vathayne and its struggle against the Kalkars, all of which was true."

"But perhaps she was an agent of the Twenty-Four, determined to trick you so that you would seek out Vathayne and lead the Kalkars to its secret location."

"I am not sure how well kept a secret is Vathayne's whereabouts," I replied. "Though the journey here was difficult, I found Vathayne's general location rather easily after merely speaking with a Va-gas. I believe there are other reasons as to why the Kalkars have not yet struck your homeland. Not only do I think your campaign against the Kalkars has wounded them more severely than you know, but they are an incompetent lot. They only achieved the successes they did in recent years as a result of Orthis' aid. Since his passing, the Kalkars have been dying a slow death. Few ships now pass between Va-nah and Earth, and those that do are in disrepair, for no one among the Kalkars knows how to maintain them or construct more."

"Are you saying my father is a liar?" Voo-rah-nee leaped up from her seat, her pale cheeks darkening.

"There are many reasons one may lie," I said. "Not all of them are nefarious. But when a man's life has been threatened and he has been thrown in prison unjustly, it is hard not to question the motives of the one who put him there."

Voo-rah-nee's eyes flashed, and for a brief moment I did not understand why my cheek had grown suddenly warm. By the time I realized the Nonovar had slapped me, she was gone from my quarters.

There I stood alone, awaiting my death sentence and with no friend left in all of Va-nah but an insatiable, flesh-hungry Va-gas.

Chapter Fourteen

A DESPERATE ACT

The Nonovar's visits to my apartments abruptly ceased, and I spent many *olas* wondering why her absence bothered me so deeply. I tried to convince myself it was because I had little hope of swaying the court in my favor and avoiding a sentence of death without Voo-rah-nee's assistance. But I knew that was not the true reason for my melancholy, for now inexplicably I cared little what judgment would be cast upon me.

The strange corkscrew-like clock in the parlor spiraled away, marking off increments of time that had seemed nonexistent during my experiences in Va-nah before I had means of measuring it. Around and around the mechanism's parts turned with dizzying intensity, or at least so it seemed to me in the funk that had fallen over me. Before long, the *ula* preceding my trial had almost expired and very soon I would be doomed to stand before the Jemadar and his court and receive their presumably foregone verdict.

Why I should care whether this maid from the Moon, princess or otherwise, should think the less of me? It was a question I could not—or dared not—answer. But I could not deny the acuteness with which her sudden departure had stung me. Had I the means of speaking with her, I might have tried to bridge the chasm that now separated us. That I did not left me with no recourse to assuage the sharp pain that gnawed at my heartstrings.

As a result, an almost suicidal recklessness possessed me in my efforts to escape my prison. I took to opening the tall window in the parlor and standing upon the extreme edge of the sill, where I gazed down the precipitous face to the keep, which upon this side dropped straight down to the bottomless well of the yawning crater. My captors had left the window unlocked, clearly confident that any attempt to escape by means of the window would result in a deadly fall into the Hoos. If only I had a confederate, I might escape by means of artificial wings and a gas bag to buoy me. But I had no ally other than No-ma-ro, who would present a ludicrous sight accoutered like a bird, even if I could convince him to give up his unending supply of meat from the flesh vats, which I knew I could not. And, of course, Va-gas were even more terrified at the thought of flying than they were of entering a body of water.

While staring out across the sheer drop, I took note that sometimes a wispy fog formed over the many inhabited tiers below and clung to the rocky walls of the colossal shaft. On several occasions, I also observed a dimly glowing bank of mist about a hundred feet beneath my window and a little to the left along the face of the keep. I concluded that this vapor must have been illuminated by artificial lighting shed through another window, though I could not see the opening from my vantage.

Knowing I had little to lose, what with my impending execution, I determined to risk all in an attempt to reach the window far below my apartments. I figured if Rapunzel could use her own hair for the purposes of scaling a tower, I could achieve a similar feat by using the materials I had at hand. Over the course of a single evening I prepared for my desperate excursion over the keep's side, tearing my bedsheets and then, when I ran out of those, the draperies into narrow strips that I tied together end to end. Using my own height as a rule, I measured out a hundred feet. After tying a heavy paperweight from the parlor onto one end of the joined fabric, I went to the window and cast down my improvised rope.

The string of linens whipped about in the strong gusts that swept across the wall, and the bob affixed to the end knocked against the keep with such force that I feared it would alert anyone who resided on the floors below. I swung the line back and forth, attempting to gauge whether it was long enough to reach the window, until at last I was rewarded by seeing the cord light up brightly with the artificial light cast from inside the keep.

As quickly as possible, I secured the top end of the cord around one of the squat legs of the room's large obsidian table, which I knew to be so heavy even my formidable muscles could not budge it. Then, with a giddiness born of the long period of inactivity in my prison, I slipped over the window ledge and began climbing hand over hand down the keep's side.

The cold, powerful winds of the lunar crater beat relentlessly against me as I descended, making it hard to maintain my footing against the wall. Several times my feet fell out from under me, and I clung solely with the strength of my arms. To fall would mean certain death.

Or would it? If I fell and somehow escaped being battered to a bloody pulp against the craggy side of the shaft, how far would I plummet before meeting my end? I imagined tumbling for half the length of the Hoos—that is, one hundred and twenty-five miles—and then being suspended in the nexus between gravity and centrifugal force that had held the *People's Glory* in abeyance until the pilot engaged the thrusters during my journey to Va-nah. There, hanging in empty space, I would go on living and breathing until starvation and dehydration at last took my life. My corpse would be condemned to float for all eternity in lunar limbo, an abiding testament to the utter stupidity of my escape attempt.

I thought of my mother and uncle and decided that no matter my low opinion of myself I did not want to dishonor them by suffering such a fate. And so with every ounce of my strength and will I clung to my fabric rope while the wind hurled me up against the wall with such violence that I cursed the very forces of nature.

Slowly, ever so slowly, I drew closer to the illuminated mist that, below and to the left, marked the location of the window I sought. When at last I came on level with the opening and tried to swing over to it, I found to my great despair that, even with the enhanced might of my earthly muscles, I could not manage to reach it. I had misjudged its lateral distance by some ten to twelve feet!

And yet I continued trying to attain the window, swinging back and forth like a pendulum, until I realized I was rapidly expending what little strength I had left. For how long I hung there over the yawning throat of the Hoos I cannot say. It is impossible to measure time in such an insufferable, interminable situation. But there was one thing I did know. I did not possess the strength to climb back up the rope to my apartments, so abused and fatigued had the harsh gusts left me.

There I hung, knowing that inevitably my spent muscles would give way and the crater would swallow me. Then, just as I resolved to summon my remaining fortitude and make one last go at it, the winds that had been buffeting me from all directions changed course and started blowing steadily in the direction of the window that was my only hope for life. So hard did the winds gust that soon I found myself clinging to a noticeably inclined line.

Now I could see the frame of the window, its ledge wide but flush with the wall. My feet were only inches from the near edge of the frame!

I knew this was my last chance to make the window ledge. Thus, even though my strength was swiftly waning and with the slightest mishap I would fall to my death in fury of the gale, I carefully loosened my grip and slid down the sharply sloped line. After uttering a prayer to God and glory of the Flag, I let go of the rope and grabbed hold of the bob I had tied on the end.

This last excruciating effort brought my legs over the window, which now I could see was open. There was only one thing I could do. I bent my legs so that they reached inside the window and let go in a leap of faith. Much to my great relief—and, I admit, to my surprise—the wind carried me through the open window and into the room beyond.

I lay there upon the tiled floor of an ornate and blessedly deserted hallway, my muscles aching and my breath wheezing from the intense exertion of the ordeal through which I had just passed. I felt like I had traveled to Gehenna and back, but I was alive—blessedly alive!

Chapter Fifteen

TU-LAV'S SECRET

I found myself in an alcove opening onto a long hallway at the end of which crossed a brightly lit corridor. It was from this corridor that light beamed down the adjacent hallway, into the alcove, and through the window, where it dimly illuminated the mist outside that I had seen from my apartments above.

I moved behind one of the alcove's recesses to conceal myself from anyone who might pass down the far corridor. There in the shadows I examined the injuries I had been dealt when the furious winds beat me against the wall of the keep. I found I was not seriously hurt beyond a number of painful though not incapacitating bumps, bruises, and minor abrasions. I sat down on the floor and leaned against the wall to catch my breath and regain my strength, but my rest was all too brief. After only a few moments I heard footsteps coming from the bisecting corridor at the end of the hallway.

I arose and peered with one eye around the corner of the alcove just in time to see two men pass down the far corridor in close succession. The first man, his wrists manacled and his skin colored a deep coppery hue unlike that of any U-ga I had yet encountered, was followed close at the heels by one of the Jemadar's soldiers. The latter held a pistol aimed at his prisoner's back.

Stealthily, I crept forward. When I reached the end of the hallway, I peeked around the corner and looked both ways. Warm light glimmered from the corridor's walls and ceiling, which were coated with the same radium-bearing substance commonly used to illuminate the interiors of habitations throughout Va-nah. To the left, the passage curved and disappeared from view about ten yards down. In the other direction, I caught a glimpse of the two men in the distance just before they turned and passed into a doorway on the right.

I lost no time and made after them. I had no weapons other than surprise and my two fists, so after a quick look to ascertain no others were inside, I bolted into the room and leaped upon the soldier who held the gun.

The man cried out when I fell upon him but before I could land a blow on him he whipped up his pistol and raised its barrel on level with my head. I have no doubt he would have fired and instantly ended my life had not the copper-hued man intervened. The man kicked the soldier in the side, causing him to fall to one knee. My fist struck the soldier squarely on the chin, felling him like an ox. He lay on the floor groaning and insensate.

I shared a smile with the handsome stranger who had saved my life, but our joy was short-lived. In the next moment, a group of armed guards surged into the room and overwhelmed us by sheer numbers, not to mention their menacing pistols and swords. Before I knew it, I had been thrown into a cell in the room along with my fellow prisoner, the barred door slammed shut behind us, locking us inside.

A man stepped forward from the mass of soldiers and sneered at me. I recognized him instantly as the leader of the group that had captured me upon the shore—Tu-lav's son, the Javadar of Vathayne, whose name I had learned was Ro-than.

"I told my sister not to trust you," the Javadar said. "Here you are, a criminal who has broken the law yet again, first by escaping your own confinement, and then by helping a known enemy of Vathayne break out of his own prison. I fear that by your own actions you have forsaken the trial my father so generously arranged for you. When he hears of your further crimes, I daresay he will not be so kind-hearted."

I laughed in the man's face, for I am not one to be intimidated by a bully, even one who possesses the ability to snuff out my life.

"Go ahead," Ro-than said curtly, clearly upset I had not been cowed in the face of his mean-spirited bluster. "Laugh while you still can." Having made his point, the Javadar turned on his heel and strode from the room along with his soldiers, leaving me alone with my fellow cellmate.

"Well," I said, "it looks like we've landed ourselves in a pretty pickle."

The copper-skinned man smiled. "I do not know what a pickle is," he said in the tongue of Va-nah, though his accent indicated it was not his first language. "Although I imagine that whatever it is, it's not so pretty after all."

"You've guessed right about that," I said. "My name is Julian 7th, of Earth. I take it you've also had a run-in with Tu-lav?"

"I am Kuvan Tal of Helium," the man said, "and you also have guessed correctly."

"Ah, how fares your alliance with Tu-lav, then?" I asked wryly. I had suspected upon seeing my companion's complexion that he was a member of the Barsoomian ambassadorial mission, but his mention of Helium confirmed it.

A look of surprise came over the man's features upon hearing my question, but then he tilted his head, his brow furrowed, and said, "Earth...I have heard the Warlord call the planet Jasoom by that name. You have traveled to Va-nah from the third planet that orbits the sun?"

"Guilty as charged," I said. "For apparently in Vathayne all one has to do to become an enemy of the state is to have been born elsewhere. And I thought the Kalkars were tyrants." I shook my head sadly, for though I had come to Vathayne in hopes of finding an ally against the brutal Moon men who had enslaved the people of Earth, I had found little to like among those U-ga I had so far encountered. Then I thought of Voo-rah-nee, who had been kind to me at first before ultimately turning upon me and leaving me to be sentenced to death at the hands of her father's court, and my heart blackened.

I must have winced at my bitter thought, for Kuvan Tal smiled kindly and said, "Do not judge an entire people based on their leaders. Would you pass judgment on the people of Jasoom for the shortcomings of your Kalkar masters?"

"You are wise, Kuvan Tal," I said. "And, of course, correct. Now tell me, how is it that a man from Barsoom finds himself in a prison cell in the interior of another world's satellite?"

"I might ask a similar question of you, Julian 7th of Earth," the Barsoomian said. "But then, one of us must speak first, and so I shall ask you to relate your story after I tell you mine."

I nodded and encouraged my companion to continue.

"I am a padwar in the guard of the Jeddak of Jeddaks, the Warlord of Barsoom," Kuvan Tal went on. "I was assigned to a post aboard a diplomatic mission to Va-nah by the Warlord himself after the Jemadar of Vathayne sent a transmission through the ether of space and contacted the scientists of my native city of Greater Helium. My people, observing through our powerful telescopes, had witnessed as the Kalkar menace swept out of the craters of Jasoom's moon and descended upon your world, engulfing it in the conflagration of war. We feared—and Tu-lav warned us—that the Kalkars would not be content with merely conquering Jasoom, and that they would use your world's plentiful resources to build a fleet of warships and attack Barsoom. This Helium would never allow, and so my people constructed a vessel to travel to Va-nah, where we hoped to aid Tu-lav and so defeat the Kalkars before they had a chance to strike Barsoom."

Kuvan Tal sighed and his face twisted into a grimace. "When my mission arrived, we were hopeful. The ambassador and the other members of our party were escorted directly into the Jemadar's presence. We had been concerned to find our transmissions disrupted by the Vathayneans, which prevented us from communicating with Barsoom and informing Helium of our well-being, but Tu-lav reassured us, saying such measures were necessary to prevent our negotiations from being discovered by the Kalkars. The excuse was reasonable enough, though I could tell the jamming of our transmissions put the ambassador on edge. Still, he is not one to be intimidated, and so we continued our dialog with the Vathayneans.

"Tu-lav spoke of his concern for the people of Jasoom, stating that once the Vathayneans and the other hidden U-ga cities had thrown off the yoke of Kalkar oppression in Va-nah, they would do the same for the Blue Planet. Soon, however, it became apparent what Tu-lav really wanted out of our exchange: the technology of Barsoom. Specifically, he sought to know and understand in exacting detail the science of the planetary rays. His people had already been experimenting with the rays, the principles of which, he told us, were known to the U-ga of ancient times but had since been lost after long ages of war against the Kalkars."

Upon hearing of Tu-lav's plans to help Earth, my heart lifted. I wondered if I had misjudged the Jemadar, but Kuvan Tal soon dashed any such hopes.

"At first, Tu-lav tried to hide what really lay behind his interest in the rays," the Barsoomian continued. "But the ambassador drew him out, asking a series of seemingly innocuous questions that roundaboutly pinpointed the Jemadar's true goal: to discover the secrets of the Eighth Lunar Ray. He did not merely wish to master the Eighth Ray for purposes of propulsion, as we have harnessed the Barsoomian equivalent upon my world—no, he wished to exploit the ray for a much more nefarious motive. With the knowledge he hoped to glean from the scientists of Barsoom, he intended to elucidate a special modulation of the Eighth Lunar Ray, creating a weapon capable of knocking down every Kalkar vessel out of the skies. of Va-nah. This, of course, would not be a bad development on its own merits. But he also meant to create an array of such devices that would continually transmit his destabilizing ray both across the inner world of Va-nah and upon the surface of the Moon, effectively sealing off the entire satellite from the rest of the solar system."

I had been sitting on the floor of the cell as Kuvan Tal spoke, but when he made this last statement I leaped up and cried, "But Earth! If such a ray utterly thwarts travel around the Moon, isolating it from its interplanetary neighbors, how will Vathayne and its allied cities help the people of Earth rid themselves of the Kalkars?"

Kuvan Tal frowned. "When the ambassador gleaned the truth, he confronted Tu-lav and asked him the same question. That, it turned out, was the end of our negotiations. The Jemadar imprisoned us in Vathayne's keep, separating the members of our party and subjecting us to unceasing interrogations. Meanwhile, I fear from the questions I have been asked that Tu-lav's scientists have dismantled our ship and are close to obtaining the information they seek even without our cooperation."

"Well," I said, "it sounds as if there is only one thing we can do."

"And what, pray tell, is that?" asked Kuvan Tal.

"Find a way out of this cell and rescue your ambassador and the other members of your mission."

Kuvan Tal laughed and said, "I admire your spunk, Julian of Earth, but at least one of those tasks is already beyond your ability."

"What do you mean?" I asked.

"The ambassador has already escaped," said Kuvan Tal. "Did you think a mere prison cell would be able to hold John Carter, Warlord of Barsoom?"

Chapter Sixteen

BETRAYAL AND TRUST

So that renowned, deathless Virginian, John Carter of Mars, was the Barsoomian ambassador! Of course, I had heard of him before—for even in the twenty-first-century nightmare of the Kalkar's domination of Earth, what child has not grown up hearing tales of John Carter's fantastic adventures on the Red Planet?

Suddenly I recalled the final, truncated words of the Barsoomian woman with whom I had spoken via Gridley Wave across the vast, cold chasm of space while in the headquarters of the Kalkars on Earth. She had said in grave tones how I must travel to Va-nah and discover the fate of "he who is worth more to me than even life itself." My mind leaped like lightning, and I could come to only one conclusion: I had spoken with the incomparable Dejah Thoris herself—Princess of Helium, and wife of John Carter, Warlord of Barsoom!

I was about to exclaim this revelation to Kuvan Tal when I heard voices coming from the hallway outside the room holding our cell.

"My father is well aware of my presence here," came the voice of Voo-rah-nee.

"Where is your guard, Nonovar?" a male voice said. "Surely you did not come to interrogate the prisoners without protection."

"Are you too cowardly to safeguard me while I conduct my business with these criminals?" Voo-rah-nee's voice carried the haughtiness of a spoiled and heartless princess, which is what I tried to convince myself she was, knowing she had abandoned our friendship and left me defenseless in the face of my imminent death sentence.

The male voice sputtered. "I am a captain in the Jemadar's army!" the man exclaimed. "I have no fear of the prisoners, O Nonovar."

It was at this point that the two walked into the room. Voo-rah-nee, her little elfin chin thrust up, regarded me with an arrogant gaze. She leveled a finger at me and turned to her companion, a strapping young man in the regalia of a soldier of Vathayne.

"Go into the cell, then, Captain," she said, "and prove you are not a coward. Beat that one into submission and then he will prove no threat to me."

The man hesitated. "Regulations say that at least two must be present when opening the prisoners' cell."

Voo-rah-nee whipped a mean-looking pistol from a holster hanging on her shapely hip, pointing the weapon's oddly flared barrel first at Kuvan Tal and then at me. "Are there not two of us?" she asked icily.

The soldier sighed deeply, then shrugged and said, "I suppose there are, your highness." He stepped in front of our cell and began fiddling with a set of keys looped on a gold ring secured to his belt.

A strange, high-pitched whine rang in my ears. The captain grabbed his head with both hands as if suddenly struck by a piercing headache, then collapsed upon the floor directly before our cell, where he lay motionless.

Voo-rah-nee stood over him and released her finger from the trigger of the trumpet-barreled pistol she had aimed at the fallen man. Instantly, the shrill whine ceased.

I knelt down and reached through the bars of our cell to retrieve the keys from the man, which had remained clutched in his hand when he collapsed.

"Quickly," she said. "The guards will come soon."

I fingered through the ring of oddly shaped keys, each of which was cast of metal of a different color and resembled nothing so much as a dog whistle.

"It's the red one," Voo-rah-nee said, seeing my perplexed expression.

I held up the key she had indicated, but still had no idea what to do with it, as I saw no keyhole in the barred door.

Grimacing with impatience, Voo-rah-nee held up an imaginary key to her lips and pantomimed blowing into it.

Ah, so it *was* a dog whistle of sorts. I held the key to my lips and blew, and though I could hear nothing but the sound of air passing through the small cylinder, the cell door sprang suddenly open. Perhaps it shouldn't have surprised me that a people whose language was based on music would use the principles of vibration and frequency in their commonplace technology.

When Kuvan Tal and I emerged from the cell, Voo-rah-nee covered us in the sight of her gun. My heart sank. For a moment I had actually dared hope she had come to rescue us.

"The keys," she said, backing up to keep her distance. "Throw them to me."

I obeyed.

"Now put these on." The woman removed a set of manacles from a hook on the wall and tossed them to me. I fastened them around my wrists and exchanged a dark look with Kuvan Tal, who still wore the shackles that had restrained him when he was thrown in the cell. Meanwhile, Voo-rah-nee approached the unconscious man and knelt before him, removing the belt which holstered his pistol and strapping it around her hips. She rose, her own gun still in hand.

"What do you mean to do with us?" I asked. "Is the outcome of my pending trial so uncertain that you would forgo the court and deliver its verdict by your own hand?"

The Nonovar's milk-white cheeks darkened. "You are a fool, Ju-lan Sev-ath!" With a rapid motion of her gun, she gestured for us to leave the room. Neither Kuvan Tal nor I wanted to end up like the fellow on the floor, so we complied.

Once we were in the corridor, the Nonovar ordered us to proceed to the right, while she followed closely at our heels, the pistol aimed straight at our backs.

We continued down the corridor, bathed in the eerie glow of the radium-painted walls. After we had gone some hundred paces, an officer of the guard appeared down the hallway, headed in our direction.

"Keep walking," Voo-rah-nee said in a low voice behind us, but we were forced to stop when the officer halted directly in our path.

"Hail, Nonovar," the man said and, standing stiffly erect, saluted by touching his right palm to his chest and then extending his right arm laterally. "Where do you go with these prisoners?"

"I am on the Jemadar's business," Voo-rah-nee said, resuming the haughty tone she had used to address the guard in the prison room. "Now get out of my way."

The man looked uncomfortable, but he moved to one side and let us pass.

We had gone a short distance when the corridor began curving sharply to the left. Soon we came to an intersection of three passageways. We took the corridor on the right and mounted a flight of stairs that wound upward, ever upward, until the muscles in my legs grew weary and I thought we must be approaching the uppermost reaches of the keep. When at last we emerged onto a level corridor, I stopped and turned to address the Nonovar.

"What are you doing?" she said. "We must go on, and quickly!"

"Not until you tell us where you're taking us," I said. "If it is to our deaths, or worse, to a place where you will torture us to learn whatever secrets your people are after, then you might as well kill us now."

Voo-rah-nee stamped her foot and uttered something in the U-ga tongue with which I was unfamiliar, but which I took to be a curse. "Very well," she said. "Let us speak in there instead of risk being spotted in the corridor." We had stopped next to an open doorway, which she motioned for us to enter. She closed the door behind us and locked it.

The room, which appeared to be a combination of library and study, was empty save for the many bookshelves lining the walls and a lounge area furnished with two comfortable chairs and a small divan. As we seated ourselves, I took note that Voo-rah-nee had returned her strange flared pistol to the holster on her hip.

"What is that, by the way?" I asked, indicating the gun. "I have never seen its like."

"Nor has anyone else in a thousand years," she said. "It's a prototype of my own making, though I cannot claim to be its inventor. Ages ago, the ancients of Vathayne harnessed the science of sound. I have pieced together enough from the old records to reconstruct some of their research. On this setting"— she removed the gun and indicated a dial near the rear sight— "the sonic gun will merely cause its target to fall unconscious. But turn it up to here"—she rotated the dial until it made a sharp click—"and it will knock a hole in the wall behind you." She returned the dial to its original setting and slid the strange-looking gun back into its holster. "I think, anyway. I have not yet tested it on its full setting.

"But enough! We are here because you are too stubborn to go on without hearing my story."

"Proceed," I said. "But first..." I held up my fettered wrists.

The woman grimaced, but she selected a key-whistle from the loop of metal she had secured to her belt and blew upon it. Instantly, the shackles on my wrists clicked open and I slipped out of my restraints and cast them onto the table before us.

Selecting a different key, she repeated the procedure for Kuvan Tal.

"I shall speak swiftly," the Nonovar said, "for the longer we stay here, the more likely it is that we shall be caught."

"Then you're not taking us to the Jemadar?" I asked, surprised.

She looked to Kuvan Tal and said, "Are all men of Earth so thick-headed?"

"Don't ask me," he said, grinning as if amused at the growing tension between Voo-rah-nee and me. "This is the first one I've met."

"I do not understand why you hate me so, Ju-lan," she said, "after it was I who stood up to my own father, the Jemadar, in your defense."

"Did you not leave me to die at the hands of the court?" I said.

"When you learn the truth," she said icily, "you will not judge me so harshly. I, however, have already passed judgment upon you, who was so quick to cast dishonor upon my name."

I rose from my seat. "Whatever do you mean?"

"When I last left your apartments," she said, "I was rightfully angry. You had insulted my father and my Jemadar, accusing him of conspiring against the people of Vathayne, withholding from them knowledge of an alliance that could save all of Va-nah from the Kalkar scourge. Eventually, however, I cooled down and considered your allegations. I went to my father and I asked him outright if what you had stated was true. He vehemently denied it. But I could not believe you would lie to me, so I went to the hangars below the keep's landing deck and began searching for evidence of the Barsoomian craft. When I came to a restricted area, I ordered the guards to let me pass on the authority of the Jemadar himself. The guards refused and said we could only resolve the matter by seeking audience with my father, but instead of escorting me to the Jemadar's court, they brought me to my chambers and locked me within.

"My father eventually came to visit me in my rooms, telling me he had acted only in the best interests of Vathayne. I asked him how it could be good for Vathayne to turn on its friends and allies, but he would hear nothing of it. He told me there are dissenting, pacifistic voices within the royal court who believe the city should remain hidden from the Kalkars and that the rebellion should be ended. These courtiers believe the Jemadar's attacks against the Kalkars risk revealing our location to the enemy. Paranoia has consumed my father. That is why he has concealed the communications of our scientists with the inhabitants of Barsoom and the existence of the Heliumites' diplomatic mission. My father trusts no one. He wants no one else to have access to the technology he hopes to obtain from the Barsoomians, as he fears it could be used against him.

"I was furious when I learned of his deceptions, but he would hear none of it. He told me I would be restricted to my chambers until he could be assured of my loyalty. I—his own daughter! But though my father is powerful, I, too, have many allies in the city, and with the help of a trusted guard, I was at last able to escape my chambers and come to free you."

"So that is why you did not return to my apartments!" I exclaimed.

"Of course," Voo-rah-nee said, raising her chin proudly and eyeing me as if I were but a lesser creature. "Did you think I would let the man who had saved my life go to his death merely because we had had a quarrel?"

"I have had little experience in matters of love," I found myself saying, and instantly regretted it.

Voo-rah-nee flushed and she leaped up from her seat. "Do not speak to the Nonovar of Vathayne about love! She despises you!"

Kuvan Tal rose and bounced on his heels, clearly amused at the situation. "Now that you two have aired your feelings, are we quite ready to go?"

Just as he uttered his question, a tremendous, deafening boom shook the apartment and plaster fell down upon us from the ceiling. I put my arm around Voo-rah-nee and huddled over her to protect her from the rain of debris, but she pushed herself out of my grasp and made for the door.

"It is as the dissenters have warned!" she cried. "Our attacks have drawn the Kalkars to Vathayne!"

Chapter Seventeen

BESIEGED

Kuvan Tal and I followed the Nonovar into the corridor outside the room where we had taken refuge. Again came a thundering explosion that rocked the ground beneath our feet and sent rubble showering down all around us.

"The Kalkars have brought their airships over the crater!" Voo-rah-nee shouted into our ringing ears. "Their bombs will pulverize the keep before my father can ready his fliers!"

I grabbed Voo-rah-nee by the arm, meaning to hurry her away to safety, but she wrenched herself free and glared at me, furious even amid the wreckage of the Kalkar assault. "Do not touch me!" she cried.

"I meant no offense, Nonovar," I said. "Where is the restricted area where you suspected your father hides the Barsoomian craft?"

The rage upon the woman's face faded as the meaning of my question settled in.

"You are right, Earth man," she said. "Our only hope is to flee upon the Barsoomian ship and rally Vathayne's allies to her defense. Come!"

Voo-rah-nee drew her sonic pistol and led us down the corridor.

"The hangars are not far," she said. "We are already on the upper levels of the keep and we only have to—"

Just then another bomb struck and the walls of the corridor directly ahead tumbled down from both sides, choking the passage with a heap of rubble. Dust from crumbling plaster filled our lungs and we fell to our knees in fits of violent coughing. I rose and, wiping the dust from my eyes, grasped Voo-rah-nee's hand to lift her to her feet. She cried out, not in anger this time, but in pain. She sank back to the floor and crouched upon one knee, clutching her ankle.

I knelt beside her while Kuvan Tal, who was uninjured, began climbing the pile of rubble confronting us looking for a way forward. "Let me see," I said. Voo-rah-nee removed her hand from her ankle, revealing a large, dark welt surrounded by her otherwise moon-pale skin.

"A piece of debris struck me," she said. "Here, help me stand again." I did as she bade, but when she placed her weight upon her injured ankle, she cried out and fell to her knees once more.

"It is no use," she said. "Leave me and get to the ship. You must summon Vathayne's allies or all is lost."

"I cannot leave you, Nonovar," I said firmly.

"And why is that, Earth man?" The haughtiness in her voice remained, despite the dire outlook of our predicament.

"Because I would never leave behind the woman I love to die while I yet lived."

Her eyes flashed with anger, but I could not mistake the tears welling them. "Don't be a fool," she said. "I have no feelings for you. That is, none but hatred!" She looked away as a single tear broke and streamed down her beautiful, dirt-caked face. "Go!"

When I made to pick her up, she picked up her pistol from where she had dropped it during the collapse and aimed the weapon at me.

I raised my hands and patted the empty air in her direction. "Easy," I said to her, then shouted up to Kuvan Tal, who was now high up on the heap of rubble. "What can you see?" Dust still hung thickly in the air, partially obscuring the Barsoomian.

"There is a way forward," he called down. "But we must hurry before another bomb strikes."

"Come down and assist the Nonovar," I said to him. "She will accept no help from me."

Kuvan Tal climbed back down and, much to my great relief, Voo-rah-nee allowed him to lift her into his arms.

"Give me your gun," I said, and held out my hand. Voo-rah-nee hesitated, but finally, reluctance writ clearly on her face, she handed it to me grip-first.

"I give it to you not because I trust you," she said, "but because I must. The fate of Vathayne rests upon our ability to get to the ship."

I grinned at her to show that her words had not stung me. Would that my grin had been a testament to the true feelings in my heart.

But I had no time to consider the Nonovar's slight against me. Every ounce of my being had only one goal in mind—to get the woman I loved to safety as quickly as possible. Although it stung me deeply to know she spurned my affections and loathed me to the core, that meant nothing in the face of the immediate danger to her person.

As we climbed up the pile of wreckage, I led the way, heaving up heavy fragments of stone and tossing them aside where they blocked the path ahead. A strange, dim light surrounded us, as the collapse of the radium-painted walls had darkened the passageway significantly, and yet the rubble glowed in irregular patches where fragments of the wall's outer face were turned upward. The way was treacherous, but at last we climbed down and stood safely upon the other side of the devastation.

The booming had stopped now and the corridor was eerily quiet as we trod onward. When we approached a stairwell leading from the side of the passage, Voo-rah-nee cried out.

"The stairs lead to the level directly below the landing deck for our winged fliers," she said. "It is there where lie the hangars of my father's experimental craft, and where I suspect the Barsoomian vessel has been hidden."

"How was the ship brought into the keep without the entire population of Vathayne witnessing the act?" I asked.

"The hangars are bored into the upper walls of the Hoos," Voo-rah-nee replied. "They open to the outer face of the volcano, so that ships may come and go swiftly. My father has long been building a fleet of aerial warships in anticipation of one day launching an all-out assault on the Kalkars. But now all his well-laid plans have come to naught."

I could hear the pain in the Nonovar's voice. It would seem that her worst fears had been realized as the last vestiges of U-ga civilization crumbled right before her eyes.

We mounted the stairs, which spiraled upward for fifty feet before opening upon one side of the stairwell. The break in the wall exposed a breathtaking panorama of the crater's interior and the many heavily populated tiers of the city below. Va-thaynean fliers, lifted by the gas bags strapped to their backs and clutching rifles and radio bombs in their hands, winged their way upward to meet the Kalkar invaders.

I stopped and peered out over the rail that ran along the stairs, craning my neck so that I might catch a glimpse of the battle above. What I saw filled my heart with dread.

A massive Kalkar airship, silhouetted by the radiant lunar clouds, eclipsed the great circular rim of the crater. Countless parachutes blossomed overhead, their thin fabric illuminated from behind by the soft rosy light cast down from the heavens. Already hundreds, maybe even thousands, of Kalkar soldiers had landed by such means upon the city's terraces. Hundreds more leaped over the side of the Kalkar airship even as I watched.

I lowered my gaze back to the terraces. Bedlam swept the streets of Vathayne as the citizens met the invaders with what-ever means they had closest at hand. The masses surged in the streets like rivers of restless souls, whipped into a hellish frenzy by the demons that fell upon them from the sky. The bright streams of tracer bullets streaked toward the descending soldiers and the airship overhead, emanating from directly above where we stood. I could only imagine the Jemadar's forces gathered atop the keep on the landing deck, offering furious resistance to the invaders. It would be upon that area that the Kalkars would concentrate their attack, which unfortunately put our party in grave peril, since we were on the level just below it.

A terrific explosion boomed somewhere beneath us, and I looked down into the Hoos to see a vast section of one of the lower terraces light up in an infernal blaze. But that was not the worst of it. After the bomb's mushroom of flame and smoke subsided, the most horrendous roar I ever heard bellowed up from below. I watched both awestruck and horrified as a mile-wide arc of the terrace collapsed into the well of the crater, carrying with it untold lives into the lunar abyss.

There I stood, overwhelmed by the ungodly sight, until Voo-rah-nee's voice broke the spell that mesmerized me.

"We must get to the hangar before the keep is overrun!" she cried.

My attention wrenched from the terror in the crater's depths, I leaped up the stairs with all the accelerated speed and heightened agility my lighter terrestrial weight afforded me. I looked back to see Kuvan Tal keeping pace close behind despite the burden of carrying the Nonovar, his own powerful muscles being accustomed to the heavier gravity of Barsoom in relation to that of Va-nah.

We reached the top of the stairs within only moments, passing through a great arch into an expansive chamber. A war claxon echoed from the high ceiling, hammering our eardrums as soldiers swarmed up a ramp leading into the gondola of a hulking airship. This was a conventional lighter-than-air dirigible, and it lay moored before a huge bay door that was being cranked open by unseen hands. Beyond the door yawned the mouth of a colossal tunnel, at the far end of which appeared a small circle of pinkish light where the shaft opened onto the exterior of the enormous mountain. I feared the airship would be doomed if the Kalkar fleet had located the opening to the hangar and lay in wait. Surely the captain of the aircraft knew this, but then, sometimes desperation clouds even the most rational judgment.

An officer ran past us, then stopped and backtracked to confront us.

"Nonovar, you are injured!" he cried in dismay, before turning and addressing Kuvan Tal. "Bring her aboard the *Tar-nath*. We leave within the *ala*," he said, using the term for the lunar equivalent of a minute. And then he turned and joined the others running up the ramp into the belly of the airship, pausing only to help a woman and her three children get inside amid the panicked fleers.

I quickly explained to the others my fear that the *Tar-nath* would be easily shot down out of the sky if a Kalkar ship waited in ambush on the other side of the mountain. I half expected Voo-rah-nee to argue with me just so she could be rid of my loathsome presence, but she agreed that the risk of boarding the dirigible was too great.

"Even so, we are doomed," she said. "If the Kalkars wait outside to pick us off, the Barsoomian ship will be shot down just the same.

"Not so!" exclaimed Kuvan Tal. "Though I am only a fair pilot, even I could evade one of these plundering gas bags were I at the helm of the Heliumetic ship."

"Then let us make haste," I said. "Where do you suspect the Barsoomian craft is moored, Nonovar?"

Voo-rah-nee pointed to a doorway at the far side of the chamber. "That is where I was denied access by my father's guard."

Together we ran for the door, Kuvan Tal still carrying the Nonovar, as the *Tar-nath*'s crew freed the airship of its moorings. The mighty engines revved and whirred, and the dirigible lurched forward into the gullet of the humongous shaft. When we reached the doorway, we could not help but turn back to see the fate of the *Tar-nath* as it emerged from the end of the shaft into the open air. We each let out a little cheer to see the craft nose up into the heavens.

Then came a terrific explosion. Our jubilant cheers turned into shouts of gut-wrenching horror at the conflagration that engulfed the *Tar-nath*. The burning hulk pitched forward sickeningly and fell from our view.

Voo-rah-nee, still in Kuvan Tal's arms, stared down the shaft as if she could not believe what we had all seen. "That officer you spoke with was my aunt's husband," she said, "and the woman and children he helped aboard were my..." A well of emotion and tears stopped her from completing her thought.

I placed my hand on Kuvan Tal's shoulder. "Come, my friend," I said. "Let us carry the Nonovar to safety and be gone from this place."

We passed beneath the arch into the adjoining chamber, whose cavernous ceiling, carved out of the rock of the Hoos, loomed over us. A broad staircase descended from high along the chamber's leftward side. From the opening at the top of the stairs came the din of gunfire and the shouts of men, doubtless resulting from the battle being waged on the top of the keep. At the far end of the chamber, across the floor of which lay scattered an array of wooden storage boxes and crates, lay a cave-like opening, some thirty feet high and fifty feet across.

My heart leaped when I saw through the breach a sleek, needle-nosed craft resting on three support legs extending from the vessel's underside. It resembled in many ways the ship that had carried me from Earth to Va-nah, though more streamlined in design and bearing a structural symmetry and elegance absent from the crude appearance of the Kalkar craft. It could only be the space ship from Barsoom, and the grin on Kuvan Tal's face confirmed it.

We ran forth and were almost halfway across the chamber when a storm of Kalkar soldiers began pouring down the stairs to our left. Spying us, they raised their rifles and unleashed upon us a deadly hail of bullets. I ducked behind a large crate, while Kuvan Tal, caught in the open, sprinted ahead with Voo-rah-nee to take a crouching refuge behind a smaller box some twenty feet beyond my position.

I opened fire with the gun Voo-rah-nee had given me, and watched as, one after another, soldiers fell upon the stairs before the sonic devastation I wrought upon them. Meanwhile, Voo-rah-nee had given Kuvan Tal the gun she had taken from the Kalkar in the prison room. The Barsoomian fired on the advancing soldiers with grim determination until his weapon's magazine had been emptied of its cartridges. Still the soldiers came on.

By now the Kalkars had reached the bottom of the stairs and were leaping into the chamber and spilling onto the floor en masse. We were mere seconds from our doom, and my companions must have known it as well. But it was then that one last, desperate hope sprung into my mind.

"Kuvan Tal!" I cried. "Take the Nonovar and run as fast as you can for your ship. I will create a distraction. Now!" And with my final word, I turned the dial on the sonic gun almost to its maximum and, gripping the weapon firmly with both hands, fired squarely into the center of the surging mass of soldiers barreling toward us.

Instead of emitting a high-pitched whine, the gun screeched like an enraged banshee and bucked so hard it almost flew from my grasp. A line of soldiers fifteen men across, blood streaming from their nostrils, toppled to the floor, whether unconscious or dead I did not know, though I suspected the latter. The men behind surged forward with no regard for the fallen soldiers they trampled over. I fired again, this time sweeping the gun's flared barrel over a broad swath of the advancing line as I bolted from behind the crate and made for the smaller box that only moments before had provided cover for Kuvan Tal and Voo-rah-nee. A row of men three times as wide fell before the sonic blast, and yet the tide of soldiers showed no sign of receding.

I glanced to my right and saw Kuvan Tal had made it safely to the adjoining chamber and, though carrying the Nonovar, was making for his ship in bounding leaps made possible by Va-nah's lesser gravity.

For a moment, I considered making such a leap myself in an attempt to reach the hangar beyond, for my earthly muscles were even more powerful on the surface of Va-nah than was the might of Kuvan Tal's Barsoomian physique. But already it was too late. A great tentacle of men had lashed out from the Kalkar throng to fill the intervening space between me and the opening to the next chamber. Too late for me, yes, but perhaps not for my companions.

Just as the mass both rushed for the hangar where the Barsoomian craft lay and converged upon me, I spun the dial of the sonic gun to its highest setting and raised its barrel to the arch of stone that frowned above the opening to the hangar beyond. For a split second I saw Kuvan Tal, standing upon the ramp leading into the belly of the needle-nosed ship and looking back in my direction. Voo-rah-nee, cradled in his arms, might have been a statue frozen in time, a marble-white hand reaching out toward me and a look of intense dismay chiseled upon her otherwise lovely features.

That was the last thing I saw before I pulled the trigger and a hellacious, keening din erupted from my pistol. The weapon flew apart in my hands even as the massive stone arch shattered in a cacophonous explosion, hurling down unfathomable tons of rock.

I had succeeded in my intent, sealing off my companions from the advancing soldiers and leaving me trapped and alone with an army of Kalkars on the other side.

Chapter Eighteen

KALKAR CITY NUMBER 1

When the soldiers came, I expected to be torn limb from limb. Instead, after about twenty brawny Kalkars piled on me and pummeled me nearly senseless with their meaty fists, heavy shackles were clamped on my wrists. A big, blond brute with a gap-toothed smile loomed over me and, lifting me up by my harness, threw me over a beefy shoulder.

"Why haven't you killed me?" I mumbled. It was all that I could do to form a coherent thought after the thrashing I had suffered.

A rumble of laughter erupted from somewhere deep in the cavernous chest of the monstrous Kalkar. "Our new Jemadar of Jemadars has ordered you to be taken alive."

"You have a new emperor?" I managed to ask.

The Kalkar spat in disgust. "I said *Jemadar of Jemadars*. Do you not know that means 'Brother of Brothers'?"

Of course, the term meant nothing of the sort, but I was too weak to protest.

"In any case," my captor continued, "it is said that our new Jemadar is not so kindly as Hralk, whom he slew to gain the throne. And the new Jemadar has taken a special interest in you, Earth man."

"Wonderful," I believe I said, though I am not sure because at that moment all went black.

I came to in what must have been only a minute or two later. I still hung like a sack of grain over the brutish Kalkar's shoulder, but now I was being carried up the stairs down which the invading force had entered the chamber. Moments later we emerged on top of the keep. A brisk breeze swirled down from the crater's mouth, waking me from my stupor.

The battle still raged furiously both in the sky and upon the city's terraces. The great Kalkar airship had descended deeper into the crater and now hung only five hundred feet above where we stood. Winged Vathayneans fired their guns into the airship's side, but their bullets merely bounced off the vessel's armor-reinforced exterior like so many corks, preventing them from penetrating the gas chambers housed within the super-structure.

The soldier carrying me dropped me roughly to the hard stone of the keep's landing deck.

"Vathayne falls before your eyes, Earth man," the brute said, and kicked me viciously in the ribs.

Groaning, I pushed myself up to my feet. I was in the process of summoning my remaining energy so that I might lay the bully flat on his back with my not-so-mean right hook, when suddenly the soldiers around me cried out in astonishment. I followed their gazes to the upper throat of the crater, where a sleek, needle-nosed craft was swooping out of the sky like an enormous barn swallow and rocketing straight for the Kalkar dreadnought.

I whooped with joy amid the throng of my slack-jawed captors. It was Kuvan Tal at the helm of his Barsoomian ship!

A large panel on the underside of the craft slid open and a large, four-barreled cannon of lustrous metal emerged from the turret. As the ship dove down, a burst of white-hot radium bullets streamed from the cannon's muzzles and tore into the crest of the Kalkar airship's envelope. For a breathless moment it seemed as if even the fierce strafing would have no effect against the dreadnought's armored hull. But suddenly the airship's envelope rent with a sickening groan, followed instantly by the eruption of a massive ball of roaring flame, which lit up on all sides the entire terraced area of the colossal crater. The airship, its aft section bending away from the main frame and hanging down like the tail of a humiliated canine, plummeted rapidly downward into the Hoos.

I ran to the edge of the keep as the sagging Kalkar dirigible rushed past our level, watching the doomed ship grow smaller and smaller, until finally it was lost in the stygian darkness of abyss.

A communal cry of elation rang up from the Vathayneans on the terrace directly below the keep. But their joy, and mine, was to be short-lived. Overhead two more Kalkar airships eclipsed the crater's mouth at angles perpendicular to one another, doubtless preparing to unleash their bombs upon the people of Vathayne, as well as upon the slender craft from another world that had momentarily given them hope.

But the plodding Kalkar airships were no match for the swift and highly maneuverable Barsoomian vessel. The latter swung low over the keep as it built up speed, a rush of air sweeping over us. I let out a cheer while around me the Kalkars reached out to the sky and shook their fists in anger. And then otherwise silent craft, propelled by the Eighth Lunar Ray, hurtled upward nose-first at a tremendous velocity in the center of the Hoos, passing out the volcano's maw and speeding easily past the dark, foreboding forms of the enemy airships into the lavender heavens.

And the Barsoomian had said he was only a fair pilot!

As I stood there watching the ship carry Kuvan Tal and the woman I loved into the clouds, a heavy hand fell on my shoulder and whirled me about. I found myself looking into the ugly mug of the Kalkar brute who had carried me up to the keep's summit. But I beheld his unpleasant visage for only a moment, as the next thing I saw was the behemoth's enormous fist smashing into my face. It would seem the brute was not

As the ship dove down...

... a burst of white-hot radium bullets streamed from the cannons's muzzles...

happy with me for cheering on Kuvan Tal's exceptional aerial talents.

Had I not been shackled I might have laid the Kalkar ogre low with my earthly muscles. Instead I found myself lying supine, staring up as one of the newly arrived airships descended to moor upon the tower that rose from the keep's center. A painful tolling rang in my ears as if my head were the clapper of a bell. I rose shakily to my feet of my own accord and allowed my captors to escort me to the newly lowered ramp, where, like Heracles in a book I once read, I passed into the belly of the beast. What else could I do? Perhaps, just like that old Greek, I might have the opportunity to rend the monster's flanks and thereby slay it, though I had to admit the odds did not favor such a happy outcome.

As it happened, my new masters were aware of my exceptional strength. Doubtless, the Jemadar had somehow learned of my involvement in Or-tis' death and hence knew of my earthly origin, for why else would he have taken a special interest in me? As a result, my captors secured me in heavy chains and locked me within a cage, the frame of which was cast out of some lunar alloy much stronger than steel. Thus I sat, morose, fatigued, and utterly defeated, as the airship carried me up out of the dead volcano and across the lunar sea to some unknown, though presumably dire, fate.

With no means of measuring time, I do not know for how long we voyaged through the clouds, but the distance we traveled must have been vast. In any case, it was lengthy enough that I grew so tired of the foul, meager gruel that was slid into my cage as an excuse for nourishment that I fairly wretched at the sight of it.

However, I was fortunate—if that term may be applied to a slave who was surely on his way to his execution, if not worse—that one side of my cage was pushed up against a porthole affording me a view of the scenery below. I looked on spellbound by the panorama that unfolded before my astonished eyes. Even the endless sea enraptured me, for though the lunar oceans are placid in comparison to those of Earth—except when Zo-al, the maker of storms, unleashes his unbridled anger upon them—their tranquil waters reflect the heavens like a mirror, displaying upon its surface an ever-shifting, kaleidoscopic mural of the lambent pink and lavender clouds above.

When at last we reached the coast and proceeded over the land, I was no less amazed by the sights I beheld. We passed over a gorge so deep I could not clearly make out its distant floor, while on either side rose steep, forbidding mountains that dwarfed the towering Himalayas of Earth by orders of magnitude. Amid the lofty peaks drifted luminous vapors that stained the crags with their amaranthine radiance. The mountains gave way to rolling hills of violet and yellow foliage, which in turn spilled onto expansive prairieland veined with wending rivers and streams that gleamed beneath the resplendent skies.

Onward we traveled through the lunar firmament as I looked down upon vistas too varied to describe here in full detail, and which impressed upon me the sheer scope of Va-nah's expansive continents and oceans. That all of Va-nah had once been fully explored by the ancient U-ga, and that its wide-ranging empire had encompassed the entire inner sphere of the Moon, seemed incredible. And yet I saw timeworn relics of that long-gone civilization several times on my lengthy voyage. In two places separated by vast distances I even witnessed what I believed to be the crumbling stone foundations of railway tracks, along which thousands of *kelds* ago electric trains had once sped to every city of the ancient empire, if the histories I had read in the library at Vathayne had any merit.

I had spied the remnants of a third such track—my gaze following the ruined railway foundation as it spanned a trackless desert made remarkable only by the myriad craters that pocked its face—when upon the curving shell of the horizon appeared a soaring mesa of gargantuan proportions. Its circular perimeter must have been at least fifteen miles in diameter, and as the tableland came slowly into view I could make out a monumental city carved out of a single, massive slab of black stone spiring from the summit. The architecture was reminiscent of that which I had seen in Vathayne, and at first I dared hope that we had come upon a far-flung U-ga metropolis—one of such immensity and might that it should fear nothing from the lone Kalkar airship upon which I was an unwilling passenger.

My hopes were soon dashed when the same blond goliath who had captured me in Vathayne's keep appeared before my cage, his cruel mien one of vindictive delight.

"Welcome to Kalkar City Number 1, Ju-lan of Earth!" he boomed. "The Jemadar of Jemadars awaits your company."

So this was the capital of the Kalkar empire! I had been taken in chains to the very city where The Thinkers had risen to power and sparked the bloodthirsty revolution that overthrew the Jemadars and nobility of the U-ga cities across the face of Va-nah. Here was the original seat of power of the Kalkar Jemadar of Jemadars and the Twenty-Four who ruled beneath him, before they were tempted away from Va-nah to plunder the riches and resources of verdant Earth.

And here, I knew, was where I would die a cruel death at the hands of the Jemadar, who undoubtedly meant to punish me for my involvement in the murder of Brother High Commander Or-tis. What hope had I to escape from such a daunting fortress amid a million soldiers of the race that had enslaved the humanity of two worlds? The only hope I retained that was not snuffed out by the sight of my new prison was that Voo-rah-nee had escaped to safety with Kuvan Tal. It was a fair trade, my life for hers, I mused. If somehow time spun backward and again placed me in the same position I had faced in the keep, I knew I would not hesitate to make the same choice as before. And, if necessary, I would do so again and again for all eternity.

And so it was that after the airship moored upon one of the mesa's ancient spires and I was led deep down into the bowels of the city and thrown into a dank cell, I faced the gloomy fate that awaited me with my chin held high and a smile upon my lips. I even took to whistling cheery tunes in the darkness of my cell, but this only seemed to infuriate my captors, who took every opportunity to abuse me both physically and verbally. These ill-tempered displays, however, always stopped short of inflicting any serious injury, either to my body or to my ego. Regarding the latter, my guards were simply too dull-witted to come up with any invective intelligent enough to even raise my ire. They refrained from the former, I surmised, because they had been ordered to keep me alive and relatively unharmed until the Jemadar deigned to come to my cell and personally wreak his own torments upon me.

I found myself in a lightless cell, fettered and secured to the floor by a heavy chain. Food was passed inside at irregular intervals through a slot that opened at the base of the door, which I could just barely reach with my fingertips, being limited by the length of my chain. If it were possible, the gruel they fed me was even fouler than that which I had been given on the airship.

The abuses I previously alluded to were made all the more hellish by the fact that the cell's utter darkness blinded me to them. These assaults consisted of either being unexpectedly blasted with ice-cold water—usually while I was experiencing the rare solace of sleep—or jabbed with a sharp implement through the small barred window set in the door. The painful prodding stopped quickly enough, however, when upon one such occasion I managed to seize the offending rod and thrust it violently back at my abuser. From the guard's cries and lisping curses, I knew I had hit the fellow squarely in the mouth with the rod's base and likely knocked out his front teeth.

As my captivity wore on, the complete and utter absence of light threatened to drive me mad. Often I held my hand up directly before my face, my eyes straining in the darkness to perceive even the barest outline of my palm and fingers. Sometimes I thought I could almost make out my hand, but then, when I moved it away, I could still "see" its faint spectral image before my eyes and I knew I had only deceived myself.

To keep myself from playing that demented game, I explored every inch of my cell by means of touch. I estimated the room was roughly ten feet in both length and breadth. The walls were completely smooth, being carved out of the same black basalt as the entire city, and therefore leaving no block of masonry that might be pried out to provide an avenue of escape, even had I the means to do so. By the sound of my voice echoing from above, I judged my cell's ceiling to be about fifteen feet high, though, of course, my chains prevented me from leaping up with my earthly muscles to touch it and see if it might afford a way out.

Eventually I became convinced that the Jemadar had no intention of either visiting me in my prison or delivering me to another location where he might further torment me. Perhaps he had forgotten me altogether. But why, then, had he gone to the trouble to have me transported via airship to Kalkar City Number 1? It seemed more likely that my isolation in the cold dankness of the pitch-dark cell was to be my punishment, and that perhaps he derived some sick satisfaction from having me suffer in his proximity, whether he witnessed my anguish or not.

Having convinced myself that I would rot in the cell for time without end, it was a great surprise when the cell door swung open with a screeching groan and a familiar, mocking voice rang out in the darkness.

"What seems to be troubling you, my dear Julian? Having a hard time seeing in this gloom?"

I heard a click and instantly a harsh, blinding light seared my eyes from a light fixture set in the ceiling. Although I had craved for what seemed an eternity for even the scantest trace of illumination, I now threw my arms over my eyes to shut out the light. My visitor—whose voice I recognized immediately, though I could hardly believe my ears—only laughed at my discomfort.

"Or-tis," I groaned. "I left you for dead in the Kalkar head-quarters back on Earth."

"Let that be a lesson for you," the man replied. "Make sure to kill your enemy when you strike him down or he will only return to wreak his vengeance on you."

Shading my narrowed eyes from the harsh light by peering through the cracks between my fingers, I could just make out Or-tis' shadowy form standing outside the doorframe.

"You," I said, "are the new Jemadar of Jemadars."

"Hralk was a good tyrant," Or-tis said musingly, "but he did not know how to run an empire."

"I thought such a form of government was anathema to you Kalkars."

By now my eyes had adjusted enough that I could make out Or-tis' cruel grin.

"Perhaps it is my terrestrial ancestry," he said, "but I do find the collectivist approach rather boring. Not that the Kalkars practice true brotherhood anyway. There is always someone at the top to reap the benefits of the masses. And why should that someone not be me?"

"How sporting of you," I said.

"But I did not come here to discuss politics." Or-tis' grin widened. "I came here to ask you whether you might like to be my guest at my forthcoming wedding ceremony?"

"What are you driving at, Or-tis?" I refused to give the vile creature the satisfaction of addressing him by his new title. "Why would I wish to attend your wedding?"

"Ah," he crooned, "because I believe you know the bride. Voo-rah-nee, Nonovar of Vathayne, will make a lovely addition to my many beautiful wives, don't you think?"

"You're lying," I said calmly, though inside I fought back a turmoil of rage and despair. "The Nonovar fled Vathayne before your forces succeeded in capturing it. I witnessed her escape with my own eyes."

"Then your eyes were mistaken." Or-tis removed something from a pouch on his belt and tossed the item into my cell. It clanked like metal on the hard floor and rolled to a stop at my feet. I reached down and picked it up.

It was a bracelet of solid silver that I was accustomed to seeing on Voo-rah-nee's wrist. When I lifted it up, I caught a faint whiff of the fragrant perfume the Nonovar habitually wore.

My fury broke and I leaped at Or-tis, intent on wrapping my fingers around the fiend's throat and throttling him until I had expired his miserable life. But the length of chain attached to the collar around my neck stopped me short.

"Now, now, Julian," Or-tis said. "I can't have a member of my wedding party acting like such a boor. I do think I shall have to reconsider your invitation."

"I will kill you, Or-tis," I said.

Or-tis laughed. "You are bold. Or stupid. Perhaps both. In any case, it is over. Vathayne has fallen and I have shot the Barsoomian craft from the skies. My scientists have learned much from studying it. It yields many innovations that are far more advanced than any that existed even in the age in which my ancestor Orthis lived. From what Tu-lav told me before he died at the hands of my interrogators, I gather that he meant to use this knowledge to create a network of devices that he planned to place all across Va-nah, and even upon its outer shell. These devices would have disabled any airship or space vessel that employed the planetary rays as a means of propulsion. By such means he meant to cripple my ships and prevent any invaders from beyond Va-nah from entering this world. An ambitious plan, I admit."

The man paused, and a gloating smile spread slowly across his lips. "But I have better use to make of the treasure trove of knowledge provided by the Barsoomian ship," he continued. "With it, I intend to recreate my ingenious ancestor's greatest invention—the electronic rifle, which, as you perhaps know from your family history, could instantly obliterate any substance to which it was attuned. The weapon was singlehandedly responsible for wiping out almost the entire International Peace Fleet in less than thirty Earth days. How long do you think it will take for the weapon to wipe out the pitiful rebellion of the U-ga cities? But my plans are not so shortsighted. I intend to build my own fleet of spacefaring ships based on the advanced design of the captured craft, each armed with an electronic rifle mounted upon its bow. With my fleet, I shall conquer Barsoom and end any threat it poses to the Kalkar collective. From there, who knows? Perhaps other inhabited worlds lie in the vast reaches of space, waiting to join cause with our brotherhood."

"You are mad, Or-tis," I said. "The Barsoomians are a warlike people and, as you say, their science is much more advanced than your own. Surely they have already invented the electronic rifle and will use it to repel any invasion you might launch against them."

"One of their scientists did," he replied. "But the nation of Helium, fearing the weapon's power, saw that it was destroyed, along with the knowledge of how to create it. Yes, the Barsoomians may strive to recreate the electronic rifle to fend off my forces, but that will take time, and by the time they do, it will be too late. I, on the other hand, have been working on the problem for most of my life and am near to unlocking the weapon's secrets. Already the new knowledge I have gained from the Barsoomian craft has made my success inevitable. Today my scientists have announced they have made a breakthrough and will deliver the electronic rifle to me within the *ola*."

You may imagine my distress when you realize that an *ola* is a period equivalent in Earth time to six hours and thirty-two minutes. Now I understood the timing of Or-tis' visit. He had waited until he was certain he could replicate the dread weapon of his ancestor. Only then had he come to me, knowing that the information, along with the knowledge that he had captured Voo-rah-nee and intended to marry her, would drive me mad.

He was not wrong, and as soon as he slammed the cell door in my face and the cell again plunged into utter darkness, I sank to the cold stone floor, utterly defeated and dispirited. Or-tis had won, and there was nothing I could do about it.

As I waited to descend into madness, as I knew I inevitably would, I heard footsteps in the darkened hall outside my cell. I groaned, believing Or-tis or one of his henchmen had come to further torment me.

I rose, ready to face whatever horror my enemy meant to inflict upon me. Again the harsh light glared down upon me from the ceiling and the cell door slammed open.

This time, having already been exposed only moments before, my eyes did not need time to adjust to the sudden light. Therefore, I saw with perfect clarity the man standing before me. It was not Or-tis, but rather a Kalkar soldier of about my same height. However, despite his uniform, the man in no way resembled any Kalkar I had ever seen before. He stood about my same height and carried himself with the carriage of a proud warrior. Clear steel gray eyes peered out from beneath shaggy blond hair, bearing an intelligence and fiery spark of initiative wholly uncharacteristic of his kind.

The man raised a key-whistle to his lips and blew into it. Instantly, the shackles on my wrists and the collar around my neck clicked open and fell away. As I stood with my mouth agape, he reached a hand to his blond head and proceeded to scratch at his scalp as if irritated by a bothersome itch. Then, his handsome features taking on a look of disgust, he grabbed hold of his mop of hair and cast it off to reveal closely cropped black hair underneath—the thick blond locks had been but a wig!

"I won't be needing that at the moment, anyway," the man said in the perfect American English of a polished southerner.

Seeming to take notice of my startlement, he smiled and placed his hand upon my shoulder in an unmistakable gesture of friendship. "Forgive me for not introducing myself sooner," he said. "I am John Carter, Prince of Helium and Warlord of Barsoom." Then, with the faintest curl of mischief upon his lips, he added, "Formerly a gentleman of Virginia."

Chapter Nineteen

AN INTERPLANETARY THREAT

J ohn Carter!" I exclaimed. "How did you manage to escape Tu-lav's prison and transport yourself all the way across Va-nah to this far-flung hornet's nest?"

My emancipator beckoned me to follow him into the hallway. "Whether it is due to the hand of Fate, bad luck, or my own folly," he said, "I have found myself behind the bars of a prison cell more times than I care to admit. However, something in my constitution has left me with no recourse but to continue fighting with every ounce of my being until I achieve liberty or die in the attempt."

We proceeded down a long, dark corridor lined with cells until we reached a door, whereupon my companion used another key to open it. Upon the other side was a stairwell whose steps spiraled upward until they were lost from sight high above. Unlike the corridor we left behind, radium covered the walls and provided an even source of lighting throughout the area.

"As for how I came to the Kalkar capital," John Carter continued, "it is an unremarkable story. I simply flew across the sea, having stolen a gas bag and a pair of those ingenious wings of the Vathayneans, and joined up with a company of Kalkars in the first city I came upon. Once there, I forged the papers that allowed for my passage aboard an airship departing for the capital. As you may have noticed, these Kalkars are not bright fellows. My simple disguise"—he held up his blond wig—"and a few clever lies were more than adequate to convince them I was a dutiful, dull-witted soldier in their collective."

I had indeed noticed. Furthermore, I had learned firsthand from my experiences infiltrating the Jemadar's army.

We mounted the stairs and began our dizzying, twining climb out of the dungeons of Kalkar City Number 1. I fingered Voo-rah-nee's bracelet, which I had carried with me from the cell. Despite my elation at being liberated, Or-tis' taunt that he intended to wed the Nonovar weighed heavily on my mind. "Where are we going?" I asked.

"To Or-tis' laboratory, of course," John Carter said. "We must destroy his work on the disintegrating ray."

"You mean the electric rifle?"

"That is what the Vathayneans call it," my companion replied. "On Barsoom, it is called the disintegrating ray. Regardless of its name, the weapon is a menace to humanity, whether that means Barsoomians, Kalkars, U-ga, Va-gas, or the people of Jasoom. A Barsoomian scientist by the name of Phor Tak invented a similar weapon using the same principle years ago. If not for the intervention of a simple fighting man in my army named Tan Hadron, the disintegrating ray rifle very well might have brought Barsoom to ruin. But the weapon Or-tis seeks is more advanced than the one invented on Barsoom. The device Phor Tak created employed shells whose charges were treated with the disintegrating ray, whereas my understanding is that Or-tis' weapon will, if completed, discharge the ray itself—thus making it an even more horrendous engine of destruction."

I did not fail to notice that this former Earth man no longer regarded the planet of his birth as his home. Could I, then, trust him, knowing he would place the safety of Barsoom above that of Earth, or Jasoom, as he called it? I did not know, but his very presence seemed to emanate loyalty and trust, and who was I to doubt the man who had just freed me from Or-tis' dungeon.

"Ultimately, I came to Va-nah because of the disintegrating ray," John Carter went on as we continued our climb. "A quarter century ago, all of Barsoom looked on in trepidation as the devil Orthis brought the people of Jasoom to their knees with the ghastly ray. We cheered from across the void of space when your grandfather, Julian 5th, destroyed the disintegrating ray rifle, though we lamented that he lost his life in the act and even so did not prevent the Moon men from conquering the planet. With the death of Orthis, however, we believed the indolent Kalkars would be unable to rediscover the principles of the ray. Thus it was with great dismay that my astronomers informed me that a man—Orthis' descendant, we believed—was attempting to do just that on Jasoom. It was not long afterward that we detected Tu-lav's signal and he reached out to us for help. I ordered the construction of an interplanetary ship and led the diplomatic mission to Va-nah.

"But the Jemadar of Vathayne is a xenophobe and had plans of his own. He did not trust that Helium or some other power on Barsoom wouldn't set its sights on Va-nah. And so he imprisoned us and began plumbing the secrets of our ship in the attempt to create a defensive weapon to isolate all of Va-nah from the worlds beyond her. Perhaps he is not wrong to do so. If we fail today in our efforts to destroy the disintegrating ray rifle, Tu-lav will be this world's last hope."

"What do you mean?" I exclaimed, stopping in my tracks on our upward climb. "Vathayne has fallen and Tu-lav is dead."

"That is what Or-tis told you, but it was only a lie to inflict further suffering upon you. Word on the streets of this city is that Vathayne repelled the Kalkar forces and its flag flies free, though it is in tatters and I fear it cannot withstand another assault. Moreover, before the invaders were driven out, they managed to capture a number of nobles from the Jemadar's court who have revealed the secret locations of the other U-ga cities. Or-tis readies his armies for war. He intends to stamp out the U-ga resistance once and for all, which the disintegrating ray will make an easy task."

"And what of Voo-rah-nee, the Nonovar of Vathayne?" I asked, daring to hope. "Was it a lie when Or-tis told me he brought her to this city and intends to force her hand in marriage?"

John Carter's grim expression told me all I needed to know.

"Then I must wish you luck finding and destroying the electronic rifle," I said. "My duty lies with the Nonovar. If I succeed in my task, I shall join you as quickly as I can in accomplishing yours."

The Warlord of Barsoom smiled. "You are a man after my own heart. I must go after the disintegrating ray rifle, but there is no need for us to part at this moment. The Nonovar of Vathayne has been locked away on one of the highest levels of the Tower of Brotherhood, the great spire that rises from the center of the city. If the intelligence I have gone to great lengths to acquire is correct, there too, on the floor above where the Nonovar is imprisoned, lies Or-tis' laboratory."

If John Carter's bemused expression was telling, I must have had the most foolish grin upon my face by the time he finished speaking.

"Let us go together, then, to the Tower of…" my companion began, but I did not tarry to hear the rest of his words and in my eagerness was already bolting up the steps ahead of him.

The Kalkar capital, constructed by the ancient U-ga during the height of their civilization and only later occupied by the Kalkars, is truly a cyclopean wonder. We must have ascended for more than half a mile before at last we saw the end of the stairwell above. John Carter bade me to stop while he fit himself with his wig and again assumed the disguise of a common Kalkar soldier. He unholstered his pistol and, pointing it at my back, told me to proceed.

We emerged in a guardroom, where the officer in charge asked my companion for his papers. The latter thereupon produced a missive, which he handed to the man. The officer scrutinized the papers with a furrowed brow. It was clear the fellow either could not read or was having a hard time of it. It seemed that illiteracy and bureaucracy went hand in hand among the Kalkars, no matter what world they dominated.

"Where are you taking this prisoner, and on whose authority?" the man asked.

"You have the papers in your hand, do you not?" asked John Carter.

"Just answer my question!" the officer said gruffly.

"Or-tis, Jemadar of Jemadars," my companion replied, "has ordered this slave to be brought to the Tower of Brotherhood, where he will assist in research vital to the security of the state. If you will check your records, you will see that the Jemadar himself has just been to the dungeons to inspect the slave."

"Of course he was!" the officer exclaimed. "I just logged his visit myself and personally escorted him from the facilities." The man eyed my companion through narrowed lids. "But why did you not take the electric lift up from the prison level with the Jemadar?"

Peering from beneath his thick blond wig, the Prince of Helium scoffed. "Do you think the Jemadar Or-tis wishes to be seen strolling side by side down the street with the former lover of the Nonovar of Vathayne, whom the Jemadar is due to wed in only seven *olas*? Can you imagine how people would talk?" And then he grinned and nudged the officer conspiratorially with his elbow.

The Kalkar grunted, and though my friend's bold lie in truth made little sense, the man nodded knowingly. But that was the way with the Kalkars, whose whole society was based on attaining power by bluffing one's way through the maze of bureaucracy. It was no wonder their infrastructure, whether that meant their space fleet or the trains running between the Teivoses of Washington and Chicago, was on the verge of collapse.

"You may pass," the officer said finally, and I breathed a quiet sigh of relief.

We were about to pass through the door that led out to the street when John Carter about-faced and returned to the officer's desk.

"Oh, I almost forgot," said my companion to the man, taking a paper from beneath his tunic and unfolding it upon the desk. "The Jemadar would like a receipt for the prisoner."

The officer's brow furrowed deeply. "A receipt?"

"Yes, and please be quick about it." My blond-wigged friend rapped his knuckles impatiently upon the surface of the desk. "The Jemadar is waiting."

Grumbling beneath his breath, the officer produced an ink pad and a stamp, and proceeded to place his mark upon the paper my friend had provided.

John Carter folded up the paper and slipped it into a fold in his tunic. Then he clicked his heels together, saluted the officer, and, permitting the man no further time to question him, escorted me out of the building.

When we had walked some distance down the busy thoroughfare, I nudged my companion. "What was that all about?"

"Oh, yes, that," John Carter said with an air of nonchalance. "I simply needed the fellow to unknowingly authorize the paperwork that will grant us entry into the Tower of Brotherhood."

"Why, you sly devil," I said.

My friend merely shrugged. "When in Kalkar City Number 1, do as the Kalkars do."

As we continued on our way, all around us shuffled the despondent citizens of the Jemadar's bleak, soulless regime. Back on Earth, I had thought that perhaps the miserable conditions of the working class were due to the fact that the Kalkars had been separated from their world of origin. Surely, I had thought, the conquered inhabitants of Earth had experienced the worst of Kalkar culture, and those Kalkars who remained on Va-nah must exist at least on a somewhat higher level of civilization. Watching the slouch-shouldered, glassy-eyed people of this city pass us by, however, convinced me that I had been quite wrong. Wherever the Kalkars ruled, they brought apathy and misery.

Of course, here I refer to members of the lower class. The Kalkars, however, pretend there is only one class, and that every Kalkar is an equal member of society. In truth, two more classes exist: on the next higher tier are those in the military, who generally fare better than the commoners because they are armed and well fed, and on the highest tier are the Jemadar and his Twenty-Four, who employ the military to beat the lower class into submission so that its members provide support for those of the tiers above.

Further down the avenue we passed a mile-long stretch of slums, though here the road was elevated and we did not mingle with the unfortunates below. When we reached the other side of the district, we boarded an electric train. No fare was required for passage, and the car in which we found ourselves was filled with both soldiers and workers alike traveling to the city's central district. After the train had gone a short distance, it came to a screeching halt. The conductor told us there had been a power outage and that we must debark and walk to the next station, the tracks of which operated on a different powerline. The passengers shuffled listlessly out of the train and onto the street. Apparently, power outages were so routine that the commuters suffered them without complaint.

On our walk to the next train station, we stopped at a communal kitchen. The food here was almost as bad as the gruel I had been fed in the Jemadar's prison, though one of the cooks, apparently hoping to gain a future favor from a soldier, slipped my friend a large fresh lunar fruit. John Carter, knowing how I had suffered in the dungeon, gave this to me. I eagerly devoured the sweet-tasting fruit, and I still believe it was the best meal I have ever experienced in all of my incarnations.

Feeling reinvigorated from our meal, we walked to the nearby station and boarded a train that took us to the central district without incident. After debarking, we filed along with the river of pedestrians flowing toward the Tower of Brotherhood, the administrative seat of the city's government and the Kalkar collective as a whole.

At the checkpoint leading into the walled area surrounding the tower, my companion produced the paperwork stamped by the Jemadar's jailor. This stated that my disguised friend was permitted to escort me, his prisoner, through the gate. The guard at the checkpoint examined the document, and for a moment my nerves were on edge, as it appeared the man was actually carefully reading the words on the paper. Literacy, it seems, increases within the proximity of the Jemadar, who must guard himself against both assassins and sycophantic supplicants.

The guard apparently found our paperwork to be in order, and with a quick bark of command he ordered the gate to be opened and let us pass inside the compound. This area, composed of spacious courts and a number of administrative buildings, was sparsely populated, as only the most trusted were permitted to enter the tower complex.

As we passed under the great arch that frowned over the entrance to the Tower of Brotherhood, an intense feeling of dread and foreboding possessed me, as if we were being swallowed whole by some colossal giant. We were only two men against a city—no, two *worlds*—full of Kalkars. If we could not stop Or-tis before he finished work on his electronic rifle, the entire solar system could fall under his thrall. There was nothing to do but continue on.

Inside the tower we stopped at another guard station. Once again, our paperwork went unquestioned and we were allowed to pass beyond the foyer. Here we found a small room with three banks of automated elevator cars. We entered one of these and my companion flipped a switch on the controls. John Carter, having meticulously planned our attack on the tower ahead of time, told me the elevator would take us to the highest unrestricted level. There we would again use the paperwork the jailor had authorized to access the secure levels above, and, ultimately, the chamber where Voo-rah-nee was being held below Or-tis' laboratory in the tower's garret.

The elevator, clanking and clattering, carried us higher and higher into the soaring spire of the Tower of Brotherhood. At last the car came to a halt and we exited into a guardroom where a soldier asked for my escort's papers. He examined these and asked my companion the reason for his visit to the tower.

"I am escorting this prisoner to the Jemadar's laboratory," John Carter said. "He has valuable information that will assist in the important research being conducted here."

The guard scrutinized the paperwork again. "It's unusual that I've not had advance notice of the prisoner's transfer," he said, and my heart felt as if it sank into my stomach. "However, I am not one to question the mark of Brother Plargh, the Jemadar's jailor. Surrender your firearm. No guns are permitted in the Jemadar's proximity." The man handed the paperwork back to my pretend captor. In exchange, John Carter unstrapped his gun belt and placed it on the counter, though he was permitted to retain his sword. It did not surprise me that Or-tis feared assassination, given that he had disposed of the former Jemadar through violent means himself.

My companion saluted the guard and, grasping me firmly by the arm, conducted me to the alcove on the opposite side of the room, which was apparently the only means of accessing the tower's higher floors. Here we mounted a winding stairway of black stone, the walls of which had been painted with a band of radium to light the way.

We were halfway to the next level when we heard the footsteps of a large party clapping the stone steps directly below. A moment later a familiar voice carried up the stairs.

"...want to be there personally so I can test the weapon myself."

It was Or-tis!

Chapter Twenty

LIKE FATHER, LIKE SON

John Carter and I shared a look of desperation, and then we leaped up the stairs with all the lightning speed that our earthly muscles could carry us in the lesser gravity of Va-nah. We reached the next level without being seen by Or-tis and whoever accompanied him, but here the stairs ended and we were faced with a choice. A corridor stretched upon either side, one curving to the left and the other to the right.

"Which way?" I whispered.

My companion looked puzzled. "I don't know," he said quietly. "The floorplan does not match the intelligence I gathered. Let us split up. If one of us is captured, at least the other will have a chance."

And having made that pronouncement, John Carter bounded down the leftward corridor while I took the other.

The hallway down which I ran carried me into a richly appointed apartment. This room stood in stark contrast to every bland, practical Kalkar dwelling I had ever had the misfortune of encountering. Thick, lavishly decorated carpets covered the floor, and upon the walls were painted breathtaking murals depicting a handsome, ivory-skinned, raven-haired people frolicking across magnificent lunar landscapes or otherwise engaged in peaceful scenes of pastoral life. In no way did this race resemble the brutish Kalkars, and I could only surmise that the artwork had been painted on the stone walls by the ancient U-ga who had built the tower untold millennia ago. That the murals were crisp and brilliantly colored, looking as if they had been painted by the brush of some master only yesterday, was a testament to the abiding artistry and workmanship of that bygone civilization.

As I entered the room, a man's voice came through the doorway opposite me.

"Come back here, you little scoundrel!"

Into the room in which I stood scampered a boy of about four years of age who, heedless in his flight, ran full bore into my legs. Startled, the child stepped back and gasped as he looked up at me.

The sounds of approaching footsteps grew louder from the other room. I smiled at the boy and then pressed a finger to my lips in the desperate hope that he might believe I wanted him to play a game of hide and seek. The boy grinned in unabashed delight and pointed to a tall window before which hung heavy drapes. I winked at my little savior and ran to the window, pulling the curtains about myself but leaving enough room between them that I might peer forth unseen from my hiding place and observe the room's interior.

A moment later a stern-looking man in the uniform of a Kalkar officer strode into the room and grabbed the child by the arm.

"I've had enough of your mischief, young man!" the man shouted so forcefully that I expected the boy to burst into tears. The little terror, however, simply folded his arms obstinately and stuck out his lower lip in a sulking pout.

"I am a captain in the Jemadar's fleet," the man continued. "If not for the tantrum you threw in front of your father, I should be leading the assault against one of the U-ga cities right now instead of babysitting a brat like you. It's simply embarrassing for a man of my accomplishments. Now sit down and let me relax in some peace and quiet!"

The man lifted the boy up into the air and deposited his rear end on a hassock. Then the man crossed the room, sat down upon a divan, and, leaning back into the cushions, closed his eyes with a deep sigh.

The boy, his arms still crossed and his lip still pouting, very deliberately turned his head in my direction until he stared straight at me. Slowly, his lips began to curl until his pout was replaced by a devilish grin.

I widened the curtain just enough that he could see me put a finger to my lips and shake my head.

Clasping his hands behind his back like a diminutive general, the lad marched across the room to the side of the dozing man and, leaning over to position himself as close as possible to his caretaker's ear, shouted at the top of his lungs, "This room is too dark!"

The man's eyes snapped open and he leaped up in anger, but the child was too quick for him and darted away from his reaching grasp.

"What's the matter with you?" the man boomed. "This room is painted with radium like all the others!" Upon making this declaration, he stalked across the room and stood directly before the drapes behind which I hid.

"Is this good enough for you, you devil's spawn?" he cried at the boy, and then pulled the curtains apart to stare straight into my smiling face with the most ludicrous expression of shock and dismay. I would have burst into laughter had I not known my life was now forfeit.

The man grabbed me by the collar and dragged me out from behind the curtain.

"Who are you?" he demanded. "Speak now or I shall summon the Jemadar's guard and they will shoot you on the spot!"

My mind raced to come up with some excuse for my presence, but before I could settle on a plausible lie, the most horrendous noise erupted from across the room. It was the boy, and he was shrieking at the top of his youthful lungs.

"Release him, Darbo!" the child shouted, and he stamped his little foot, tears of rage streaming down his cheeks. "He is my personal slave!"

"What is this about?" the man asked incredulously.

"My father gave him to me for a plaything," the boy said. Then he turned to me and asked, "Isn't that right, Klabar?"

"That is right, young lad," I said, and jutted out my grinning chin to show Darbo that he had been bested.

"No," the man said firmly to the child. "You can cry all you want, but we are going downstairs to sort this out with the captain of the guard. He will know who is authorized to enter these apartments. Come with me, Klabar...or whoever you really are." He grabbed me roughly by the arm and yanked me toward the doorway that opened onto the corridor leading to the stairs.

The boy screamed in anger and ran to the doorway, spread-eagling himself in its frame to prevent us from passing through.

"You will not take him, Darbo!" he shrieked. "I will tell my father and he will skin you alive!"

"Get out of my way!" the man shouted, his face flushed with fury. "I don't care who your father is, you snot-nosed brat! You will do as I say!" And he raised his arm to strike the little boy with the back of his hand.

But the blow never landed. At least *his* did not. Mine, on the other hand, struck the man squarely in the jaw. The fellow toppled with a thud to the plush carpet.

I looked to the boy to make sure he was all right, but I need not have been concerned. By all appearances, he was not frightened in the least. On the contrary, there he stood in the doorway, howling with laughter.

I shushed the little monster, for I did not want his loud-mouthed mirth drawing anyone to the apartment. "Let's let old Darbo sleep it off, shan't we?" I said quietly, and winked. The boy nodded and managed to reduce his boisterous peals to a quiet snorting. Relieved that the boy was behaving, I dragged the unconscious man across the room and deposited him behind the divan, where he could not readily be seen.

I returned to the door and knelt beside the child. "Thank you for saving me," I whispered with a grateful smile. "What is your name?"

The boy grinned and puffed out his little chest with pride.

"I am Or-tis," he said, "son of the Jemadar of Jemadars."

Chapter Twenty-One

A FIGHT FOR THREE WORLDS

With the help of the boy, I found Darbo's scabbarded sword hanging on a post in the adjoining room. I strapped the weapon on my hip and left behind the apartments of the Jemadar, hoping I would be able to accomplish what I must before the young spawn of Or-tis became bored and tattled on me to the guards or some other adult.

This time I took the corridor that John Carter had chosen to explore, which curved halfway around the side of the tower until it ended at a stairway. To one side of the steps, an arched wooden door stood ajar. A trail of fresh blood ran from the door and passed up the stairs.

I examined the gruesome scene carefully. The droplets of blood grew smaller as they proceeded up the steps. Whoever had committed the bloodshed had done so in the room and then fled up the tower.

Cautiously, I approached the door and peered inside. Beyond was a small room, against the far wall of which stood a table holding an uncorked ceramic jug and three pewter goblets. The corpses of three men lay on the floor where they had died with swords in their hands during a violent encounter.

As I backed away from the room and made to head up the stone steps, an alarm claxon began clamoring in the tower. A few moments later, the whine of sirens broke out all across the city.

My heart sank. We had been found out and now the entire resources of the Kalkar capital had been called to the Tower of Brotherhood and directed against us.

I drew my sword and bolted up the stairs following the winding trail of crimson. I had ascended perhaps twenty feet above the previous level when the grisly spoor led me to a closed door, behind which I heard the clanging of steel against steel. Without hesitation I swung the door wide and leaped into the room beyond.

A spectacle unlike anything I had ever witnessed was playing out in the high-ceilinged chamber before me. Four men with swords faced off against a single opponent who was backed into a corner—it was John Carter, his blade running red with the blood of his adversaries! The corpses of three Kalkars lay heaped up one atop the other on the floor before the Warlord of Barsoom, whose fighting smile could only be a testament to their deaths at his hand.

One of the Kalkars he now fought cried out in dismay as a clever flourish of John Carter's blade flung the man's sword out of his grasp. I could not perceive the fatal stroke of the Warlord's sword, so fast it was, but I did see his opponent fall and become the fourth corpse on top of the grim heap.

I whooped a battle cry and leaped to engage the nearest swordsman. The others turned, surprised at my unexpected attack. John Carter used their startlement to his advantage and leaped in the lesser gravity of Va-nah, vaulting clear over their heads and landing at my side to slash his blade across the throat of one of our staggered enemies. The man fell, leaving us now with only two opponents, whom we proceeded to engage with the utmost determination.

John Carter flashed me a smile as he riposted his assailant. "What kept you?"

"Oh," I replied, deflecting a blow, "just babysitting the Jemadar's brat of a son." I lunged, but my partner was no mean duelist and knocked me back with a beat parry.

Out of the corner of my eye, I saw my companion flick his blade and make a small cut to his opponent's cheek. A moment later, with a seemingly effortless motion, he repeated the action, slicing the opposite cheek of his foe. The Warlord of Barsoom seemed to be uncannily calm as he faced the Kalkar's slashing blade. But even more so, he appeared to be enjoying himself.

"Or-tis," I called to my friend as we fought side by side, "have you seen him?" We had heard Or-tis ascending the stairway behind us, and yet after John Carter and I separated, I had not encountered my nemesis in the apartment where I had found his son. He could only have come upstairs to the very room we now occupied.

"He has locked himself in his laboratory yonder," John Carter said, pressing his opponent toward a door set in the room's far side. "He has taken the Nonovar of Vathayne with him as a hostage or I might have killed him before he escaped."

My blood ran cold, and I renewed my attack against my adversary with savage fury.

John Carter's opponent cried out and fell before him, where he lay unmoving at his feet. The Warlord had no sooner dispatched his foe than three more men ran into the room from the stairwell. One of these was Darbo, the airship captain I had knocked senseless in the apartment on the level below. He must have come to and been found by the other two guards when they came up to investigate the cause of the alarm.

The man whipped out a pistol that had been tucked under his belt and aimed it at John Carter. I cried out in warning, but I was too late. The man pulled the trigger at the precise moment I drove my blade into the heart of my adversary.

I looked up from the glazed eyes of the lifeless man before me, expecting to see my friend lying dead with a bullet hole in his forehead. I instead saw Darbo's severed hand, the pistol still clutched in its fingers, flying through the air, a stream of crimson fanning out in its wake. The shocked man, his eyes fairly bulging from their sockets, held up his arm and gazed in disbelief at the blood-spewing stump of his wrist, where only a moment before his hand had been. Then, before I could even understand what I was seeing, steel flashed under the glow of the radium-covered walls, and the man's head separated from his shoulders and rolled like an ungainly ball across the stone floor.

John Carter, impossibly still very much alive, snatched up a second sword with his off hand from one of his fallen foes and bounded over Darbo's headless corpse. Before my unbelieving eyes, he took on the two remaining Kalkars at once, dual-wielding his swords. Never had I seen a man so skilled with a blade, nor have I ever since. I have heard John Carter called the best swordsman of two worlds, but I can attest that during that fight in the Tower of Brotherhood, he was the best swordsman of at least three.

Suddenly I comprehended the miracle that must have transpired. It could only be that Darbo's gun had misfired. In truth, it should not have surprised me so greatly, since the gunpowder of the Kalkars, as a result of the routine inefficiency of their munitions facilities, is often of inferior quality.

Why Darbo should have been permitted a sidearm in the restricted area I did not know. Perhaps he was afforded special privileges in the course of his duties to protect the Jemadar's son, though that seemed unlikely as, thankfully, the man had been unarmed when I first encountered him. Peradventure he had obtained the gun from the guard station on the lower level in response to the alarm. In the end it made no difference—Fate had intervened, and that was all that mattered. I only thanked Providence that the other soldiers did not carry firearms, for if they had, John Carter and I would certainly have been dead men.

But all of these thoughts did not cross my mind in the heat of combat, or if they did, they streaked like lightning not through my intellect but through my nerves, for to hesitate in contemplation amid battle is to court one's odds of meeting a swift death. And that I could not abide while my princess was yet in peril.

I sprang to my companion's side and drew the attention of one of his adversaries. My friend's off-hand blade clattered to the floor as he cast it away and closed on his opponent, a brawny giant of a Kalkar who was seven feet tall if he was an inch. As I fought my own combatant, John Carter moved with a celerity that barely seemed human, outmaneuvering his foe with deft swordplay and bounding leaps that saw him alternately lunging beneath the Kalkar's nose and jumping out of the lunar giant's reach before he could land a blow.

For my own part, I owed my life to the relentless hours of sword training my uncle had imposed upon me from a young age. But perhaps even more so, I owed the deadly talents that I inflicted against my enemies to the Kalkars themselves, for it was they who had burst into my family's home in the dead of night and torn my beloved grandmother forever from my life. In so doing, they had lit the wick of vengeance in my breast, which now burned all the more furiously and motivated each murderous swing of my blade.

And so John Carter and I fought on—one of us determined to end the Kalkar threat before it reached across the chasm of space to wage war against his beloved Barsoom, and the other driven to strike back against the vile scourge that had tyrannized his family and spread like a pestilence across green Earth, and that now sought to rob him of the woman he loved and decimate her people. Truly was it a tale of three worlds—Earth, Barsoom, and Va-nah—each struggling to resist the dread menace of the Kalkars. But here and now, teetering on the edge of the razor-thin plank that spanned the dark pit of defeat, stood only two men. Atlas had been burdened with only one world—my friend and I endeavored to hold up three while balancing on a tightrope!

The goliath confronting my companion seemed only to grow more enraged at the acrobatics that kept him from stamping out his puny opponent. I had pegged the slovenly, low-browed giant for a dimwit, like so many Kalkars I had encountered who had been bred exclusively for size and brute strength.

But then the fellow surprised me. While John Carter was leaping back from a long-armed swing, the dowdy ogre of a Kalkar grabbed a wooden bench sitting against the wall behind him and hurled it—not at the Virginian, but at me! Though I saw the piece of furniture flying at me out of the corner of an eye, I had been busy with my challenger, recovering from a clever feint. Thus I had no time to react and the bench hit me square on, knocking me to the floor and precipitating me some distance across the room.

Meanwhile, John Carter also seemed to have been taken by surprise at the unsportsmanlike move. Though I did not see how the Kalkar giant had accomplished the feat, my friend had been disarmed and now lay supine on the hard floor. The colossus crouched over the Warlord of Barsoom, one meaty hand wrapped around his throat, and was squeezing the life from his frame.

I scrambled to my feet, my shoulder throbbing where I had slammed into the floor, my ribs tender and bruised from where the bench had struck me. Already my own opponent was barreling across the floor at me, his sword raised to end my life.

What in heaven's name was in my hand? I looked down and saw Darbo's pistol in my grasp—I must have picked it up from the floor while I lay prone.

Almost without awareness of the act, I raised the gun and pulled the trigger. This time it did not misfire. The running man fell dead at my feet.

I seized the man's sword from where he had dropped it and flew across the room to confront the Kalkar brute assaulting my friend. However, I might have stayed where I had been, for when I got there, the giant lay bleeding out on the stone floor.

John Carter rose from the slain goliath, wiping a dagger clean with a kerchief. He slipped the knife in his belt and retrieved his sword.

The sound of men's voices clamored up from the stairwell. Reinforcements were coming.

John Carter walked calmly to one of the soldiers who had fallen before my arrival and removed something from a ring looped around the man's belt. He tossed it to me. It was a key.

"Go save your princess," John Carter said. "I will hold off the others."

"You'll be killed!" I exclaimed.

But the Warlord of Barsoom was already at the top of the stairs, his gray eyes sparkling as if in anticipation of the fight to come.

"Just make sure to destroy the disintegrating ray rifle," he said. "If you do, you will save *my* princess, and her world as well." And then, a cool smile upon his lips, he turned to face an army of Kalkars singlehanded.

I sounded the key and swung open the door.

Chapter Twenty-Two

THE MADMAN OF LUNA

I found myself in a spacious chamber with a high, vaulted ceiling. All manner of experimental apparatus lay before me, many of which I had no reference for. Lab tables lay heaped with spools of coppery wire. The open drawers of cabinets revealed trays full of delicate instruments resembling surgical tools. A large blueprint schematic with numerous pencil marks scrawled upon it lay unfolded across two wide desks. Life-sized armatures, like those used by a sculptor, stood in various poses about the room, many with portions of their limbs cleanly severed off. But nowhere in the room did I see Or-tis, Voo-rah-nee, or any other.

I approached one of the armatures. The remnants of a linen sheet were wrapped around the upper part of one of the metallic arms. The cloth looked as it had been cut with great precision. Another armature was fitted with armor, but the upper half of the suit was missing. It was not that the pieces of the suit that dressed the torso were entirely absent from the frame; rather, the upper portions of those pieces were present, but they appeared to have severed cleanly through and had their lower extremities removed, as if someone had taken a sawblade to armor, cutting horizontally through one rerebrace, then sawing across the plackart, and again cutting through the rerebrace on the other arm.

As the sirens clamored all about me, a shiver ran down my spine. Since my childhood, I had heard of the electronic rifle that had been conceived in the demented mind of the archfiend

195

Orthis. It was said that the weapon could generate a beam of radioactivity on a modulating scale, such that it could be adjusted to any number of unique vibratory rates corresponding to specific forms of matter. This resonance excited the electrons of the matter, destabilizing it to such a degree that the target of the beam was essentially transformed into ether.

Or at least, that is how it was explained to me. Regardless of the science behind the weapon, its effect was clear—adjust the electronic rifle to the vibratory rate of iron and direct its beam upon an object composed of that metal, and that object would instantly dissipate before one's eyes.

Having examined the two armatures nearest me, I instantly understood their purpose. They had been draped with different substances—in one instance, linen fabric, and in another, tempered steel—and then subjected to the corresponding modulation of the disintegrating ray. In both cases, the experiment had been successful. Or-tis had managed to recreate the electronic rifle—the same superweapon that allowed his ancestor to obliterate the International Peace Fleet and conquer Earth.

As this fact dawned on me, a voice rang out from some hidden place on the other side of the room.

"Ju-lan, beware!"

It was Voo-rah-nee, and had she not shouted in warning, I should have died on the spot.

I dived behind a lab table just as a horrifying hiss sizzled through the air beside me. A gaping hole opened up in the floor where only a moment before I had stood—a five-foot area of stone composing the space where I had just been standing had simply vanished into thin air.

Cruel laughter broke out from across the room. I looked around the corner of the table for the source. Or-tis emerged from behind a cabinet, Voo-rah-nee struggling in his grasp. He held the electronic rifle, its stock crooked under an arm. The weapon was sleek, with a long barrel and a dial on one side near the trigger, while a series of antennae feathered from behind the sight.

"Come out, Julian," Or-tis said, "or I shall simply disintegrate the table you cower behind."

"I'm no fool, Or-tis," I replied.

"Oh, I think you are."

Or-tis raised the rifle and discharged it, but I was already running even as the table I had been using for cover disappeared as if it had never been there. Or I should say, all of it vanished except for the table's surface, which was made from a different material from the wooden base. The tabletop, its support now missing, slammed down and shattered against the stone floor.

As I ran, I looked back at Or-tis. I saw him turn the dial on the gun as he swept its barrel toward me. Voo-rah-nee, freed from his grasp while he performed this task, threw her whole weight against him just as he pulled the rifle's trigger.

Again the air hissed. This time the beam went astray, hitting the wall behind me and cutting away a broad swath of stone some five feet high and twenty feet across. With a tremendous crash, the entire wall collapsed, hurling large chucks of black stone into the chamber.

Dark gray dust billowed from the devastation, swirling about me like an apocalyptic maelstrom in the gusting wind. I lay prone on the floor where I had fallen, coughing the fine powder from my lungs. Slowly the pall lifted as the dust settled or was carried away on the wind.

I wondered why Or-tis had not simply adjusted the weapon to disintegrate me. Perhaps madness had simply overcome his reason.

A cold draft swept up from behind me. I pushed myself to my feet and peered through the thinning haze for any sign of Or-tis or Voo-rah-nee.

The wall that had been struck by the beam, as well as part of the ceiling and floor adjoining it, had toppled to the court-yard a thousand feet below. An entire side of the building now stood exposed to the open air, casting the eerie violet light of the clouds upon what remained of the room's interior.

Across the city, the sirens still blared. In the sky over the capital hung many dark forms—enemy airships besieging Kalkar City Number 1. Beneath these ominous hulks billowed clouds of black smoke where bombs had been dropped.

"The forces of Vathayne come," came a voice from behind the murk obscuring what remained of the room. "But they are too late."

The dust cleared and I saw Or-tis standing before me armed with his electronic rifle, which was aimed straight at me. Voo-rah-nee was again in his grasp.

Behind them, smoke rose from a long row of filing cabinets. The destruction wrought by Or-tis' ray had knocked over a number of test tubes and started a chemical fire.

"From what I see," I said, "Tu-lav stands a good chance of taking the city. You will be defeated, Or-tis. Drop the gun and release the Nonovar."

Or-tis only laughed. "An entire navy of airships isn't strong enough to stand against the electronic rifle," he said. "I'll shoot them all down from the sky. But it is sad, I admit."

"What are you talking about?" I asked.

The air was now clear enough of dust that I could plainly see Or-tis' smirk. "You call her 'the Nonovar,'" he said, "but your eyes betray your love for this woman." He shoved Voo-rah-nee roughly and she fell to her hands and knees upon the hard stone floor.

Voo-rah-nee rose with dignity and walked to my side. She slipped her arms around my neck and nestled her head against my chest. "I am sorry it has come to this, Ju-lan," she whispered to me. "Perhaps we shall meet again in another incarnation and things will be different."

"I am sure of it," I said, and kissed her upturned lips.

"Ah, it is too bad my scientists did not finish the gun so that it might destroy organic flesh and bone," Or-tis went on, seeming to take pleasure in the tender scene unfolding before him. "Oh, do not fear. It will wreak utter destruction upon the Vathaynean navy, instantly disintegrating the frames of its airships. I can barely contain my anticipation at watching Tu-lav and his soldiers fall in terror from the sky as their ships come to pieces around them. But yes, it is a shame they did not complete work on *all* of the rifle's modulations. Otherwise, Julian 7th, I should very much like to dissolve the bones of your precious Voo-rah-nee right before your very eyes until she is nothing but a sack of flesh." He snickered. "And then I should do the same to you. All in the name of science, of course. After all, aren't you curious how long one can live without a skeleton? I'd lay odds on less than a minute before the lungs collapse completely and stop feeding oxygen to the brain. A pity that I shall have to delay the experiment. But then, I'll gain almost as much satisfaction disintegrating the building beneath your feet and watching as you're crushed to death under a thousand tons of rubble."

Finished with his speech, Or-tis raised the electronic rifle and, aiming the barrel directly at the floor beneath our feet, pulled the trigger—and cried out in shock as the gun rattled apart in his hands, breaking up into a dozen or more pieces that clattered to the floor!

I had no idea what had happened, but I did not hesitate. I had dropped both my sword and my pistol when Or-tis had pulverized the wall behind me. Although I did not see the pistol anywhere, I spied my sword lying near the edge of the broken floor. Now, before Or-tis could recover from his surprise at the sudden loss of his rifle, I leaped for the blade and snatched it up.

Or-tis, seeing me advance upon him, whipped out his own blade and parried my blow just in time to save his life.

The man fought like a cornered dog, his sword slashing at me savagely, every blow powered by the half-earthly muscles of his mixed heritage. But my own earthly birthright enhanced my strength as well while I was within Va-nah, and we found ourselves almost evenly matched.

Or-tis employed every dishonorable trick he could manage to his advantage, and several times I felt his blade nick my flesh. But my uncle had not taught me the niceties of traditional courtly fencing, but rather how to survive by any means possible. Thus, for every wound that Or-tis inflicted upon me, my own blade dealt two upon him.

At last he could no longer stand the punishment I exacted against him. Screaming in rage, he lunged at me with reckless abandon. But this action was to be his undoing, for I had kept my composure and, when he sprang, I landed a hit that dug deeply into the flesh and bone of his right shoulder.

Still, Or-tis did not drop his blade and somehow managed to transfer it to his other hand. Bleeding profusely from his wounded shoulder, his teeth biting back the pain, he cried, "You have not defeated me, Julian 7th! We will meet in battle again, in another life, and next time it will be you who lies a corpse bleeding out upon the floor!"

He leaped at me, but I beat back his sword with ease and drove my blade into his evil heart.

Chapter Twenty-Three

THE CIRCLE OF LIFE

I looked for Voo-rah-nee, but she was already at my side, where she had remained throughout the fight with Or-tis.

I threw down my sword at her feet and knelt before the woman I loved more than life itself. "My Nonovar," I said, gazing at the floor in my reverent bow. "I understand that I have wronged you and that I was a fool ever to doubt your friendship and loyalty. So, too, do I understand that I can never redeem myself in your eyes, but know that this lowly warrior is forever at your service, no matter how you regard him."

"You are indeed a fool!" came the haughty voice of Voo-rah-nee. "Rise, Ju-lan of Earth, and look upon the judgment of the Nonovar of Vathayne."

I did as commanded—and found myself staring, stupefied, into the smiling face of the Moon maid.

"Yes, you are a fool, Ju-lan," she said teasingly as she slipped her arms around my neck, "but you are *my* fool." Our lips came together, and for that brief and yet also somehow eternal moment, the war that raged in the sky about us disappeared. At last, I knew peace in my heart.

But then the blissful moment ended and I knew we were still very much in danger. Still, one mystery needed solving immediately. "There is one thing I cannot understand," I said. "How is it possible that the electronic rifle fell to pieces even as Or-tis discharged it upon us?"

"It is nothing so incredible," Voo-rah-nee said. "I simply turned the dial on the rifle as I struggled with Or-tis. When he pulled the trigger, he expected to disintegrate the stone beneath our feet and hurl us to our deaths. But Or-tis did not realize I had set the gun to disintegrate the very same metal alloy that made up its own barrel and various parts of its frame. When he discharged the electronic rifle, his own action destroyed it."

I shook my head in amazement. "Then you knew all along the rifle would fail?"

"I did not *know* for certain, Ju-lan," Voo-rah-nee said. "But I hoped." And again she kissed me.

The chemical fire that had been raging on the other side of the room still burned fiercely, though fortunately the wind blowing through the gaping opening in the side of the building dissipated the noxious fumes and provided sufficient air to breathe. By now the blaze had consumed the entire row of filing cabinets. Voo-rah-nee assured me the cabinets had held the sum of Or-tis' research into the electronic rifle. I breathed a sigh of relief upon hearing this news, for it meant Tu-lav would be denied the information necessary to recreate the super-weapon.

"Let us go," I said. "But stay behind me, as a tremendous fight is being waged at the top of the stairs leading up to the next room." I knew I must get to John Carter's side in all haste. Our only chance of escape lay in fighting our way out of the tower against impossible odds and somehow making our way to one of Tu-lav's airships.

"I will come," Voo-rah-nee said, "but I am a warrior just as you, and I will not cower in your shadow." She went quickly to Or-tis' corpse and took up his sword, holding it with the ease of one practiced with a blade. "I am not as good with a sword as I am with a pistol, but it is not as if I have not had training. If we must die, it will be side by side."

I could not help but grin at her courageous spirit. I was quickly learning that there is no one made of sterner stuff than the Nonovar of Vathayne.

"Then let us go die," I said, and Voo-rah-nee grinned back at me.

But even as I spoke, a clamor arose in the adjoining room. Before I could react, John Carter leaped into the room, a dozen soldiers dressed in the regalia of Vathayne at his heels. Among them was Tu-lav, who, with tears in his eyes, ran to his daughter and took her in his arms.

"You seem to have taken care of Or-tis easily enough," John Carter said as he approached me.

"Oh, it was not all my doing," I said, and nodded in the direction of the Nonovar. "I had a little help."

The Prince of Helium placed a hand upon my shoulder and we turned away from Tu-lav and his daughter. In a low voice, so as not to be overheard, he said, "Tu-lav has perfected his defensive weapon and turned it against the Kalkar fleet, disabling their engines. Already half the fleet of the Jemadar of Jemadars has surrendered to the ships of the united cities of the U-ga, and those of the other half have either turned tail and run for the hinterlands of Va-nah or will surrender shortly as well."

"You don't trust him," I whispered.

"Do you trust the man who imprisoned you and put you on trial as a traitor?"

"Perhaps more than I would trust Or-tis," I replied, "but not much more. What then shall we do?"

John Carter frowned. "There is not much we can do but wait and see. For now Tu-lav seems pleased that his daughter is safe, Or-tis has been defeated, and the Kalkars have been struck a devastating blow. Perhaps the well-being of his daughter and his decisive victory will make him more magnanimous than he has been in the past."

"Perhaps," I said, and turning back to regard the Jemadar reuniting with Voo-rah-nee, I wanted to believe it.

The Warlord of Barsoom left my side and went to speak with Tu-lav, and I was about to do the same when I felt something tugging at my harness. I turned and looked down at the little boy I had encountered in the apartment below.

"Now that you have killed my father," he said, "who will take care of me?"

My heart nearly broke upon hearing the boy's question. As I sought in vain for some reassuring reply, he looked up at me with his brow furrowed in perplexity.

"It is the oddest thing," he said.

"What is odd?" I asked.

"When you came to the apartment of my father," he continued, "you were a stranger to me and I was sure that I had never seen you before in my life. But now..."

"Yes?" I prompted, even as a little chill ran down my spine.

"Only moments ago," he said, "why, perhaps at the very moment you ran my father through, I had the strangest feeling. It suddenly occurred to me that I have known you for a very, very long time."

I drew away from the boy as an ominous feeling swept over me, and I am not ashamed to say that I shuddered.

"I must go find my mother," the boy said, and he scampered away. But when he reached the door leading into the next room, he stopped and looked back at me with a peculiar regard.

"Ah, yes, I'm beginning to remember now." A devilish grin stretched slowly across the boy's lips. "Until we meet again, Julian 7th."

And then Or-tis, son of Or-tis, passed through the doorway and was gone.

Chapter Twenty-Four

THE MOON KING'S DECREE

I shall not tire you with a detailed account of the days following my confrontation with the Jemadar of Jemadars in the Tower of Brotherhood. Suffice it to say that within a matter of days Kalkar City Number 1 fell to the Vathayneans and their allies. Any pockets of resistance that were met throughout the metropolis either surrendered or fled onto the plain to be rounded up by infantry deployed by Tu-lav's airships.

Fortunately, such incidents of resistance were few, being limited mainly to military officers who had more of a stake in retaining their allegiance to the Kalkar regime. Those of the working class, who had suffered most at the hands of their keepers, put up no fight whatsoever, and in fact welcomed the invading forces with open arms. In several instances, the workers even went so far as to aid their conquerors in securing various quarters of the city from the holdouts among the soldier class.

Though witnessing such acts heartened me, I admit I held some reservations about the ultimate fate of this newly conquered population. Would Tu-lav accord them full citizenship in the U-ga alliance or rather subjugate them and make them slaves to the nobility? I did not know, and even Voo-rah-nee was unable to ascertain her father's intentions in this matter. Vathayne and the other hidden U-ga cities had a long history of aristocracy and had endured centuries of conflict with the Kalkars. I was relieved to see no cruelty directed at those who had surrendered.

All the same, war is war. I knew from reading the forbidden histories of Earth that the resolutions to such conflicts are rarely simple and the unintended consequences of even the most noble of military triumphs are impossible to predict. Only time would tell the character of the victors.

One of Tu-lav's first acts after his forces burst into the upper level of the Tower of Brotherhood was to order an exhaustive search of Or-tis' laboratory. Fortunately, his people found little of value that had not been consumed by the chemical fire. This development sent him into a fury, and I am unsure he believed his daughter when she told him she had not been privy to any of Or-tis' research into the electronic rifle and its deadly modulating ray.

Of course, I knew differently. Or-tis had forced Voo-rah-nee to help him carry forward his experiments, and she was indeed intimately acquainted with many details that might be helpful in recreating the superweapon. But having seen firsthand the weapon's devastating destructive power, she knew as well as anyone its awesome potential for annihilating life and the Pandora's box it would open no matter who wielded it. I loved Voo-rah-nee all the more for her absolute silence concerning the matter and chastised myself severely for ever doubting her loyalty. It was a mistake I would never make again.

Tu-lav's next act was to secure the Barsoomian vessel that Or-tis had shot down out of the sky as it sought to escape the Kalkar attack on Vathayne. In a secret bay deep beneath the city we found the ship's pilot, Kuvan Tal, whom Or-tis had put to work repairing the damaged ship. The Barsoomian had not been harmed, and he was overjoyed to see that Voo-rah-nee was safe and I was alive. Even more elated was he to reunite with the Jeddak of Jeddaks.

Ever fearful of Tu-lav's motives, I was greatly relieved when I learned the Jemadar had put John Carter in charge of repairing the ship and delivering it back to Vathayne. When we were in private, I spoke with the Prince of Helium about the matter.

"Perhaps you and Kuvan Tal," I said, "should take this opportunity to leave Va-nah and return to your world while you still can."

"I cannot do so while my crew are yet captives in Vathayne," John Carter replied. "Besides, Tu-lav's airships patrol the skies around this city. While my ship is fleeter and more maneuverable than the dirigibles of the U-ga alliance, we have already seen how easily the latter disabled the engines of the Kalkar airships. As the *Tara*'s engines also employ the planetary rays for propulsion, it would be a simple matter for Tu-lav's fleet to render our ship inoperable. No, I fear we are at the mercy of the Jemadar of Vathayne."

"That assumes he has any capacity for mercy," I replied darkly.

One of Tu-lav's soldiers entered the room at this point in our conversation, and John Carter smiled at him. "We shall see," the Warlord said to me. "But for now, my friend, I have much work to do." Without further word, he entered the adjoining hangar where repairs were proceeding apace on the Barsoomian craft.

Within a couple weeks by earthly reckoning, the ship was ready for flight. Voo-rah-nee and I, along with John Carter, Kuvan Tal, and a small group of Tu-lav's soldiers—the latter doubtless sent along to keep an eye on the rest of us—boarded the *Tara* and rose into the pink and lavender skies above the former Kalkar capital. Flanking us on all sides were Vathaynean dirigibles, including the Jemadar's flagship—a show of force clearly meant to intimidate the crew of the *Tara* and prevent her from escaping.

Although our ship could have reached Vathayne in but a matter of earthly hours, we proceeded at the pace of our much slower escort. Therefore, I had much time to consider our options in the face of whatever decision Tu-lav would inevitably make about our fates. Voo-rah-nee, for her part, insisted she would endure alongside me whatever judgment her father imposed, no matter how harsh it might be. That, of course, I could never let stand, though it was pointless to tell her so. She had made up her mind, and I daresay I have never met a soul as determined as my Moon maid.

At last the great cone of the volcano La-fal-nah rose up out of the placid, shining sea and our ship descended into the vast crater. As we dropped down toward the landing deck on top of the keep, I saw that efforts were already well underway to repair the damage the city had suffered during the Kalkar attack. Much to my great surprise, the industrious people of Vathayne had somehow miraculously rebuilt the foundation of the mile-wide stretch of the terrace that had collapsed into the Hoos as a result of the Kalkars' bombs. While I marveled at the sight below us, Voo-rah-nee told me proudly that the city's architects had doubtless employed the advanced techniques of her ancient ancestors to achieve the feat.

We finally came to a rest on the top level of the keep. Tu-lav's airship had landed ahead of ours, and so when we disembarked from our craft, I was little surprised to meet the Jemadar of Vathayne and his soldiers at the bottom of the ramp. His regal eyes were stern as they passed over me and alighted upon his daughter.

"Come, Voo-rah-nee," he said. "I have indulged you enough. Now it is time to return to our home."

"And what, Father, will become of Ju-lan, and what will be the fate of the Prince of Helium and his men?" Voo-rah-nee asked, moving not a step from my side.

"They will await the decree of the council," Tu-lav said. "It is as our laws insist, as you well know, Daughter."

Voo-rah-nee's gray eyes glimmered with steely conviction. "No," she said. "It is as *your* laws insist, for *you* are the maker of laws in Vathayne. I have studied the ancient laws in detail, Father, and there is nothing in them that would have you pass judgment on these warriors who stand before you. They are our friends. Have they not risked their lives to defeat our enemies and keep our city free?"

"Indeed they have," Tu-lav replied. "And for that reason, they shall be judged all the more mercifully by the court of the Jemadar. Now come with me, Daughter." And with Tu-lav's pronouncement, his soldiers moved in to escort Voo-rah-nee away from me and our party.

Voo-rah-nee reached for the gun at her hip, but I placed my hand upon her own and, drawing her close, whispered into her ear: "This is not the time." I feared for Voo-rah-nee's safety, for Tu-lav could have had his men slaughter us at a mere word. I looked to John Carter, whose hand was upon the hilt of his sword, but he gave me a knowing nod and released his grip on the weapon.

Voo-rah-nee kissed me and said loudly, so that her father could clearly hear, "We will be together again soon, my Ju-lan." And then she walked proudly to her father's side and said firmly, "They will *not* be harmed."

"Of course not," Tu-lav said, but already had his daughter turned a cold, beautiful shoulder to him. The Jemadar nodded to the commander of his guard, who approached John Carter, Kuvan Tal, and myself. The soldier bowed in deference, and then gestured for us to follow, which we did willingly.

The Jemadar's guard led us back into the keep, where we soon found ourselves back in my old apartments. I was not surprised to discover that the window I had previously used to escape the keep was now sealed fast, replaced with a solid granite wall.

"Well, that is that," I said, eyeing the cold stone. "There is nothing more for it but to hope for the best and await the Jemadar's verdict."

But Tu-lav did not prolong our detention for long. After a not-so-restful sleep and a breakfast that I barely touched consisting of fine and sumptuous Vathaynean meats courtesy of the flesh-vats, a contingent of guards arrived to deliver us to the court of the Jemadar.

Tu-lav appeared to be in good spirits as he sat upon his stately throne. He smiled at us and bowed his head as we entered the grand chamber, the cold regard of the former kings and queens of Vathayne carved in bas-relief upon the walls seeming to pass judgment upon us. Upon the thrones positioned slightly behind Jemadar were the stunning queen of Vathayne and the royal couple's children, Voo-rah-nee and her brother Ro-than. The former half rose from her regal seat upon seeing me, and I smiled broadly to reassure her that I was well. She sat back down, her eyes glittering beneath the luminous ceiling and filled with concern for my well-being.

The guard commanded us to kneel before the Jemadar, but neither John Carter, Kuvan Tal, nor I would comply. When the guard made to force us to our knees, Tu-lav raised his scepter and ordered his men to stand down.

"Let us not mince words," said the Jemadar of Vathayne. "I do not brook outsiders interfering in matters of state, and so do you stand accused—and guilty, I might add—before my court."

"Father!" Voo-rah-nee shouted out in anger.

"Silence, Daughter!" Tu-lav cried. "You will hear out the judgment of the Jemadar, as the ancient laws do in fact decree."

Voo-rah-nee pursed her lips, and I could see her pale knuckles whiten further as she grasped the arms of her throne.

"Yes," Tu-lav went on, "these men do stand guilty of questioning the will of the Jemadar of Vathayne and his council, and of fostering machinations against my people. Do you deny, John Carter of Helium, that you broke out of my prison and sought to sabotage my plans to use the technology of your vessel to secure the peace and security of Vathayne."

"Only after you imprisoned me and my people," John Carter said. "It was you who betrayed a willing ally who was ready to risk his life and the lives of his warriors to defend you against the Kalkars."

"Nonsense!" came Tu-lav's fiery reply.

"What, then, is your evidence to the contrary?" John Carter said coolly.

"The Jemadar needs no evidence," Tu-lav said. "I have witnessed your actions with my own eyes. But I am eminently fair-minded. I do not deny that sometimes our interests have paralleled. Ultimately, you have provided a great service to my nation by aiding in the destruction of Or-tis and his capital. While the Kalkars have by no means been wiped from the face of Va-nah, they have been set back upon their heels. No longer do they hold supreme dominion over our world, and it is my intent to weaken them even further while they are thus wounded. This is not a little thing, and I owe much of it to you, John Carter. Even more do I owe to Ju-lan Sev-ath, slayer of the villain Or-tis. And while, as a result of your past actions, neither of you can be trusted, I must still weigh your crimes against the good you have accomplished."

Tu-lav rose from his throne, his scepter held high. "John Carter, you and your warriors are free to return to your world upon the *Tara*. But know that you are not welcome to return here. Even should you try, only death will await you, for my network of emitters will prevent any ray-propelled ship from functioning in the skies of Va-nah or over the exterior of the great crust that surrounds our world like a shell. Go now, John Carter, while my patience remains."

The Warlord of Barsoom stood his ground and did not so much as blink. "And what is to become of my friend, Julian 7th of Earth?"

Tu-lav face took on a friendly smile. "Fear not for your friend. I promise you he will return to Earth alive and well."

John Carter turned to me and clasped my shoulder in a Barsoomian gesture of friendship. "I do not trust him," he said in full hearing of the Jemadar.

"And yet we must," I said. "What other choice do we have? Besides, perhaps we should take him at his word, at least in this matter. Your world is no longer a threat to his own in the face of his emitters, so what does he lose by allowing you to return to Barsoom and letting me go back to Earth." As I uttered this sentiment, I admit I felt as if my heart had sunk into my stomach, for I could not imagine a life without Voo-rah-nee, nor could I imagine her father would allow her to return to Earth with me. I said nothing, however, for I feared that Tu-lav's mercy would turn to retribution should his will be questioned, and that this was the last chance for John Carter to return to his beloved Dejah Thoris. "Further," I continued, "as Tu-lav has said, the Kalkars are no longer an interplanetary menace, and so your mission in Va-nah is complete. You must go home to your world while you still can. Your princess awaits you."

The Warlord of Barsoom regarded me for a long moment before turning his gaze back to Tu-lav. "My warriors and I shall return to Barsoom as you wish, Jemadar," he said. "But know well that your threats carry no weight with me. I shall be monitoring your activities both within Va-nah and without through means of which you have no knowledge, and I shall employ the powerful telescopes of my scientists to ensure that you keep your word about the safe return of Julian 7th to Jasoom. If I discover that you have betrayed your promise, you will have great cause to regret it. I have spoken."

The cold tone of John Carter's terse words sent a little shiver down my spine. I wondered if John Carter were merely bluffing about his secret monitoring capabilities. I decided that, whatever the case, were I in Tu-lav's shoes, I should not like to gamble against the Jeddak of Jeddaks.

Having said his piece, John Carter turned on his heel with a whirl of his cape and strode from the throne room, Kuvan Tal flowing close behind. That was the last I ever saw of either man, at least in that lifetime, though in a later incarnation... But I get ahead of myself and must task myself with finishing the tale at hand before launching into yet another.

After the departure of the Warlord and Kuvan Tal, the Jemadar returned his attention to me. "And now it is time to pass judgment upon you, Ju-lan Sev-ath," he said icily. "You have not yet been tried for killing my personal mo-lah-kar, who was very dear to me and accompanied me on many hunts. Moreover, while you were being held for trial on suspicion of treason, you escaped my prison."

At this point, Voo-rah-nee leaped from her throne and leveled an accusing finger at her father. "How can he have committed treason if he is not a citizen of Vathayne?" she cried.

"I do not wish to implicate you in cavorting with this criminal, Daughter," he said, "but I shall if I must for the sake of Vathayne!"

For a moment, Voo-rah-nee looked as if she had bloody murder on her mind. Then her anger seemed to evaporate in the face of pride and her expression suddenly grew as cold and hard as alabaster. With regal deliberation, she dismounted the dais and walked slowly to my side. She took my hand and smiled up at me, then looked back to her father.

"I stand with Ju-lan Sev-ath," she said coolly.

The Jemadar sighed and shook his head as if tired of dealing with an unruly child. "Ju-lan Sev-ath," he said, "I have weighed your crimes against the state against your aid in our time of need. I hereby banish you from Va-nah for the rest of your mortal existence. You will never return to this world, nor will you ever again look upon my fair daughter, the Nonovar of Vathayne. Even should you see her again—which I guarantee you will not—you will not recognize her, for as part of your punishment, my doctors will subject you to a mental technique of the ancients that will erase your memory. Not only will you not remember ever having left Earth and your subsequent experiences in Va-nah, but any incarnation that you shall ever live will hold no memory of your current incarnation. From the vantage of your other lifetimes, it will be as if you had never existed, either before your trip to Va-nah, your experiences after arriving here, or the remaining days of your life after you have left. I cannot risk that the people of Earth should gain any advantage from what you have learned during your stay in Va-nah, lest they ever free themselves of the Kalkars' shackles and venture here. But know that the removal of your memory is my gift to you as well as my punishment, for you will be blissfully unaware of anything you have lost from your time in Va-nah." He lowered his gaze knowingly until it fell upon his daughter.

A single tear ran down Voo-rah-nee's cheek. "You are truly a monster, Father," she said, trying but failing to steady her voice. "I am ashamed that the same blood runs in our veins."

"You will think differently, child," he said, "once you have had time to consider my wisdom. Do you think that the Nonovar of Vathayne could ever be happy with this lowly barbarian from another world?"

"You are no better than the Kalkars, Father," Voo-rah-nee replied. "You cling to your precious nobility just as they deceive themselves by clinging to their imaginary sense of brotherhood. But you are both misguided. It is what a man or a woman actually does that determines his or her worth, not some vague or grand-sounding philosophy." She squeezed my hand firmly. "Ju-lan is more noble than any man I have ever known, no matter his heritage, for the deeds he has done and the good life he has lived. Would that I could say as much for you, the so-called Jemadar of Vathayne!"

"I have heard enough!" he cried. "Guards! Separate them! Escort the Nonovar to her quarters and place her under armed guard. And take the prisoner to my dungeon, where he will await my mind-wizards. There he will remain until he has been subjected to the treatment and the ship has been readied to take him back to Earth!"

Voo-rah-nee screeched in anger and dismay but it was to no avail; the Jemadar's guards swarmed around us and tore us from one another's grasp.

"Ju-lan," Voo-rah-nee pleaded as she was pulled away, "I cannot go on! I refuse to endure a life without you!"

"You must live, Voo-rah-nee!" I cried, chilled by the implication of her words. "Your father cannot make me forget you, no matter the ancient techniques he employs. I *will* remember, whether it takes me a thousand incarnations in the attempt— I will find a way!"

And then she was gone, carried away by her father's soldiers.

Meanwhile, I was thrown in shackles and brought deep down beneath the keep to the Jemadar's dungeon. For how long I sat there alone in my bleak and dreary cell, I do not know, but eventually the door opened and, much to my surprise, I was escorted back to the Jemadar's throne room.

Gone were the courtiers and soldiers who had presided over my last visit, nor was the queen present or her two children, Voo-rah-nee and Ro-than. Only Tu-lav sat upon the dais, and when the guards brought me before him, the Jemadar, slouching in his throne, dismissed them with an exhausted wave.

Indeed, Tu-lav's entire countenance seemed to have changed since our last encounter. No longer was he the prideful, arrogant monarch of Vathayne—rather, he appeared to have transformed into nothing more assuming than a pitiful, wrinkled old man.

"Why have you summoned me?" I asked. "And where is Voo-rah-nee?"

Tu-lav slowly raised a limp hand and pointed to the back of the chamber. I looked where he indicated and saw something lying to one side of the door that I had not noticed when I entered. I am not ashamed to admit I shuddered in both fear and dread, for what lay there in the shadows resembled a human form.

I leaped up and crossed the room in but an instant, where I knelt beside the lifeless body of a woman. My palms cold and sweating, I brushed back the long locks of midnight-black hair from her pale, beautiful face. It was Voo-rah-nee.

"She told me she could not live without you," Tu-lav said wearily, "but I did not listen."

I rose from the cold, dead corpse of the woman I loved and walked back to the throne.

"I am ready for the treatment," I said. "I do not wish to remember."

Tu-lav merely nodded and called for the guards to take me back to my cell to await his mind-wizards.

I had been back in my cell for what must have been only minutes when the door opened once again. I did not even look up, for life had lost all meaning for me. What did I care if it was the wizards or an executioner? Both would relieve me of my suffering.

"Ju-lan, my friend," came the basso voice, "it is good to see you again, though you look as sorrowful as I would had a great earthquake hurled the flesh-vats into the Hoos and there was no more meat to eat in all of Va-nah."

"It is worse than that, No-ma-ro," I said.

The Va-gas grunted and, pacing back and forth, rubbed his flanks up against the bars of my cell in a doglike gesture of affection. When he was done, his broad, proud face looked up at me, his eyes twinkling strangely, as if they held back a secret.

"I hear they are sending you back to the Place Deep Beneath the World," he said, which was as close as a Va-gas could come to understanding Earth's place in the cosmos. "I shall miss you, Earth man, but I have left you a gift in honor of our parting. It is a pity that you will never know that it was I who gave it to you after the Jemadar's wizards are finished with you. But perhaps that is as it should be. As the Va-gas saying goes, a true gift is not given for the benefit of the giver."

"I do not understand," I said.

No-ma-ro grinned as widely as the Cheshire cat and then turned about and was gone. Only a short time later the mind-wizards came, and that is my final memory of Julian 7th in Va-nah.

Epilogue

TIME AND FATE

I leaped up from my seat, where for the past several hours I had been listening with rapt attention to my visitor recount his remarkable story.

"Surely that cannot be the end of the tale!" I exclaimed. It was now well after six o'clock on the next morning. We had stayed up all night as my guest had narrated his singular account, and yet I felt neither groggy nor fatigued. "I must know what happened after you—I mean Julian 7th—returned to Earth," I went on. "You dealt the Kalkars a devastating blow in Va-nah, but what was the result of that victory on Earth? Moreover, after you returned, did you ever regain your memory of..." I let the last sentence trail off, suddenly keenly aware of the pain my question might inflict upon my visitor.

Julian 3rd merely smiled and said, "Yes, there is more to the tale, though it is still strange for me to call up the memory, for the Julian who returned to Earth knew nothing of the events he had experienced within the Moon. Further, I—my current incarnation, I mean—could not recall anything pertaining to the incarnation of Julian 7th, including the parts of that incarnation's life that occurred before and after the trip to Va-nah, until after my visit to the monastery in the Himalayas. It is all rather like a dream within a dream, though the visceral sort of dream that makes one believe the events have really transpired. As, of course, I know they someday will."

I shook my head at the strangeness of it all and then en-couraged my guest to continue his story, which he related in his own words as follows:

My next memory is of being rattled awake by what seemed to be the furious shaking of the entire world. It took me a few moments to understand that my initial impressions were mis-placed. I was not upon the Earth, but rather in the belly of some kind of vessel plunging downward through the atmosphere. A belt was strapped around my waist and another across my chest, securing me fast within a half-reclined, cushioned chair. Beside me in the cramped cabin another chair was affixed to the floor, a small, cloaked form belted into it. Tongues of flame flickered and lashed outside a small port in the wall beside me and thunder boomed in my ears as the metal plates that composed the cabin shuddered so violently I thought they might shake free of their rivets.

After a few minutes, the rattling and rumbling ceased and the steep angle of our descent leveled out. Now, instead of the orange and red flames that had raged outside the portal, silky white clouds flitted beyond the glass, and at times I saw the azure of the sky emerge from behind the vapor.

I was on a ship flying through the heavens! How had I come to be here? My last memory had been of helping Henry clean out the horse stalls behind the house on our little farm in Oak Park. I could not explain it.

I called out to my companion in the seat beside me, asking for an explanation of our whereabouts and the reason for my presence in such a strange setting. The figure turned its head slightly toward me in response, and the cloak was drawn back just enough that I caught a glimpse of the gentle curve of a woman's cheek and long, dark eyelashes. Then she turned away, drew up the hood of her garment, and withdrew a small compact of makeup from beneath her cloak. She opened the case and began applying the cosmetics to an unusually pale white patch of skin on the back of her otherwise richly tanned hand.

We flew through the sky without speaking for about half an hour. I looked out the little window and saw that we were now cruising at an altitude of only a few hundred feet over expansive plains of greenery below, upon which twilight was rapidly falling. We continued to descend until the familiar skyline of war-ravaged Chicago loomed silhouetted against the horizon's waning glow to the portside of our ship.

Within minutes the craft set down gently upon the ground, and a man with skin as white as porcelain emerged from the forward cabin. I recognized him as a U-ga, one of the native humanoid races from the interior of the Moon—hereditary enemies of the Kalkars. He went first to the woman seated beside me and ensured that she was all right after the rough descent through the atmosphere. He helped her out of her restraints and then knelt on one knee, his head bowed, as if presenting himself before royalty.

"You must hurry," the man said. "I do not believe the Kalkars witnessed our landing, but I cannot be sure."

The woman stood and told the man to rise. After he obeyed her command, she said, "You understand our agreement, Dotak? You can speak no word of this when you return to Va-nah or your life and the lives of your family will be in extreme jeopardy."

"I understand," he said. "But I must ask you one last time: Do you really mean to go through with it? I am willing to return you to Vathayne and take our chances that the Jemadar will be merciful when you reveal your deception. Think nothing of my life. I am but a servant, but you—you are..."

"Shoosh, Dotak." The woman reached up and cradled the man's cheek with affection. "Your family has faithfully served my own for a hundred generations. I know it is your duty to try to dissuade me, but I have made up my mind. You must leave us here and depart before the Kalkars come and we are all as good as dead."

The man bowed to indicate his assent, but I could not mistake the pain upon his face. He opened a door in the side of the craft, pulled a lever in a niche in the hull, and looked on as a ramp lowered to the ground below. At a motion from Dotak, I unbuckled myself from the chair and joined the woman at the doorway. Her face still hidden beneath her hood, she took my hand in her own and together we descended until we stood upon the firm ground of Earth.

Though I could not remember the circumstances under which I had left the planet of my birth, nor my time away from it, I yet experienced the strong feeling that I had been gone for a long, long time. I drew into my lungs the rich, humid air of summer, reveling in the familiar smells of the district of Oak Park in the Teivos of Chicago. I was home.

Still holding hands, the woman and I watched as the ramp retreated into the hull of the sleek craft from which we had just emerged. Then the vessel lifted swiftly and silently into the air and glided off into the twilit sky until we could see it no more.

When the ship was gone, I looked down at the woman in puzzlement about what had just transpired. "What now?" I asked. "I don't even know your name."

She drew back the hood of her cloak and I saw before me the most beautiful face I had ever looked upon.

"You may call me Victoria," she said. "I understand it is a regal name upon your world, and as such it will remind me of home."

"You are a U-ga?" I ventured. I rubbed my hand to indicate that I had seen her daub makeup upon her own hand to give the deception that her skin was deeply tanned.

"Yes," she replied, "but no one must ever know. Do you promise to keep my secret?"

"I will never let the Kalkars hurt you," I said, without knowing why I felt such a strong compulsion to protect this strange woman whom I had never seen before that very day.

Out of the darkness came the whinny of a horse. The girl drew close to me and shuddered.

"What kind of creature is that?" she asked. "Is it dangerous?"

I laughed. "No, that's just old Betsy, a dam from my own stables. I'd recognize that whickering anywhere."

Victoria relaxed. "A pet of yours?"

"Not a pet," I explained. "A horse. There's a difference, you know?"

"Perhaps you can teach me about...*horses*." Though she spoke English, she pronounced the word strangely. "I need a job, after all."

Again, Betsy's neighing peeled through the night.

"She's about to foal," I said.

"Foal? Like a Va-gas?"

I couldn't hold back a snicker. "Something like that."

"You should name the new offspring No-ma-ro," Victoria said decisively.

"No-ma-ro?" The odd combination of syllables rang with a familiar cadence to my ears when I spoke it aloud, though I could not explain it. "Why?" I asked.

"Because you owe him. We both do. If No-ma-ro hadn't told me about the mur-laks and raced off to the wilds to bring one back to Vathayne before you were returned to Earth, then I never would have been able to fool my father into believing..." She stopped herself and smiled. "Forget what I have just said. The less you know the better."

"Whatever you say, Victoria," I said, and laughed again.

We stood listening for some time as the crickets chirped merrily in the failing light. I, for one, did not want the moment to end, so content did I feel with this strange woman from another world. And somehow I got the feeling that she, too, felt happy in my company. At last, however, Victoria made a little shiver as the chill of the evening began to settle in. I put my arm around her to warm her and she nestled closer to me.

"Let us go," I said. "I want to introduce you to my mother and aunt and uncle."

"Will they welcome me?" Victoria asked hesitantly.

"I am sure of it," I said, and then walked hand in hand with my future wife back to the farmhouse.

Julian 3rd sank deep into his chair, his eyes now closed. Though he must have been weary from the telling of his long tale, his expression was one of placid contentment.

"Now that is an ending!" I cried. "You are indeed a lucky man, my friend."

"And why is that?" My guest's eyelids remained gently shut.

"Why, there are few men besides yourself, if there are any, who can honestly claim to have met the very same love of his life twice for the first time!"

The man seated before me snapped open his eyes and perked up. "And yet at the same time, I have never met her, for she exists only in the future."

"But you shall meet her one day," I exclaimed, grinning.

"You are a romantic, old man," my companion said. "But you are right. We should all take the good where we can, for many challenges still lie ahead waiting to confront us."

Suddenly my good mood evaporated. "They are coming, aren't they? The Kalkars..."

For more than a minute we sat together in silence, brooding over the grim fate that awaited the human race in only a few short decades.

"I have spoken to the President," I said finally. "He is a good man. He listened earnestly to what I had to say, and I have earned a measure of respect in my position as Secretary of Commerce. And yet the tale I told him would be difficult for anyone to believe had he not heard it directly from your lips. I admit that I, too, succumb to doubt at times. But then I consider that events of the past few years have unfolded exactly as you have told me they would, and with such precision that my doubts fall away in the face of the threat that looms before us. Tell me, is there nothing we can do to prevent the horror of the Kalkar invasion?"

Any hopes I had that my guest would say something to ease my fears died when I saw the man's grave expression, only to be resurrected a moment later when the corner of his mouth quirked into a lopsided grin.

"There is always hope," he said. "Have I not already told you the events of the life of Julian 20th, the Red Hawk?"

"Indeed you have," I replied. "And I have not forgotten the tale, for how could I? But all that humanity will suffer in the interim between now and the twenty-fifth century...can it not be prevented?"

"After all the strange and wondrous things I have seen, both in this life and in those preceding and following my current incarnation, who am I to deny the unexpected? Unfortunately, so far I have seen no evidence to suggest that humankind can do anything to alter the course of events of which I have foreknowledge from my future incarnations. Still, I do not believe that I would be telling you my story if some part of me did not yearn to alter the future. I have heard the hypothesis that the existence we experience takes place in but one of an infinite array of universes. Is it possible to jump the rails, so to speak, and leap from our own dismal reality into another whose future will bring peace and prosperity? A universe in which the Kalkars are defeated before they ever leave Va-nah to assail Earth? Or perhaps better yet, a reality that decrees mutual peace between the Kalkars, the U-ga, and the inhabitants of our own world, without the need for the bloody throes of war in the first place. I do not know if such is possible, or if we have perhaps already 'jumped the rails' but are unaware of it. Perhaps in some other reality, Earth made contact with Mars in, say, the early twentieth century. How would history have unfolded differently were that the case? Again, I do not know, and these questions I pose are but idle speculations. In the end, we must face what we must and make our decisions for the future as best we can, all of our actions based on the shadowy displays we see dancing upon the walls of the dimly lit cavern we call human knowledge. It is truly all that we can do."

"Then you must describe those shadowy displays as best you can," I said. "For it is all we have to go on. Tell me, did Julian 7th ever return to Va-nah?"

"No, he did not," my companion replied, and then added with a grin, "at least not to my recollection, and as you have seen my memory is not exactly to be fully trusted in regard to that incarnation. But I did—*he* did, I should say—lay the foundation for the revolution that will one day free humanity from the shackles of the Kalkars. Alas, his life was not an easy one after he returned to Earth, and one year the house burned down under mysterious circumstances—fortunately, not before Voo-rah-nee, the woman who came to be known as Victoria, risked her life rescuing Old Glory from the inferno. But Julian 7th was undaunted and rebuilt the farmhouse with his own hands, this time constructing a sturdy foundation composed of bricks and stones recovered from the ruins of old Chicago. And all the while he laid the groundwork for rebellion—efforts that did not go to waste when the time was right and his ancestors eventually rose up against their masters."

"And what of the defeat of the Kalkars within Va-nah?" I asked. "Will Tu-lav's triumph against them—aided as it was, or will be, in no small part by the valiant actions of Julian 7th and John Carter—be a lasting victory? What will occur within the Moon in the intervening years between the incarnation of Julian 7th and that of Julian 20th, who, as you have told me will end the war between his people and the Kalkars? Will the U-ga rid Va-nah of the Kalkar scourge, and will either race send their ships to Earth following the victory of the Red Hawk?"

My guest leaned back in his chair and grinned knowingly. "That," he said, "is a story for another time."

ACKNOWLEDGMENTS

Many thanks to all the good and hardworking people at Edgar Rice Burroughs, Inc., for their help with this novel, the completion of which fulfills my major childhood ambition to write and have published an authorized novel continuing the epic tales of ERB. In particular, I thank Jim Sullos for his willingness to listen to my story proposal and his eagerness for the project; Tyler Wilbanks for managing the book's production; Scott Tracy Griffin for his assistance in promoting the book; and Cathy Mann Wilbanks for handling the company operations as the book went forward.

I also thank my first readers, Win Scott Eckert and Joshua Small, for vetting my ideas, keeping me in line, and making this a much better story than it otherwise would have been without their help; Gary A. Buckingham and Robert T. Garcia, and Scott Tracy Griffin for their invaluable help with the text; Chris Alan Peuler and Mark Wheatley for their awe-inspiring artwork; my uncle Thomas S. McGraw for introducing me to the works of Edgar Rice Burroughs in my formative years; Jason Scott Aiken, Henry G. Franke III, Jim "The Red Hawk" Hadac, Bill Hillman, Chuck Loridans, Rudy Sigmund, John Allen Small, and Jess Terrell for their friendship and enthusiasm for all things Burroughsian; the members of The Burroughs Bibliophiles and the Edgar Rice Burroughs Chain of Friendship for keeping the flame alive; and Robert R. Barrett for his support of this project, for his informative and insightful correspondence on the Moon series, and for consulting ERB's original manuscript of *The Moon Maid* to determine once and for all that the correct singular form is "Va-gas" and the correct plural form is "U-ga."

Of course, my greatest debt and gratitude lies with Edgar Rice Burroughs, without whose timeless works I would not have written this or likely any other book.

The Wild Adventures of

Edgar Rice Burroughs® Series

Swords Against the Moon Men

Christopher Paul Carey is the coauthor with Philip José Farmer of *The Song of Kwasin*, and the author of *Exiles of Kho*; *Hadon, King of Opar*; and *Blood of Ancient Opar*, all works set in Farmer's Khokarsa series, which was inspired by the timeless works of Edgar Rice Burroughs. He has also scripted two comic books from Dynamite Entertainment featuring iconic characters created by Edgar Rice Burroughs: *Pathfinder Worldscape*: *Lord of the Jungle One-Shot* and *Pathfinder Worldscape: Dejah Thoris One-Shot*. His short fiction may be found in anthologies such as *The Avenger: The Justice, Inc. Files*; *Doc Ardan: The Abominable Snowman*; *Ghost in the Cogs: Steam-Powered Ghost Stories*; *The Many Tortures of Anthony Cardno*; *Tales of the Shadowmen*; *Tales of the Wold Newton Universe*; and *The Worlds of Philip José Farmer*. Carey is a senior editor at Paizo—working on both the award-winning Pathfinder Roleplaying Game and Starfinder—and he has edited numerous collections, anthologies, and novels. Carey holds a master's degree in Writing Popular Fiction and lives in Western Washington.

COVER ART
Chris **Peuler** is a genre illustrator based in Chicago, working primarily in fantasy and science fiction. A traditionally trained digital painter, Chris has created vivid imagery for various gaming and book publications. His first full wraparound dust jacket painting for Edgar Rice Burroughs, Inc., was the cover art for Lee Strong's novel, *A Soldier of Poloda: Further Adventures Beyond the Farthest Star*.

INTERIOR ILLUSTRATIONS
Mark Wheatley holds the Eisner, Inkpot, Mucker, Gem, Speakeasy awards and nominations for the Harvey and the Ignatz as well as being an inductee to the Overstreet Hall of Fame. He has designed for Lady Gaga, The Black Eyed Peas, ABC's *Beauty and the Beast*, and *Square Roots*, as well as *Super Clyde*, *The Millers* and *2 Broke Girls* on CBS. His works include Doctor Cthulittle, Breathtaker, Return of the Human, Ez Street, Lone Justice, Mars, Black Hood, Prince Nightmare, Hammer of the Gods, Blood of the Innocent, Frankenstein Mobster, Miles the Monster, Skultar and Titanic Tales as well as Tarzan, The Adventures of Baron Munchausen, Jonny Quest, Dr. Strange, The Flash, Captain Action, Argus, The Spider, Stargate Atlantis, the Three Stooges, Torchwood and Doctor Who.

PUBLISHED BY
Edgar Rice Burroughs, Inc., Tarzana, California

About Edgar Rice Burroughs, Inc.

Founded in 1923 by Edgar Rice Burroughs, as one of the first authors to incorporate himself, Edgar Rice Burroughs, Inc. holds numerous trademarks and the rights to all literary works of the author still protected by copyright, including stories of Tarzan of the Apes and John Carter of Mars. The company has overseen every adaptation of his literary works in film, television, radio, publishing, theatrical stage productions, licensing and merchandising. The company is still a very active enterprise and manages and licenses the vast archive of Mr. Burroughs' literary works, fictional characters and corresponding artworks that have grown for over a century. The company continues to be owned by the Burroughs family and remains headquartered in Tarzana, California, the town named after the Tarzana Ranch Mr. Burroughs purchased there in 1919 which led to the town's future development.

www.edgarriceburroughs.com
www.tarzan.com

Sci-Fi

BOOK SERIES #5

A Soldier of Poloda

FURTHER ADVENTURES
BEYOND THE FARTHEST STAR

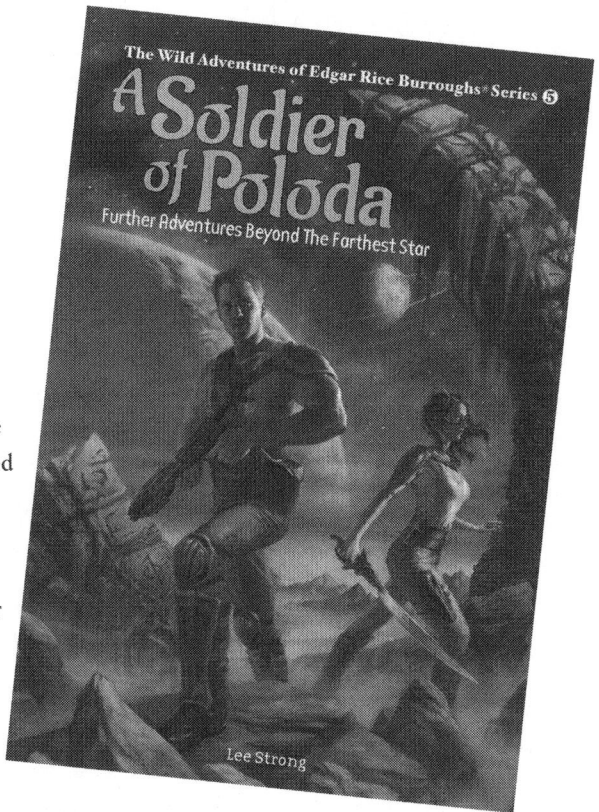

Worlds at War! American intelligence officer Thomas Randolph is teleported from the World War II battlefields of Normandy into the belly of the evil Kapar empire on the planet Poloda. The Kapar's only passion is to conquer and destroy the outnumbered Unis forces who had been engaged in a century-long struggle to survive. Rechristened Tomas Ran, the Earthman now understands that the same fierce determination to defeat Hitler must now be used as a weapon to defeat the fascist Kapars – a merciless foe bent on global domination.

Available at
www.ERBurroughs.com/Store

MarkWheatleyGallery.com

a gallery of art
by **Mark Wheatley**
Pulp Art, Comic Art,
TV Art & more

portrait of
Edgar Rice Burroughs
by Mark Wheatley

Made in the USA
Middletown, DE
05 July 2020